One December Morning

BOOKS BY EMMA DAVIES

Lucy's Little Village Book Club
The House at Hope Corner
The Beekeeper's Cottage
The Little Shop on Silver Linings Street
My Husband's Lie
The Wife's Choice
A Year at Appleyard Farm
After the Crash
The Little Island Secret
The Midnight Bakery

THE LITTLE COTTAGE SERIES
The Little Cottage on the Hill
Summer at the Little Cottage on the Hill
Return to the Little Cottage on the Hill
Christmas at the Little Cottage on the Hill

THE ADAM AND EVE MYSTERY SERIES
Death by Candlelight
Death at the Dinner Party
Death on the Menu
Death at Beresford Hall

CLEARWATER CASTLE SERIES
Secrets of Clearwater Castle

Letting in Light

Turn Towards the Sun

The Mystery of Montague House

EMMA DAVIES

One December Morning

bookouture

Published by Bookouture in 2025

An imprint of Storyfire Ltd.
Carmelite House
50 Victoria Embankment
London EC4Y 0DZ

www.bookouture.com

The authorised representative in the EEA is Hachette Ireland
8 Castlecourt Centre
Dublin 15 D15 XTP3
Ireland
(email: info@hbgi.ie)

Copyright © Emma Davies, 2025

Emma Davies has asserted her right to be identified as the author of this work.

All rights reserved. No part of this publication may be reproduced, stored in any retrieval system, or transmitted, in any form or by any means, electronic, mechanical, photocopying, recording or otherwise, without the prior written permission of the publishers.

ISBN: 978-1-83790-319-1
eBook ISBN: 978-1-83790-320-7

This book is a work of fiction. Names, characters, businesses, organizations, places and events other than those clearly in the public domain, are either the product of the author's imagination or are used fictitiously. Any resemblance to actual persons, living or dead, events or locales is entirely coincidental.

To the young man in the red Mini, without whom this story would not exist...

1

22 DECEMBER

Peg paused by the garden gate, captivated by the change in the scenery. The world had been transformed overnight. Gone were the muted greens and mud browns of winter, and in their place a layer of sparkling, iridescent white. What was stark and bare now stood in shining splendour.

True hoarfrosts were rare and those she remembered the most were from her childhood, when she'd been fascinated by the wonder of a spider's web made crystalline, and the curve of holly leaves on the bush at the bottom of her garden, each one seemingly dipped in sugar. But then she grew up and work replaced the wonder, marriage and a family replaced the fascination. They had still been there, but faded into the background of Peg's busy life. Now she was older she had time to stand and stare.

Inhaling the crisp morning air, Peg turned back to look at the woman who had been such a huge part of her life and now, even in her eighties, still capable of the fiercest hugs. Peg didn't want to think about how her aunt's ample figure felt a little less round each time she visited, or how the corners of her house stayed a little more dusty, and focused instead on Mim's big, wide smile which lit up her pale blue eyes and set them twinkling with mischief. They were the same blue eyes Peg had inherited, as had everyone on her mother's side of the family – even Peg's children had been blessed. Peg always reckoned she'd inherited her indomitable spirit from her aunt as well, and more often than not she greeted the day as Mim did – full-on, staring it straight in the face.

There had been a time though, not that long ago, when Peg had struggled to get out of bed at all. For months. And it wasn't that her memories of Julian had faded; more that these days she had learned to be grateful for them instead of seeking to push them, and the pain they caused, away.

She raised her arm and waved, knowing that despite the coldness of the day and Peg's entreaties to stay inside, Mim would stand on the doorstep and wave until Peg's car had reached the end of the road and she turned out of sight.

Peg's heart lifted at the thought of what awaited her at the other end of her journey – the Cotswold village where she had lived for the last thirty-odd years, with its leafy lanes and jumble of golden stone buildings. Green verges and thatched cottages, gabled roofs and the hotch-potch of chimneys on the old vicarage. But even as she pulled open her car door and climbed inside, the thought had already become tinged with sadness. She couldn't go on pretending that everything was fine, or putting off the decision for another year. Mim wasn't getting any younger, and her last illness had shaken her confidence badly. However much it broke her heart, this Christmas would be Peg's last at Bramble Cottage, and she had known it for some time. She dug out her brightest smile and waved again as she slowly drove away.

Peg was deep in thought as she pulled into the petrol station. It was her last chance to buy fuel before the motorway, but that wasn't the only reason she stopped in this village. She'd been doing it for as long as she could remember. Smack bang in the centre of the village, John and Julia Clements' shop was part convenience store, part delicatessen, part hub of all village gossip, and had the added benefit of a large helping of charm thrown in for good measure. So what if their petrol was a few pence more expensive than elsewhere? For Peg, who avoided 'corporate' at any cost, it was a rarity to find a business like this still open. Where else could she be greeted by a six-foot-high tree with an animated 'mouth' which grinned as it sang 'Have a Holly Jolly Christmas'? Where else could she buy chocolates made by Julia herself, with fondant centres of raspberries, strawberries and blackberries from her own garden? Where else would she be treated like a friend rather than a customer? And where else would a doe-eyed Irish Wolfhound nuzzle her hand on the lookout for treats? Not on the motorway, that much was certain.

The place was busy today and Peg felt another surge of longing for home. The main street in her own village would be bustling, the brightness of the morning bringing people out to run last-minute errands, yet still stopping to chat at the bus stop beside the village green. Fairy lights would be festooned from every tree and window, and an enormous wreath would be hung on the pub door, garlanded with bright red ribbon. She sighed with contentment as she pulled alongside one of only two petrol pumps and began to fill up her car. She would be there soon.

The shop was loud with voices as Peg pushed open the door, smiling as the Christmas tree burst into song. Other people might be tempted to rip its plug from the wall in the first half hour of use, but not the Clements. And not Peg. It was as much a part of her Christmas now as the first ritual playing of her Michael Bublé album.

Of the people inside, probably only one other had come to

pay for petrol – the rest were there for newspapers, or loaves of bread, fat with olives, forgotten jars of cranberry sauce or iced gingerbread men freshly baked that morning. Some, like her, were there for Julia's chocolates. It always did to keep a box in the house at this time of year, just in case of unexpected visitors bearing gifts, or, in Peg's case (knowing full well that any unexpected visitors she *did* have were not the kind to bring gifts), so that she could eat them herself.

She stood back to let a man move past her, his face harried as he squeezed through the gap. He was clutching a phone to his ear while trying to unscrew the top from a bottle of water and neither action was going particularly well. She opened the door for him and smiled in sympathy as he pulled a rueful face at her. She'd spent far too many Christmases of her own in the past worn to a frazzle, dazed by the sheer number of things there seemingly were to do; but now that she knew better, she rejected the seasonal hysteria. It was far simpler and far nicer. Every year the cover of the magazine she wrote for screamed that this would be the *Best Christmas Ever!* and she winced in dismay whenever she saw it. Expectation was a dangerous thing, in her opinion.

In the end, she bought two boxes of Julia's chocolates. She couldn't decide between the lure of her favourites or the opportunity to try some new ones, so she shrugged and carried both to the till. Life was too short.

Outside, a car was waiting for the pump, so Peg pulled forward into one of the parking spaces the shop reserved for customers. She wanted to check her phone before the last leg of her journey and fetch a packet of Werther's from her bag in the boot. Once she was on the motorway there would be no stopping.

The harried man from the shop was parked in the space beside her, and was now rubbing ineffectually at his windscreen with a small piece of tissue. It had no doubt been fished from his pocket, probably already crumpled and next to useless even before he'd applied it to the window.

'Beautiful day, isn't it?' she remarked cheerfully as she climbed from her car. Receiving no reply, she stopped and indicated his screen. 'I have a cloth if you'd like to borrow it,' she added.

The man looked up, all manner of expressions crossing his face. Eventually his lips twitched in what might have been a smile. 'I wasn't expecting this today,' he said. 'My water jets are frozen solid. And with all this muck on the roads, I can't see a thing... I bought some water from the shop to try to clear it but it's freezing on the screen.' He grimaced. 'Mind you, it was from the fridge so it's halfway there already.'

Now that she looked, Peg could see the glass was covered in a layer of crusty brown. 'I think it's all the grit they've put on the roads,' she said. 'It stops us sliding about but I agree, it's mucky stuff.'

The man looked pointedly at Peg's windscreen which, in contrast, gleamed in the weak sunshine. She laughed. 'I unblocked my jets before I left,' she said. 'Hang on, I've got something which might help.'

She edged between the two cars and opened the passenger door, taking out a large flask which was propped on the seat. A cloth sat beside it and she fetched that too, handing both to the man.

'It's just tepid water,' she said. 'But it will clear your screen, and if you trickle it onto your water jets as well it will hopefully unblock those, too. It might take a few goes to melt the ice, but...' She trailed off. 'Sorry, I'm not trying to tell you what to do, I'm sure you're more than capable...' She stopped again. The man had enough on his plate already by the look of things; he didn't need her life story as well. To her surprise, though, he laughed.

'Are you always this organised?' The weary look was replaced by one of amusement.

Peg pulled a face. 'I am, I'm afraid. I'm—' She was about to say 'on her own' but she stopped. 'Just made that way, I guess. But I've got a couple of hours' journey ahead of me and I didn't want to get caught out.'

'Yeah, me too. The journey, that is, not the part where I should have planned for it. Are you driving home for Christmas?'

She nodded. 'How about you?'

'Yes, but to someone else's home,' he replied. 'My son's. And daughter-in-law's.' There was something about the way he said it which caught Peg's attention, but she didn't want to pry.

'I've been to visit my aunt,' said Peg. 'Who I love to bits, but I'm very much looking forward to being back in my own front room, cat on my lap, sitting beside a roaring fire with a book in my hand and a pot of tea on the go.'

He unscrewed the cap from the flask. 'And I'm holding you up,' he said.

'No, it's fine, honestly, I don't rush these days. In fact, I quite enjoy the journey. I put my music on, turn up the heating, and smile every time I see a car go by loaded up with presents. It's a bit like that feeling you get on Christmas Eve when you're a child. I love the anticipation.'

He gave her a sideways look. 'If you say so,' he replied, but then the corners of his mouth twitched, softening his remark. 'I can't say I particularly enjoy the drive, but at least, thanks to you, I stand a chance of getting there in one piece.' He poured some water on the screen and held out her flask. 'Thanks, that was a lifesaver.'

Peg looked at the dribbles of liquid cutting a trail through the murk. 'Now you're just trying to be polite,' she said. 'But I've got plenty of water – another whole flask full – so please, use what you need. I'm not going to leave until I know that you're sorted and your water jets are unblocked. Otherwise you'll be five minutes down the road, your windscreen will be practically opaque and you'll never be able to clear it because your wiper wash is still frozen. I need to check a couple of things on my phone before I start driving, so take your time.'

She pulled open the car door and climbed inside, leaving him with no choice but to carry on. It was Christmas, after all, season of goodwill to all men...

She watched him for a moment, surreptitiously, while she checked the traffic news. Izzy, the eldest of her two children, and easily the most critical in terms of people's appearance, would have made the comment that he had dressed in the dark. She smiled to herself thinking that, although perhaps not the kindest expression, it was quite appropriate in this case. His blue corduroy trousers ended several inches above his boots, revealing socks which, admittedly, were both green, but which were definitely not from the same pair. His jumper, also blue, was clearly a favourite – bobbly and well worn – but also on back to front. How did you not notice something like that? Wouldn't it feel weird? His scarf, in contrast, looked brand new, and was slung loosely around his shoulders, getting in the way and almost trailing on the ground... Given the rest of his attire, and his direction of travel, she would hazard a guess that the scarf had been a present, either from his son or, more likely, his daughter-in-law, and was being worn today for tactful peace-keeping reasons. She smiled again. He looked as if he was a good soul, a kind soul.

After a few minutes there was a gentle tap on the window and she put down her phone to find him grinning at her. 'I have used nearly all your water, but it did the trick. Really, thanks again, that was such a help.'

She opened the door again to take the flask from him. 'No problem. Like I said, I have another one.' She smiled. 'Well, you never know, and you can't be *too* organised.'

'So it would seem... I—' He broke off as his phone began to trill. 'Sorry, I'd better take that, it's my son...'

She nodded, indicating that he should answer his call. Then, stowing away the empty flask in the boot, she retrieved the Werther's from her bag and pulled open the packet.

'One for the road?' she offered.

He took one, smiling briefly, but his attention was already miles away, the harassed look back on his face.

'Have a safe journey,' she mouthed, almost silently.

He cupped a hand around his handset to muffle his voice. 'Yes, you too.'

A minute later, Peg reversed out of the parking space. The man was still speaking, a hand planted anchor-like on top of his head as he stared into space. She wondered if without it he was scared he might float away.

'Happy Christmas,' she whispered.

2

Peg was well over an hour into her journey by the time the first flashes of brake lights came, a whole line of them stretching into the distance, vivid in the rapidly darkening afternoon. Five minutes ago it had been bright sunshine, but now the sky looked leaden. She frowned. There wasn't any snow forecast – the weather had been one of the things she'd checked when she'd stopped for petrol. Sub-zero temperatures, yes, but dry all the way home. She wriggled in her seat, sitting slightly more upright, and drove slowly on, matching her speed with those of the cars ahead.

She was cautious but not unduly worried. Such was the nature of motorways; it was probably just someone stuck in the outside lane when they shouldn't be. But ten seconds later she had slowed her speed by half. Indicating, she changed lanes, moving across to the slow lane where there was the least amount of traffic. By the time she had completed the manoeuvre, however, she was almost at a standstill, and now all three lanes were filled with cars, bunched up and crawling. It was scary how little time it took for that to happen.

Glancing in her rear-view mirror again, she could see the

spaces behind her dwindle to nothing as more vehicles slowed and pulled up behind. She switched off her music and came to a complete stop. The rear of the car in front was filled with bedding, piled high so that only a slender gap between it and the roof remained. A child's duvet cover decorated in dinosaurs lay uppermost, and although she couldn't see the occupants of the car, it was Christmas Eve the day after tomorrow – it didn't take a genius to work out that they were either going on holiday or would be staying with relatives come their journey's end. She glanced around her, wondering how many other families were in the same situation. The delay wouldn't make that much difference to her, but what about everyone else? She hoped for their sakes they would soon be moving again.

Every car held a different story, had a different destination – hundreds, if not thousands of lives crossing and interconnecting – and it drew her memory back to past journeys, previous Christmases when the children were small. When the drive was filled with cries of 'are we nearly there yet?' and feverish excitement that inevitably led to petty squabbles and bickering. And Julian, who always drove on such occasions, never minded. He never once lost his temper with them, or told them to be quiet, and she was reminded anew that she never understood then how precious those times were, how fleeting they would be. She always thought there'd be more years, the infinite supply that youth imagines, but they had slid by with alarming speed until, suddenly, the children were grown and gone, and then, not nearly enough years later, Julian had gone too. Only he was never coming back.

She examined her thoughts for a moment, wondering fleetingly why those memories had come to her now. But she knew why. She understood only too well how poignant this time of year could be, how every car around her held lives in motion. And lives in motion were subject to change. The smallest thing could deflect them from their original trajectory, sending them spinning, pushing them off course. Sometimes to a better place, but not always.

The cars in the other two lanes were still crawling past, inching their way forward, but it was clear that whatever was holding everyone up was big enough to affect all the traffic, and she shivered. Please God, let there not have been an accident.

Peg had done this journey so many times she knew the route like the back of her hand, but she still had the directions mapped out on her phone. Just like she'd told the man at the petrol station, you could never be too careful. And when she looked at the snaking line of the M5 motorway on her screen, it was red. She moved the map with two fingers, following the red line first one way, and then the other. Already the queue behind her stretched for some distance but in front... She peered closer, frowning. There seemed to be no end to it.

She looked up, alerted by something else, a sound which, as she waited, grew louder. Moments later, her wing mirror filled with flickering blue light as a police car flashed past on the hard shoulder, followed almost immediately by an ambulance. She dropped her head and turned off the car's engine.

It was bitterly cold outside, and now that the engine was no longer running, the warm air from the heating disappeared, too. She could feel the cold air seeping towards her and she shivered. She had taken off her coat at the petrol station – it was too bulky to drive in comfortably and irritated her after a while – but she would be glad of it now. It was clear she might be stuck here for quite some time. She unclipped her seat belt and reached around to fish it from the back seat.

As she did so, a car in the far lane caught her eye. Like the others, it was still inching forward, as if desperate to claim every bit of space available to it. Didn't people realise it would make no difference? She turned back to watch its progress as it moved slowly past her, craning her neck in an attempt to see around the other vehicles. It came to rest two cars ahead of her, still in the outside lane, and although with such limited vision she couldn't be sure, she was fairly certain the driver was the man she had encountered earlier. It was the same colour car, and he was wearing a bright orange scarf over a blue jumper. She couldn't see the curls of messy dark hair which fell across his forehead, but she could imagine they were there. She smiled. What were the chances?

Tussling with her coat in the confined space, she wriggled herself into it, and then sat back with a sigh. She turned her music back on but almost immediately turned it off again. It seemed incongruous now she was no longer moving. And she was peckish, too. Perhaps another Werther's would help. But then again... She glanced at her watch. She'd made herself some sandwiches for the journey and hadn't planned on eating them just yet, but she could have one – that wouldn't hurt, surely? The tinfoil-covered package glinted in teasing fashion from the passenger seat.

An hour later, Peg was bored. Bored, cold and hungry. She tapped her feet in an effort to keep warm and shoved her hands under her armpits even though she had already thrust them into her gloves quite some time ago. It was no good; she couldn't just sit there. Neither the cold, her hunger or the thoughts in her head were going to go away unless she did something about them. The book she was halfway through reading was packed in her bag, and it was only in the boot, she could fetch it in an instant, but the thought of reading irritated her, and she didn't know why. She felt restless, not anxious exactly, but unsettled nonetheless, and the idea which had come to her only moments before was taking up far too much room in her head.

She turned on the car's ignition and flicked the wipers, sending a wash of water over her windscreen. Her view cleared somewhat but, predictably, her situation didn't. It was ridiculous to think that it would. Everyone had turned their engines off now, so even the glowing red dots from people's rear lights had disappeared. Picking up her phone, she navigated to the site she used for road traffic information, closing her eyes briefly as she read the information on the screen. It was official. Their section of the M5 was the site of an 'incident' and they would be subject to several hours' delay while it was closed. She took a deep breath. It was time to find out if she was about to make a complete fool of herself.

Climbing from the car, she pulled open the rear door on her side, collected several things from the back seat and began to thread her way between the rows of cars. She paused a moment, but only to get a better view. She wasn't bothered what people might think of her, she gave up worrying about things like that a long time ago, but she was keen to see if her deductions had been right. Reaching the car in question, she bent a little and tapped on the passenger window. *Okay, Peg, try not to look deranged...*

The face which greeted hers was startled, but, she was pleased to see, flickered with recognition. She'd been right about the orange scarf and blue jumper, and the dark curly hair. The man from the petrol station clearly knew who she was, too. He quickly wound down the window and leaned across to see her better.

'I thought it was you,' she said. 'What are the chances?'

He shook his head, smiling. 'Crazy,' he replied. 'Although right now it does seem as if the entire world is stuck on the motorway. There's been a spillage of some sort, did you know? We could be stuck here hours.'

'Which is why... I've brought these. Mince pies, would you like one?' She lifted the tin she was carrying to show him, not that easy given all that was under her arm. 'I've also got sandwiches, some tea and a bag of crisps... Sorry, I came prepared.'

He leaned across to open the door. 'So I see. Here, let me take them.'

She passed him the tin first before unloading the rest of her packages one by one until she was able to slide into the seat unhindered. She held out her arms to take them back again.

'You're not a serial killer, are you?' she asked. 'I just need to check before I get settled.'

'Would I tell you if I was?' he replied, the arch in his eyebrows registering his amusement.

'Fair point,' she said. 'I'm not one either, just in case you were wondering.' She held out a gloved hand. 'I'm Peg, by the way.'

'Henry,' he replied. 'It's nice to meet you. And this is really very kind of you.'

'I was worried it was an accident,' replied Peg. 'But a spillage doesn't sound so bad, does it? Do you know what it was?'

Henry shook his head. 'Could be anything. It also depends what caused the spillage in the first place. Whether another vehicle was involved.'

'Oh yes... I hadn't thought of that. For some reason I'm envisaging tins of paint, I don't know why. I've got visions of cars dripping in the stuff.'

'I hope it's a nice colour,' said Henry. 'Not just magnolia. Or grey. What *is* the fascination with that at the moment?'

'Farrow & Ball, Breakfast Room Green, nice and calming,' she said.

They smiled at one another. Peg pursed her lips.

'I'm not sure why I'm doing this,' she said. 'I know we've both agreed we're not serial killers but it's probably not very sensible. Despite it being Christmas.'

'Does that make a difference?' he asked.

'It should,' she replied. 'Nothing bad should ever happen at Christmas.' But Peg knew only too well that wasn't the case.

'Nothing bad should ever happen at all, but alas...'

Peg dropped her head to hide her smile. She didn't know anyone who used the word *alas*. She liked it, though. Alas and alack... one of those old expressions which you scarcely heard any more. And both words meaning virtually the same thing, like saying I'm very very sorry, but with a little more charm.

'Yes, sadly, that's not the world we live in, is it?'

He shook his head. 'More's the pity. So how come you did venture forth then?'

She wrinkled her nose. 'In the spirit of honesty I should probably tell you that one, I was bored, and two, I thought you might want something to eat, and possibly drink...'

'On account of me not being very organised?'

'Was I right?'

'I'm starving. But I've been told not to spoil my appetite. My daughter-in-law is cooking dinner for me tonight.'

'Ah...' said Peg knowingly. 'The daughter-in-law... Does she have a name?'

'Sofia. With an "f" instead of a "ph" – that's very important. It's from the Greek and means wisdom, but...' The corners of his lips twitched.

Peg laughed. 'Was that irony I detected?'

Henry slid her a glance. 'I couldn't possibly comment.' He eyed the tin of mince pies. 'May I?'

'Please do. I've got some sandwiches as well. Cheese and beetroot. They taste nice but don't travel all that well. They've gone a bit pink, sorry.' Peg began to open the tinfoil-wrapped packet. 'Which would you rather?'

'I haven't had cheese and beetroot in years. I might... just half, though. Are you sure you don't mind? Isn't this your lunch?'

'Yes, but I've already eaten half a bag of sweets, I'm hardly faint with hunger.'

'In that case, thank you. I'll save the mince pie for dessert.'

'So,' she said, once they were settled and busy eating. 'Your son and daughter-in-law. You're staying with them for Christmas?'

'Hmm. I do so every year. The twenty-second to the twenty-seventh. And not just my son and daughter-in-law, it's her mother too – Blanche.'

'So that would be your son's mother-in-law... sounds like a winning combination for any Christmas gathering.' She raised her eyebrows.

'It's not so bad...' He broke off with a wry glance. 'Actually, sometimes it's awful, but I get to see my son – Adam – and that doesn't happen all that often. And for all that I make rude noises about Sofia, she's a good cook, and... I don't imagine having her mum and father-in-law to stay is her favourite way of spending Christmas either. Blanche can be a little... spiky. She's a good ally at times, when she's in the mood. When she's not, she hardly speaks. Sometimes I think they only invite me so that I can talk to her and they won't have to.'

Peg studied him. 'Do you mean that? Because if you do, that's rather sad.'

Henry stared through the windscreen ahead. 'Do I mean that?' He paused. 'No, not really. But, like a lot of things we often jest about, it has its basis in truth. My son and I have lost something along the way. We were always very close before but now we're like strangers, well-meaning but awkward and uncomfortable in one another's company. But I'm his dad, and it's Christmas, so...' He left the sentence hanging the air.

Peg understood exactly what he was getting at – duty – one of those horrible words which seemed to raise its head far more at certain times of life. These days the tables had turned – no longer did Peg feel it towards her children, but instead they now felt it towards her. And it was a horrible reminder of age, of changing circumstances. It's also one of the main reasons why her children had gone skiing for Christmas, because Duty went hand in hand with Burden, something she'd only recently begun to think about. She thrust her thoughts away, turning them back to what Henry had said.

'So why the change between you and your son? You said you were close *before*. Did something happen to change that?' She checked herself. 'Sorry, it's none of my business.'

Henry picked up a fallen crumb from his lap and absently ferried it to his mouth.

'No, it's fine, no great shakes. I got divorced. And for perhaps the first time in his life, my son was forced to look at his parents as individuals, as people rather than simply a presence in his life. There was also an element of taking sides, something his mother was keen to see happen, which, given that she now lives in Canada, is somewhat ironic. But my son looked, and I don't think he was overly taken with what he saw.'

Peg winced at his words. 'That sounds rather harsh.'

Henry shrugged. 'The truth often is. I *do* think he's been listening to his mother rather more than is good for him, and before you ask, no, I'm not bitter at all...' He broke off, giving a reticent smile. 'But since the divorce it's as if he goes out of his way to prove that he's different from me, so what does that tell you? It's as if he's suddenly lost the ability to see me as he always has, and instead has turned me into a stereotype who bears no relation to me at all.'

'Does that happen often?' asked Peg, made curious by his words. 'The stereotype thing, I mean. Do you think people treat you differently now you're divorced?'

'All the time,' replied Henry, not even taking a moment to think. 'They make assumptions, too. My friends all assumed my wife had an affair, and her friends all assumed it was me.'

'And did you? Or she?'

'Nope. On both counts. It might have been easier if we had. People seem to prefer it when they can pick someone to blame.'

Peg nodded. 'It's odd, the assumptions people make. I almost lost my best friend after my husband died. It was the strangest thing – as if I'd changed my personality overnight. I agree some things *are* different – how could I not be affected by what happened? But I'm fundamentally the same. I didn't chase after her husband when mine was alive, and I certainly didn't want to after he'd died. That's what she thought, though – that I'd suddenly become some kind of predatory merry widow. It really hurt when I worked out the reason why she had been keeping her distance, more so because it was then that I needed her friendship more than ever.'

'Hmm. It's nonsensical, but I think we're all programmed to see stereotypes to some degree. Women think divorced men are all going through a midlife crisis, are weak, fairly pathetic, oh and chauvinistic, lazy, self-obsessed... whereas men think we're living the good life.'

It wasn't something Peg had given much thought to in the past, but she could see how easily she could assume such things, possibly already did. 'And so by extension, a divorced woman is either a man-hating feminist or a poor downtrodden victim depending on your persuasion.' She frowned. 'That's appalling.'

'That's human nature,' Henry replied, shrugging. 'And my son has definitely placed me firmly in the box labelled weak and fairly pathetic, and so in an attempt to ensure that he turns out nothing like me, has married a woman who expects nothing less than perfection and now lives his life in a permanently conflicted state.' Henry's sigh echoed around the car. 'It's also, I suspect, down to the fact that I don't altogether approve of his choice of partner. Not that I say anything, of course, but I reckon he's worked it out. He thinks I should have no opinion because my own marriage failed, so what do I know? Whereas I think I'm blessed with that awful affliction parents have and should never let their children see...'

'Wisdom?'

'Not sure it's that in my case. Simply that I've had a lot more years on the planet than he has and time has given me a broader scope of experience. It's also that from a distance I can see things that, up close, are hidden from my son...'

Peg made an apologetic face. 'We're complicated creatures, aren't we?'

Henry smiled. 'That we are. If you don't mind me asking, how long have you been on your own?'

'Four years...' She swallowed. 'Almost to the day. My husband died on the twenty-sixth of December, Boxing Day.'

3
———

Henry could kick himself. What a stupid thing to have asked. What did it matter when her husband died? The fact that he had was bad enough. And now here they were, only days from the anniversary. Henry hadn't had a hugely fun time of things when he and Linda divorced, but at least she was still alive. 'I'm sorry... I shouldn't have asked.'

Peg smiled. 'And yet it's *me* who's embarrassed *you*. I didn't need to offer the exact date he died, so it's me who should apologise. You wouldn't feel like you do if I'd said he died in August.'

A poignant hush settled in the small space. Peg scratched her head and Henry risked a look at her. He hoped he hadn't upset her. She was nice. She was the first person he'd spoken to in a long while who seemed to understand.

'Sorry...' she said, crinkling up the tinfoil from the sandwiches. 'Forgive the pun, but death is such a conversation killer, isn't it? Shall we have a mince pie?' She paused a moment. 'It's never an easy subject to talk about, but doing so with a perfect stranger who you're never going to see again feels easier somehow.'

'I guess it does,' agreed Henry. It certainly explained the

urge he had to keep on talking. 'Perhaps it's because you can say all the things you want to knowing that you won't have to face that person again. It's not like when you talk to family, and whatever you say is forever going to occupy a huge space between you, like the proverbial elephant in the room.'

Peg cranked the lid off the tin which was sitting on her lap, filling the car with the most incredible smell. 'Would you like one?'

The thought of buttery pastry was too much for Henry's willpower and he readily helped himself.

'How long do you think we're going to be stuck here?' Peg asked.

'Hard to tell. I guess much depends on what was spilled – if it can be picked up, or whether they're currently hosing Farrow & Ball's Breakfast Room Green off the motorway.'

Peg laughed, a deepish chuckle. 'Let's hope it's the first option. Although maybe now is a good time to mention that even if we manage to eat all the mince pies, I have a stash of sausage rolls in the boot too. Plus, a ginger and date cake, some cheese biscuits, a yule log and a Christmas cake.'

'That's taking being prepared to the extreme.'

'I've spent the last couple of days baking for my aunt. She's in her early eighties and although she's very fit, an arthritic hip means she can't stand for any length of time. It's put an end to her days of cake making, sadly, so when I visit I make all her favourites and while I'm at it, an extra batch for me.'

Henry nodded, thinking. 'So... just out of interest, how long do we have to stay here before we move on to the sausage rolls?'

'I can get them now, if you like.'

'No... honestly.' Henry held out an arm to stop her from getting out of the car. 'I was just kidding.' He peered at the tin of mince pies. 'Although these *are* incredibly good.'

Peg indicated that he should take another. 'My daughter has been known to eat five of these in one sitting, so I've made rather more than I can eat on my own. I'm glad you're taking them off my hands.'

'Now *you're* just being polite,' said Henry. 'But thank you for attempting to make me feel less greedy than I am.' He bit into the pie, showering his lap with flakes of pastry and icing sugar.

'So, tell me about your Christmas,' said Peg. 'About your son and Sofia with an "f" and no "ph". What's it like?'

'Drawn-out, overly complicated and like something out of *Homes and Gardens.*'

Peg suppressed a snort of amusement. 'Go on...'

'I'm serious. I arrive today so I can acclimatise, because Christmas is like a military operation – a four-day affair which starts tomorrow with a posh lunch at the golf club, then a special breakfast on Christmas Eve and a party in the evening, and finishes about 9 p.m. on Boxing Day after a lavish brunch with a few special friends and a trip to the theatre to see *The Nutcracker*. There's so much food, and ritual... themed decorations and enforced activity.'

Peg's mouth dropped open. 'Wow... and you do that every year?'

'Uh-huh... with a few extra embellishments here and there.'

'Just wait until they have kids, that'll put an end to it.'

'Oh, I don't think it will. Sofia will have them thoroughly trained, like the Von Trapp children in *The Sound of Music...*' He trailed off, running a hand through his hair. 'I'm being cruel,' he added. 'Which isn't fair. Sofia's heart's in the right place and she works incredibly hard to make sure everything is perfect, but I think she's labouring under a false expectation of what that is. It's not really her fault either; she's of the generation who are glued to social media and brainwashed into believing all they see. But I wish she understood that I go to spend time with them because they're my family. I don't care whether the napkins match the bows on the backs of the chairs.'

'Bows?' mouthed Peg, eyes widening. 'That's... hardcore.' She winced. 'Would now be a good time to tell you that I used to be an editor for exactly the type of magazine which preaches the Christmas perfection message? It's a myth which exerts a huge amount of pressure on people, needlessly in my opinion. Leads to a lot of heartache, too. Especially when people have little enough money as it is and can't afford what are laughingly referred to as "must haves".' She took a deep breath. 'Thankfully I got out of that game while I still had my sanity intact. Now I'm retired, I still write for a magazine, but only occasionally and mostly about gardening and nature.'

'So, I'm guessing Christmas is a very different affair in your house then?'

'Well, for starters, there'll just be me this year, so yes, you could say that. My children have always loved skiing, something they shared with their dad, and as holidays together are few and far between, I insisted they go off to have some fun. Besides, I'm not a fan of hurtling down a mountainside and having bits of me snap off, so it's a win-win situation – it prevents them from worrying about me being on my own, while also ensuring I get to have a lovely quiet time of things. So, tomorrow I shall go into the woods behind my house and gather armfuls of holly to decorate the house, then I'll make some mulled wine for me and a special suet cake for the birds, before walking down the lane on Christmas Eve to enjoy the carol service at the local church. I'm not at all religious, but the vicar doesn't mind in the slightest. He says any place gets a bit holy if it's left on its own to think for a while and I agree with that. You can feel it, and that's what I like. That, and a good sing-song.'

'It sounds like heaven... no pun intended.'

'It's not for everyone, but I enjoy it.'

'How many children do you have?' asked Henry.

'Two,' replied Peg. 'Both girls.' She was about to elaborate when a loud shrilling filled the car.

'Sorry,' said Henry, taking up his phone. 'Hold that thought a moment.'

It was Adam, again. He knew it would be.

'Hi... yes, still here,' he said into the phone. 'We haven't moved in almost two hours now. A container load of something has spilled further up the motorway.' He glanced at Peg, smiling as he listened to his son's reply.

'Well it can't be helped,' he said. 'I guess I'll get there when I arrive. And it could be worse. It could have been an accident.' He nodded. 'Yes, I'll let you know what time I think I'll be arriving just as soon as it looks like we're on the move again.'

He wondered whether Peg could hear what his son was saying. He hoped not. 'I know it's inconvenient,' he replied to Adam's next comment. 'And I'm sorry. I also know Sofia's gone to a lot of trouble, but if I'm not there by dinnertime, eat without me, don't let anything go to waste.' He paused, listening. 'I don't mind, beans on toast will suit me... well, then I'll have whatever Sofia *does* think is suitable. I really don't mind, Adam.' He picked a flake of pastry off his trouser leg and put it in his mouth. 'Yes, I'll ring again when we get going. Oh, and I'm absolutely fine, by the way. It's no bother at all being stuck in a traffic jam which is going to double the length of my journey.'

Henry couldn't help himself. This was... he counted them up in his head: the fifth phone call he'd had from Adam today, none of them for any reason other than to fuss. To convey some thought or other that Sofia had had – most of them concern that he was going to disrupt all her plans. Not once had any thought been given to how he was faring. Peg's quiet yet joyful Christmas was beginning to sound more and more idyllic, and he suddenly found himself longing for his life to be different. He was enjoying sitting in a car with a total stranger, eating cheese and beetroot sandwiches and mince pies. Part of him would like to tell Adam all about her, but he knew full well what his son would say and he didn't want to hear it. So he wouldn't be sharing any details of what he was doing right now. The hold-up might only last a couple of hours, and if they were going to be the best few hours of his day, then Henry wanted them all for himself.

'Listen, I'll ring as soon as I can, okay? As soon as I have any news.' He ended the call, a little embarrassed by his snarky comment. 'Sorry about that,' he said to Peg. 'You were saying, you've got two children.'

'I have. Izzy, my eldest, and Phoebe, who's younger by just over a year.'

'And are you close?'

'Emotionally or geographically?'

Henry smiled. 'Whichever.'

'Well, geographically Izzy is the furthest away from me now, but it's varied over the years. University took them both away from home first, then their jobs did, but they're more settled now, though neither of them has a partner. They'd hate to admit it, but they're too much like me – far too independent for their own good. We are close though, emotionally speaking, and I think losing their dad has brought us even closer. I also think it's the first time they've begun to think about me in terms of my age, and I'm not sure I like that.'

'You're worried about becoming a burden?'

She smirked. 'Maybe not just yet. I think, well, hope I've got a fair few years left in me before I get to being that but, ultimately, yes. My mother used to say she didn't want to be a burden and I invariably told her not to be silly. Now I understand just how she felt because, whichever way you want to look at it, I guess my children always thought their dad would be around and that we would be there to look after one another. Now that onus has fallen on them.'

'One which I'm sure they're happy to take on. I might be making assumptions here but it doesn't sound as if you visit your aunt every year out of duty – you do it because you want to.'

Peg nodded. 'I don't know what I'd have done without Mim over the years. My dad isn't around and my mum died in my early twenties so for a long time, Mim was all I had.'

'There you go then. And I'm sure your children feel the same way.'

'Yeah, I know,' said Peg lightly. 'But Julian's death changed the dynamics within the family, and I don't think any of us realised that would be something we'd have to navigate. Grief, yes, but... You must feel it too, in your situation?'

Henry licked his lip, chasing away a last crumb of pastry. 'I have wondered in the past whether the reason Sofia tries so hard is because I'm on my own, because Adam's mum isn't around now and she feels she has to make up for that in some way.'

'We're back to that elusive perfect family Christmas again, aren't we?' Peg smiled. 'But I think you're right. Have you ever tried explaining that to her?'

'Not in so many words... She's not someone I find it easy to talk to, and I don't think we could have that kind of conversation.' He took a deep breath, conscious not to let it out in one sighing rush. 'And I'm worried that if I do, I'll ruin Christmas, and my son will never speak to me again.' He stopped, fingering the edge of his scarf. 'Sorry, I'm being dramatic.'

'I don't think you are. These are the things which worry us, aren't they? And Christmas has become a time of such expectation, it heightens those feelings.'

'It must be especially hard for you at this time of year.'

'The first anniversary certainly was. My girls went skiing because being at home was too much for them. They wanted me to go along, but conversely I didn't want to be anywhere *but* at home. I knew it would be hard, but I felt as if I'd be abandoning Julian if I went anywhere else. So that's what we did.

And it was fine. I mean, that first year we just got through it as best we could but, since then, it has got easier.

She gave a small smile. 'I actually love Christmas. And I love *my* Christmas. There's peace in solitude, in being alone, and I found out to my cost very early on that wishing for things to be different doesn't make them so. So you reconcile yourself to your present. You invite Grief in because she's a part of your life now and isn't going anywhere, so you might as well make her welcome. Besides, she's a little like me – she's mellowed a bit with age, and although she sometimes lies in wait for me around a corner, jumping out at me when I least expect it, for the most part we get on well. We even have a laugh together sometimes, thinking about the past.'

Henry thought about Linda. About all the complicated thoughts he still held towards her. 'I think that's wonderful.'

Peg smirked. 'Oh, I've had my fair share of down days, too. Days which were filled with anger – anger at a world I wanted to burn to the ground for having the audacity to exist, *carrying on* when I couldn't begin to imagine how that was possible – anger at Julian for dying and leaving me on my own, which wasn't at all what we'd agreed – and anger at whatever entity it was that I'd been praying to, who rudely told me I couldn't have what I wanted. I railed at the injustice of it all. The unfairness. But after a time even that dissipated, and I realised that even though Julian had died, it simply wasn't my time. I was alive and I had better get on and live. We never know what's around the corner, do we?' She pointed out of the window. 'Or what's up ahead... Is it snowing?'

Henry peered up at the sky. 'No, it can't be. The sun's coming out again, look.' But even as he spoke tiny specks of white began to mill about, like petals drifting on a breeze. 'It's okay though, it's fairy-tale snow. Not the great big clumpy stuff which settles in minutes and makes travelling a nightmare. We'll be fine...' He broke off to indicate the line of cars ahead of them. 'And hopefully this lot will clear soon.' Henry smiled, although he wasn't altogether sure he wanted it to. He hadn't talked to Peg for nearly long enough yet, plus, by the time he arrived at his son's house, the damage would already have been done. His late arrival would no doubt set the mood for the entirety of the Christmas festivities, and if it weren't for the fact that he'd get to see his son, he'd consider turning around and going back home... provided they ever got moving, of course.

'Have you got much further to go?' he asked.

Peg shook her head. 'Only another hour or so. Straight down the M5 and then turn off towards Stow-on-the-Wold.'

'Yeah, me too. Although I turn off a bit sooner, towards Evesham. Where are you headed?'

'Lower Steeping. Do you know it?'

Henry stared at her in surprise. 'I used to go to school there. So your little church where you sing carols now is where I used to sing them in my youth. My family left the village before I started secondary school and moved up north to Stoke. It's where I still live now. But my son lives in Bishop's Coombe.'

Now it was Peg's turn to look astonished. 'That's only about fifteen minutes away from me. What are the chances?'

'I'd say about the same as bumping into someone at a petrol station and then meeting them again seventy miles further on down the road.'

Peg shook her head. 'I don't believe it. But then again, it is Christmas... If this were a film, one of us would be saying something about a Christmas miracle.'

Henry laughed. 'Christmas coincidence doesn't have quite the same ring to it, does it?' He was about to add that he wasn't a ruggedly handsome hero either, when he caught something out of the corner of his eye. He peered through the windscreen. 'Hang on... isn't that...?'

Peg leaned forward too. 'What did you see?'

'A light, I think. Way off, but...'

'It is! It's a brake light. Does that mean...?' She smiled into his face. 'I think we might be moving.' But then her mouth opened into a round 'O' of surprise. 'I'd better get back to my car or I'll be in trouble.'

He began to help her, putting the lid back on the tin of mince pies, and gathering up a fallen glove while still keeping a watch on the traffic in front. The cars directly ahead were all starting their engines now, and Peg gave him a panicked look, then laughed.

'Shit, I'm all of a dither now... Listen, have a safe journey and a good Christmas and...' She rolled up the top of the bag of crisps and shoved them under her arm, then handed them back to Henry. 'You have them... I'll only drop them.' She clambered from the car, pulling her car keys from her pocket. 'It's been lovely meeting you!'

'Yes, you too, Peg. And thank you, for the food, the chat, for everything...' He was gabbling. There was so much he wanted to say. 'And have a lovely Christmas!'

Her face was split by a wide smile as she ducked back down to look at him again. 'Yes, you too. Oh, I hope so and... just... look, if it all gets too much—'

'Yes?'

Peg was backing away. 'My house is the one at the far end of the green and—'

Henry leaned sideways, craning his neck to see her as she began to run back along the line of cars.

'Just c—' Her voice was snatched away by the sound of engines roaring into life.

'What?' he shouted. 'Just *what?*'

But Peg was gone.

4

Henry glanced at his watch again. He was five minutes away from Adam's house and just in time for dinner. Maybe things would be okay. Maybe they would... He was about to tell himself that things would be different this year, but they wouldn't be. The more pressing problem was that something *had* changed, though. Somewhere along the M5, and he couldn't say exactly where, something had changed, within *him*. And he needed to think. He needed some space to work out what it was, and what he was feeling, because the minute his son opened the door, any time and space he had available to him would disappear, swept up in a flurry of greetings and arrangements and...

He'd spent the last leg of his journey going back over his conversation with Peg. Thinking about all the things she'd said, and all the things he'd said. Realising that, as he drove, he was smiling. That he could still see her face, and hear her voice. That her black hair, shot through with silver, was in plaits, for goodness' sake, and he'd meant to say how much they suited her. How her mince pies were the best he'd ever eaten... But most of all he'd thought about what she'd said as she was leaving. What he couldn't be sure about, but what he hoped might have been some sort of an invitation. She'd told him where her house was, but what was the rest of it? *Just c—* was all he'd heard. Was she telling him to come over? And if it wasn't that, what else could it have been?

He swiped a hand over his face and slowed the car, wondering whether he should pull over for a moment, but the clock was ticking. And the one thing he absolutely could not be, was late. And so Henry drove the last couple of miles trying to thrust thoughts of Peg from his head and turn them instead to the days ahead of him. To all the things he should say, and do, to ensure that everything would go according to plan. To ensure that his son wouldn't think any less of him, and that another invitation to visit might be forthcoming. Christmas might be something of a trial, but the alternative – not seeing his son at all – would be infinitely worse.

The front door opened before Henry had even finished getting out of the car, and any hopes he had that Adam had rushed out to greet his father out of pure affection were dashed the moment Henry received his perfunctory hug.

'Great, you made good time in the end then?' Adam didn't wait for a reply. 'Let me grab your bag. Is it in the boot? Dinner's just about to be served.'

Henry nodded, unmoving, and feeling a little dazed. Even without the milieu of thoughts about Peg swirling around his head, he was still tired from his journey – a journey which had gone from two and a half hours to just over five, and all of them cooped up in the car. He couldn't work out if his legs felt leaden or like jelly. He fetched his coat from the back seat, locked the car and slowly followed Adam up the path.

'Let me take your jacket, Dad,' said Adam once they were inside. 'You know where we are, just through here.' He pointed towards the vast kitchen which led into the dining room.

Henry licked his lips. The heat was stifling. 'I could do with a quick pit stop, if that's okay? Long drive... I'm desperate for the loo.'

'Right... yes, of course. Well, you know where that is, too. I'll just go and...' He didn't finish the sentence, leaving Henry alone.

With a resigned smile, Henry pulled open the door to the cloakroom and stepped inside. He wouldn't have been at all surprised to find Adam waiting for him, ready to whisk him away once he'd finished washing his hands, but, mercifully, the hallway was empty, save for the array of coats and shoes stored neatly in a purpose-built unit, and copious decorations, of course.

A huge swathe of greenery and baubles snaked its way up the banister. A wreath matching the one on the front door hung on the inner doorway to the living room and a small, twinkling tree stood on an oak console table with a tasteful tableau of frosted pine cones and berries beside it. His bag, he noted, stood on the floor at the foot of the staircase.

Straightening his jumper and hanging up his scarf, Henry rolled his shoulders around and stretched out his neck before walking through to the kitchen, the largest smile he could muster fixed on his face.

'Sofia... hello.' She turned from the island unit where she was standing arranging vegetables in a serving dish. He walked forward to greet her, kissing her on the cheek as was customary. 'Merry Christmas.'

'Merry Christmas,' she replied, turning back. 'Adam, could you take these to the table, please?' She handed her husband the dish. 'Come and sit down, Henry, the food's ready.'

'Good job the traffic got moving when it did then,' he said.

Adam stepped forward. 'What was it in the end?' he asked. 'Did you find out what caused the stoppage?'

Henry was about to make a joke about it being Breakfast Room Green, when he stopped himself. They wouldn't understand and he didn't want to explain. He shook his head. 'No idea. There didn't seem to be anything obvious when I drove on. Just one of those things, I guess.'

Adam took the dish of vegetables.

'I'm just thankful it wasn't an accident,' added Henry. 'That doesn't bear thinking about, especially at this time of year. Losing a few hours is nothing compared with losing a life, is it?'

Sofia looked at Adam. 'No, of course not. Come and sit down before the food gets cold.'

Henry stared at his heaped plate. Under other circumstances it would have looked lovely, but Henry felt rushed and ill prepared to eat a large meal only minutes after stepping from his car. Plus, perhaps foolishly, he had taken the edge off his appetite by sharing Peg's sandwiches and eating several of her mince pies – both things he was perfectly within his rights to do. A flicker of irritation soured his stomach.

'You really shouldn't have gone to so much trouble, Sofia,' he said. 'This looks lovely, but you must have been cooking for hours.'

'Nonsense. I know how much you enjoyed the poussin last year,' she replied. 'And I'm not having you come all this way with just beans on toast to greet you at the other end. Besides, Adam and I always eat a proper dinner.'

Henry nodded and picked up his knife and fork. 'Well, thank you. It looks wonderful.' He cut up a small amount of meat and popped it in his mouth. The mushroom sauce was incredibly rich; laden with wine and heavy with cream. 'Mmm, tastes it, too.' He nodded. 'You both look well.'

'Tell him about your promotion,' said Sofia, smiling at her husband.

And just like that, all mention of his journey was over. However much he was proud of his son, he didn't particularly want to listen to his news just now. What he wanted to do was tell them about Peg, about her husband, and what the festive season meant for her. How hard it must be, and weren't he and Adam and Sofia lucky to be alive and healthy and together and... But he wouldn't tell them any of those things, so he just smiled, told Adam it was wonderful news and took another mouthful of food.

'Of course, it isn't just the money,' said Sofia a few minutes later. 'Although it's absolutely what Adam deserves. It's the recognition of how hard he works. Plus, it'll mean a lot less time in the classroom, wasting hours dealing with bad behaviour and sorting out stupid squabbles.'

Henry frowned. 'But I always thought you enjoyed the classroom?' he said. 'Didn't you say it was why you went into teaching in the first place, not to push around bits of paper?'

'Yes, but ideology will only get you so far,' replied Adam. 'And that was when I was fresh from training, and far too naive. Teaching isn't like it was when you started, Dad. Things are different now, and whether you agree with it or not, paperwork is a massive part of the job. Exam results, league tables...'

'I'm *still* teaching,' replied Henry mildly. 'I understand all that.'

'You lecture, Dad, it's very different. Schools are all about performance, and taking on the role of Head of Humanities now, as well as English, will mean I get to really shape the curriculum, to correct all the strategies that have been holding us back and put new ones in place. I'll be helping to take the school to the next level, and in terms of my career that can only be a good thing.'

Henry sliced a green bean in half, wondering how to phrase what he wanted to say. Or, rather, how to hold back what he wanted to say and still appear supportive.

'Well, that all sounds very exciting. Well done.'

'You could be a little more enthusiastic.' Adam was staring at him, a challenging look on his face. It was a look which Henry was beginning to see more and more these days.

'No, I'm really happy for you,' he replied, determined not to bite. 'But I'm also very tired. It's been a long, slow journey over and your old man's not as young as he used to be. As long as *you're* happy, I'm more than pleased. It's a great position to attain.'

'Of course I'm happy, why wouldn't I be?'

Henry deliberately filled his mouth with food so he couldn't reply, instead giving a nod of acknowledgement.

'Plus...' said Sofia. 'You remember our friends from Cheltenham?'

'The ones who come to the theatre on Boxing Day?'

She nodded. 'They've not long secured a villa in Spain on a new development and there are a couple of plots left, apparently. We think we might take a look after Christmas. I quite fancy being able to jet off over there whenever we want to.'

Henry stole a look at her as he lifted his wine glass. She was positively glowing. 'Well, let's drink to that then,' he said, raising a toast to them both. 'Sounds wonderful.'

'It's a little better than two weeks trudging around a rain-sodden campsite, anyway,' added Sofia, smiling sweetly.

Now that hurt. Those were Adam's childhood holidays, not hers. Holidays which Adam had always seemed to enjoy, which they had all enjoyed. Henry sipped his drink and forced in another mouthful of food. 'And how about you, Sofia? How's life in the world of interior design?'

The poussin was followed by a plum tarte tatin, and by the time the meal was finished, Henry was feeling nauseous. The food was too heavy and the heat in the room unbearable. And it wasn't even seven o'clock yet – there were hours to go before he could retire to his room. He found himself wishing that Adam had a dog so that he might offer to take it for a walk. Linda had got custody of theirs, and he missed Meg dreadfully. Her gentle, undemanding presence and her silken ears and coat so soothing in times of stress. It wasn't just that though; the thought of cold, dark and quiet streets was suddenly rather appealing.

'We're having a few neighbours over in an hour or so,' said Adam, as they moved from the dining room into the living room. 'Not for long, just for a couple of drinks and a few nibbles. We thought having a party on Christmas Eve might be a bit much for Blanche this year, so we're having our usual get-together tonight instead.' He lowered his voice. 'Between you and me, she's struggling a little with her hearing. And then tomorrow, there's our annual lunch at the golf club. I'm not sure Blanche will want to come to that either, but you're invited, obviously. And if you don't fancy it, I'm sure Blanche will be glad of the company.'

Henry sank onto the sofa which, out of the two in the room, was slightly further away from the roaring log burner. 'Oh, right, that sounds lovely.' He cleared his throat. 'Could I possibly have a glass of water?'

5

23 DECEMBER

Peg didn't think she'd ever seen such perfect weather for Christmas. Clear skies overnight had meant the silvery coating of ice from the day before had remained, but an early sun and slight rise in temperature had brought a warming glow to the morning. Water droplets had begun to form on the ends of branches and the day positively sparkled. And, out here in the woods behind her house, all was still.

She breathed in the cool, clear air, relishing the verdant smell of the undergrowth which would follow her home, clinging to her coat and hair. It was just one of the wonderful aromas which she loved at this time of year, like cinnamon and oranges, cloves, the spicy smoke from her log fire and fresh pine from her tree. Even the scent of her old copy of *A Christmas Carol* which she read every year had its place in her memories of the season.

With the rest of the day stretching ahead of her, Peg took her time, enjoying the feeling of the air on her skin and the physicality of walking, so different from the day before when she'd been confined to the car for so long. Her encounter with Henry was still on her mind, too.

There were so many things she should have asked him. She felt as if she'd done all the talking and none of the listening, but Henry had been so easy to chat to, that was the thing. It was such a rarity for her these days. At social events she mostly found herself making polite but awkward conversation with people she had no desire to know any better. That was one of the benefits of getting older, she supposed – that you knew your own mind, and could spot instantly the people you'd make a connection with. But she didn't even know what Henry did for a living. Whether he was retired or still working. What his life was like back home. She knew the type of Christmas he had with his son and daughter-in-law wasn't much to his liking, but what was?

She took a pair of secateurs from her pocket and snipped at a bough of holly. It was pointless thinking about it now. She'd had her chance and... She stopped, staring at the greenery in her hand. A chance at what, exactly? The Christmas miracle they had joked about? She shook her head, annoyed with herself. On the motorway it had seemed a plausible thing to say, but here in the woods, miles away from where they'd been, it felt ridiculous.

Twenty minutes later, with her arms full of everything she needed to decorate the house, she made her way slowly back home. Julian had bought this patch of woodland over fifteen years ago now, and there wasn't a day when she didn't congratulate her husband for having such a sound idea. The wood had originally belonged to the estate which bordered it, but when it had come up for sale, Julian had jumped at the chance to buy it. Peg had spent so many hours walking there, or drawing the plants, that he reckoned she should have it as her own, and even though it was Julian who technically owned it, it had become known locally as Peg's Wood. It was one of the reasons why she swore she would never leave her cottage. With the children gone, it was too big for her really, but even after Julian had died and its memory-filled corners had seemed almost too much to bear, she told herself she would only regret it if she moved. And time had proved her right. Now those same echoes of the past were a source of comfort, not pain.

Opening the back door, she waggled her feet until her wellies dropped off and, kicking them unceremoniously against the wall, she padded across the floor to pile her greenery onto the table. Doubling back, she removed the thick gloves she had worn to protect her hands from the holly prickles and shrugged off her coat, hanging everything on a series of hooks which were mounted beside the door. Rolo was right where she'd left him, curled into his basket beside the stove. He opened a sleepy eye as she passed, but seeing no food was in the offing, let it close, stretching himself into an impossible position as only cats could. It might not be time for lunch yet, but with her mind very firmly on the cup of tea she was about to make, the ringing of her phone took Peg completely by surprise. She slipped it from her pocket as she returned to the table.

'Mim... I wasn't expecting to hear from you today, is everything okay?' She frowned as something rumbled in the background.

'No, I'm cross.'

'Oh...?' She wedged the phone against her shoulder and carried the kettle to the sink. 'And why's that then?'

'It's this blasted wrist of mine, and it's Christmas, for goodness' sake. It's most inconvenient.' Peg nodded, filling the kettle with water. Her aunt didn't usually complain about her aches and pains though. Peg never usually found out she'd been having problems until long after the event.

'Is it hurting? I know you don't like taking painkillers, but a couple of paracetamol every now and again won't harm you.' She paused, readying her response for when her aunt argued like she usually did whenever medicine was mentioned.

'Mim... are you still there?' Alarmingly, it sounded like there were voices in the background. 'Mim?'

'Yes, I'm here, dear. Hang on a minute while I talk to this nice young man.'

'What nice young man? Mim...? What's going on? Who have you got with you?' All kinds of scenarios began to play in Peg's mind. Her aunt was usually very careful when callers came to the door, and if it was someone she didn't know, they got very short shrift. There was a muffled noise and what sounded like a radio in the background, full of static like the kind the police used...

'Mim?' Peg put down the kettle and slid the phone into her hand.

'Hello, is this Peg?'

'It is. Who's this?'

'My name's Joel and I'm a paramedic with the Staffordshire ambulance service. I'm with Miriam. She's your aunt, I believe?'

Peg's stomach dropped away in shock. 'She is, yes... Is everything okay?'

'Your aunt's taken a bit of a tumble and...' Peg could hear Mim in the background telling him what to say. 'She's told me to tell you she's fine. And she is... although in a degree of pain which we've given her something for. She'll have to be taken to hospital, though, I'm afraid. We're fairly certain she's broken her wrist and, given her age, they'll want to give her a quick check over as well. But the hospital will be able to confirm that, and—' He broke off, Mim's voice clear behind him. Despite the circumstances, Peg couldn't help but smile a little as her aunt demanded the phone back.

'You're not to worry, Peg. I'm going to be perfectly all right. We're just waiting for Dot next door to get me some things together – you know, in case I have to stay in. I'm not having anyone I don't know rifling through my underwear.'

'Good, I'm glad she's with you, but listen, tell Dot not to

worry about packing stuff for you.' She had visions of Mim's neighbour filling a bag for her as if she were going on holiday. 'I'm not sure they *will* keep you in, and if you do need anything from home, I can sort that out later. The most important thing is that you do what the paramedic says and get off to hospital, okay? I'll see you soon.'

'No, Peg. That's why I'm ringing. You're not to come up, because it's Christmas and you're too far away. I shall be perfectly all right and—'

'And you're my only aunt. There's no way I'm letting you go back to your house on your own. You need someone with you, and don't argue because I know Dot is going away tomorrow to stay with relatives until after Christmas. Can you put Joel back on, please?' There was a momentary pause. 'Joel, hi, yes, you'll have to be firm with her, she can be quite stubborn when she wants to be. And tell her neighbour not to worry about what she might need, I can sort all that out later if necessary. I'm going to leave now, but I'm over two hours away. Can you just give my aunt my love and tell her I'll see her soon. No, I won't speak to her, you'll never get going if I do... thanks so much. Bye then.'

By the time the call ended, Peg was already mentally running through what she might need to take with her. And fifteen minutes later, she was ready to go. She'd even checked her route to see if there were any hold-ups – she didn't want a repeat of the day before, but it was also Christmas Eve tomorrow, and the roads would be mayhem. She snatched up the tin of mince pies from the side, permitting herself a small smile as she remembered sharing them with her miracle man. She tutted. She must stop calling him that. Leaving the greenery from the woods still heaped on the table, she closed the back door behind her.

Judith's car was thankfully still in her drive, and Peg's knock at her door was answered almost immediately. She threw the door wide and stepped back to let Peg in.

'Sorry, Judith, I'm not stopping...' She held up a box of Heroes. 'I'm really sorry... These are to say thank you for looking after Rolo while I was up at Mim's...' She pulled a face. 'And also in down payment... I've just had a call to say that she's had a fall and they think she's broken her wrist. I've got to go back.'

Judith pushed the box of chocolates away and then pulled her friend into a hug. 'Don't be silly, I don't need these and of course you must go. Don't worry about Rolo, or the house, I'll sort them.' She pulled back, searching Peg's face for clues as to how she was feeling. 'You okay?'

Peg nodded. 'You know Mim, she's as stubborn as they come, but this is the second fall she's had now, and that's a worry...' She held up her hands helplessly. Judith knew how anxious she would be.

'I know, but you can worry about that later. For now, just take it easy. You've a long drive ahead of you, but there's no need to hurtle up there, she'll be looked after until you arrive.'

'I know.' Peg nodded again. 'Thank you, Judith, so much. I don't know what I'd do—'

'We both know you'd do the same for me if ever it was needed, so go on, go, and drive carefully.'

Relief washed over Peg. Judith had been a good friend for so many years. She didn't know what she'd do without her. She pushed the box of chocolates back into her hands.

'I will, thank you. Oh, and Happy Christmas, Judith.'

Perversely, when it was driving on the motorway which Peg was worried about, it was only when she turned off it that her anxiety levels rose. Once Peg was back on a single carriageway, with traffic moving both ways, she felt as if she was swimming upstream, fighting against the tide of traffic. The road wasn't even that busy, but she couldn't shake the feeling that she was struggling to get to a destination that would forever be just out of reach.

She knew that Mim was in relative good health for her age, and that a broken wrist wasn't all that serious, even for someone in their eighties, but she was only too aware of the date. If anything happened to Mim, she wasn't sure she would be able to bear it.

And what made it worse was that, when she finally arrived at the hospital, Mim hadn't even been seen and was sitting in A&E, hunched and clearly in pain. The nurse was sympathetic and resolute that the doctor would get to Mim as soon as possible, but there was nothing more she could do. All Peg could do was nod and smile; there were clearly a lot of other people unlucky enough to be in the same situation.

She made her way back to the waiting room and tried not to think about Christmas four years ago. Tired posters were pinned to the walls and lacklustre decorations swayed gently against the heating ducts. It was totally devoid of charm, and even though understandable, it made the poignancy of the date even harder to bear. With a sigh, Peg sat down, took hold of Mim's good hand and resigned herself to being patient.

6

All hope of a quiet cup of tea went out of the window as soon as Henry entered the kitchen. He'd deliberately risen earlier than usual, thinking that Adam and Sofia's sunny conservatory would make for a peaceful spot to start the day, but a camera tripod of all things stood in the centre of the room, and Sofia was bustling – something which experience had taught him he needed to avoid at all costs. He was about to slink back upstairs when Sofia hailed him from across the room.

'Morning, Henry. I'm going to need you to stay out of here, I'm afraid. I'm a bit busy doing some photo shoots. But I've put some coffee in the living room. And some cereal. I hope that's okay?'

Photo shoot? Henry stared at his daughter-in-law, utterly bemused. But, being Henry, he smiled, and turned on his heel. The living room might not be sunny, but it might at least be quiet.

The long, low coffee table had been pressed into service as a breakfast buffet bar, and Henry felt bizarrely as if he'd wandered into a B&B by mistake. A jug held orange juice, another, milk, and an assortment of plastic containers had been filled with muesli, cornflakes and Weetabix. A pot of coffee, two mugs and a small tray holding cutlery made up the collection. He perched on the sofa and thought unaccountably of Peg.

She was only fifteen minutes away; he could see her if he wanted, even if he didn't quite know why. Perhaps it was simply the fact that her Christmas sounded so idyllic compared with his. He glanced around the room – at the towering Christmas tree, one of three in the house, already lit with what seemed like hundreds of tiny, star-shaped white lights; at the fireplace, with an extravagant arrangement of candles and bows and foliage draped along the mantel; and at the bay window, which was festooned with even more lights, hung with decorations and playing host to what he could only describe as a winter tableau. He sighed. Everything seemed so *complicated*...

His breakfast was interrupted by the arrival of Adam, who had found some toast from somewhere and was still munching his way through a slice. Henry eyed it enviously. Cereal never sat quite right with him of a morning. For lunch, yes, or even as a snack at night, but too much milk this early always made his stomach feel a little queasy.

'Morning, Dad,' said Adam, taking another bite of his toast. Henry wondered if Sofia knew he was eating it without a plate. 'I'm going to pick up Blanche in a few minutes, if you fancy a trip out? Sofia's a bit busy this morning, and it will give us a chance to catch up. We didn't get much opportunity to talk yesterday, did we?'

Henry swallowed the last of his coffee and nodded. It would appear Sofia wanted them both out of the house, or at least for the hour's round trip to where Blanche lived. He returned his mug to the coffee table.

'Should I wash these things up first?' he asked.

Adam frowned, and shook his head, throwing the last of his breakfast into his mouth. 'Best not,' he said. 'We can do it later.'

. . .

'Good news about the promotion then,' said Henry, as soon as Adam had navigated his way through the gated development where they lived and turned onto the main road. 'I didn't realise there was one in the offing.'

Adam checked his rear-view mirror and accelerated away. 'Um, no... it wasn't something I applied for. The post is the result of a restructure within the school. It's a little complicated.'

Henry nodded, stroking the wale of his corduroy trousers so it lay flat. If he didn't know better he'd say that Adam was looking for some advice.

'And how do you feel about taking on Humanities as well? Quite an ask, I would have thought.'

There was a long pause. 'Well, it won't be all of them. Probably not, anyway... Probably just history. I think someone else might be getting geography and religious studies. And it's not definite yet, anyway. It was a bit last-minute – I only had the conversation with the head the day before term finished.'

'Oh...' Henry scratched his head. 'I thought Sofia... I thought it was all agreed.'

'It probably is, in fairness. I've got the holidays to decide before we talk again in the new year. It won't come into effect until Easter, though. There are still a few things to be worked out.'

'The restructuring you mentioned?'

Adam nodded. 'Schools are having to be more creative about how they make the curriculum work with less money.'

'But you'll be getting a pay rise?'

There was silence for a few moments as Adam concentrated on a junction. He slid Henry a glance. 'It's not about the money, Dad.'

'Is that a no?'

'We didn't really discuss it. But I'm sure there will be. It's a much bigger managerial role, and, like I said, there are still details to be worked out.'

'So what's happened to the current Head of Humanities?'

'She left in the summer, but they've struggled to replace her, so I think this is a new solution to make things work. It's been a bit hit and miss this term.'

'I see...'

'What, Dad?' Adam was beginning to sound irritated.

Henry needed to choose his words carefully. 'Nothing... I'm just interested in what you're going to be doing. You're not a history teacher, after all.'

'Yes, but I won't be teaching the subject, just taking responsibility for it.'

'And you're getting more time out of the classroom for that?'

'That hasn't been decided yet.'

'Right... Sorry, but I thought Sofia said—'

'I might have intimated that I'd get more management time...' Adam frowned, taking a deep breath. 'But only because it's what Sofia expects. It's kind of how she measures promotion, but that's only because she doesn't really understand teaching.'

'Because she thinks time in the classroom is less important than being stuck in an office making policy?'

Adam made no comment.

'Okay...' said Henry slowly, thinking for a moment. 'So last year they made you Head of English, which meant you had overall responsibility for a department of six teachers. And that responsibility meant that your teaching commitment was cut by a quarter so that you could perform your new duties. Now, I don't know how many teachers are in the Humanities department, but even if you just take on responsibility for the history staff, it will still be an increase. That sounds like an awful lot more work, and yet from what you say there might not be any extra time made available to do the job, or indeed extra money.'

Henry gave his son a sideways glance. 'Are you certain this is something you want to do?'

A loud tut echoed around the car. 'Yes! Because it's a great opportunity. Honestly, I don't know why I bother telling you these things.'

Henry raised his hands in submission. 'I'm not being critical, Adam, just trying to be a sounding board – playing devil's advocate, if you will.'

Adam nodded. 'Okay, but it's all about results these days, Dad. I'll be responsible for raising attainment levels across the board and whether you like it or not, that's how the field of education views success. That's going to be the thing which takes my career to the next level.'

'Or takes advantage of it. I work in education, in case you'd forgotten, and while I'm sure there are many differences between higher and secondary education, there are an awful lot of similarities as well. Don't be so anxious to do your master's bidding that you hand yourself to them on a plate. You still need to ask yourself the same questions – am I happy with what I have now? And will I still be happy if I take the promotion?'

'Of course I'm happy. This year has been great. Becoming Head of English has been tough, but no one takes on a promotion thinking it's going to be easy, do they? That's not the point.'

He turned to Henry and smiled, but Adam had never been very good at hiding how he was feeling when he was a child and he was no better at it now. Admittedly, the glimpse Henry got of Adam's face before he turned his attention back to the road had only been momentary, but his smile was superficial at best; it didn't go anywhere near as far as his eyes.

'In any case, what kind of message will it send if I *don't* take the job?' added Adam. 'If you're not a team player, then you're nobody.'

'Perhaps what you are is someone who cares about their mental health and recognises that, while it might be a massive boost to their career, it will only be that if the new post is hailed a success.' He held up his hand. 'And before you argue, I'm not saying you wouldn't make it a success – I have every faith in your abilities – but it's a massive ask, and the cost to you personally might be higher than you're prepared for.'

'You sound like Sam,' said Adam, irritation clear in his voice.

'Who's she?'

'Head of Foreign Languages. She'll probably be the one picking up religious studies.'

'Well, maybe Sam recognises the sense in being cautious.'

'Yeah, but it's different for women, isn't it?'

'Is it?' countered Henry. 'Really...? Even now?'

'We're still expected to bring in the money.'

Henry couldn't help but wonder if Adam was speaking for all men, or just himself. Sofia's business might be doing well, but the philosophy of only ever wanting more and more never stops. There's always more to be had.

'That's a lot of expectation,' he replied. Adam was fidgeting in his seat, becoming riled. 'Look, I'm not throwing cold water on the idea,' Henry continued. 'But I'm your dad, it's my job to worry about you. All I'm saying is that if the school doesn't get the results it wants, even though what they're asking of their staff seems an incredibly tall order, what then? No one's ever a failure if they're set up to fail. But no one ever sees it like that either.' He studied Adam's expression. 'Well at least you have the holidays to think about it. That will give you and Sofia plenty of time to talk things over.'

'I've got a tonne of reports to go through, Dad.'

'Okay, it will give you *some* time to talk things over. But make sure that you do, and... I know I don't see you all that often, but I *am* here for a few days. I'm always happy to listen.'

Adam didn't reply. It was, perhaps, the natural place for the conversation to end, but Henry was very well aware that wasn't the only reason. He changed the subject, and they spent the remainder of the journey talking about which books they had recently read. This, at least, was a safe topic of conversation.

Blanche elected to sit in the back once they were ready for the return journey, so Henry's opportunities to talk to her were few, beyond the usual pleasantries. She did, however, lean forward just before they turned onto Adam's drive and give his shoulder a squeeze in solidarity. He appreciated that. Maybe this Christmas wouldn't be too bad after all.

Sofia appeared to have changed outfits while they'd been away, and a lot more besides. She wasn't in what Henry would have called casual attire before, but now she had on a long red velvet skirt and a fluffy white jumper with short sleeves, decorated with some sort of sparkly beads. Her hair was curled and her lipstick was an exact match for the shade of her skirt.

After giving Blanche a hug, and a kiss which didn't quite meet her cheek, Sofia led them through to the kitchen with an expansive wave of her arms.

'Adam, why don't you get everyone a drink while I just take care of this quick video?'

Henry's eyes followed the direction of her hand to the dining room where the table had been laid for a bacchanalian feast. It was heaped with holly and trails of ivy which curled around a charcuterie board and another one piled with cheeses, grapes and the kind of savoury biscuits his grocery budget would never allow him to buy. Creamy-coloured candles had been placed at regular intervals along the table, together with a huge glass bowl which sat in the centre, full of fresh roses, the colour of which incidentally also matched Sofia's skirt and lipstick. A tripod stood in one corner of the room where a waiting camera was already fixed to capture the scene.

'Oh...' Henry turned to Adam in confusion. 'I thought you were going out for lunch. Isn't today the golf club do?'

Sofia bustled past him. 'This isn't for us... It's our Christmas Day dinner. I won't have a minute of time on the day itself to record this, so I'm doing it now. Then I can just upload it to my socials when I'm ready.'

Henry glanced at Blanche, but she looked just as bemused as he did.

'I've started a blog on my website,' Sofia explained. 'And it's surprised me how popular it's been. I mean, really popular. People can't get enough of aspirational content these days, and because I cross-post to Instagram and TikTok, it's led to such an increase in business that I can't neglect it. But it's not always that easy to find things to say, especially at this time of year when everyone expects to hear about all the wonderful Christmassy things you've been doing.'

'So this is all fake?' said Blanche.

Sofia shot her a murderous look. 'No, it's not fake. I'm just managing my time more effectively.'

Adam cleared his throat. 'And speaking of which, we wondered if you might like to go to church tomorrow evening? What do you think? The setting is just perfect for the kind of photos that will look great on Sofia's blog. If we get a bit of frost as well, it will look even more amazing.'

'Or snow,' put in Sofia. 'That would be incredible.'

'Mainly though, it struck us that it could be a lovely thing to do. Something you might enjoy a little more than another party.'

Henry glanced from one to the other. Adam sounded as if he was bribing a small child with sweets, while Sofia looked a little embarrassed at having to make it clear that the outing was entirely for their sake, and nothing whatsoever to do with her new-found desire to be an influencer.

'Sounds great,' he said, smiling and nodding, even though he was certain that somewhere an elf had just died. He should stop being so cynical, and Adam was right – whatever his and Sofia's motives, it was a far nicer option than making small talk over canapés for hours.

'Excellent, that's settled then.' Adam looked at his watch. 'Hadn't we better get ready for lunch?'

Sofia looked down at her sumptuous skirt. 'I am ready, darling. All I need to do is film a quick video and then pop this lot away. It won't take more than a few minutes. Could you just press the button for me while I...' She trailed off to pick up a stack of gleaming white plates from the counter.

Adam, on cue, moved behind the tripod, pausing for a moment while Sofia got into position before pressing the appropriate button. He then exited the dining room in the other direction, moving through the connecting door into the sitting room, out into the hallway and back into the kitchen, where he came up behind them. Not a word was said during the entire manoeuvre. It was clearly a practised procedure.

Making no reference to what had just happened, Adam busied himself opening a bottle of wine which he took from the fridge, leaving Henry and Blanche to gape at what was happening in the room next door. Sofia swept – Henry could think of no other word for it – around the room, adding a plate to each of the settings around the table, almost as if she were leaving a gift there. Once finished, she crossed to the dresser at the back of the room, also heavily decorated, and lifted something from it. Henry was astonished to see they were place cards, annotated in a dark, swirly script. Sofia placed one in the centre of each of the plates, adding a sprig of red berries for extra... he couldn't quite think of the word.

Blanche caught his eye from across the room and raised her eyebrows – just a tad – but enough for her meaning to be clear. Maybe this Christmas was going to be even more ridiculous than the last.

7

'Here we go, Blanche, another cup of tea for you.'

Henry put down the tray he was carrying on the table beside her chair and removed his own mug from it. Another cup of tea... he was already sick of the stuff.

'Are you warm enough?'

'Yes, thank you.'

Henry nodded. Right... All there was left to do was turn on the television and hope to find something which he and Blanche might have some common ground over. Either that or sit in awkward silence. He took a seat opposite her and picked up the remote control.

'You didn't fancy it then?' said Blanche, leaning forward in her chair. 'The golf club do? Can't say I blame you. It wouldn't be my cup of tea either, even if I had been invited.'

'No... nor mine. I might be wrong but I get the feeling they wouldn't be my kind of people.'

'Hmm...' Blanche looked at him over the rim of her mug. 'So, looks like you drew the short straw again and got stuck babysitting me instead.'

'Babysitting?' queried Henry, with a wry expression on his

face. 'How old are you, again? You can't be that much older than me; our kids are almost the same age.'

'I'm seventy-five,' announced Blanche. 'Sofia was a rather late addition to the family. I didn't have her until I was forty-two.'

'Well, that's... positively ancient.' Henry was pleased to see a corresponding twinkle in Blanche's eye.

'Although Sofia often makes me feel twice that age. She doesn't actually say as much, but like so many things she doesn't say, the implication is there just the same – that I'm a doddery old fool who can't be trusted on her own.'

Henry wasn't sure how to reply. Despite Blanche's admission, he didn't want to be overly critical of her daughter. But he had also had enough of biting his tongue, of trying to do and say the right thing in order to be the perfect guest. So he decided to tell the truth.

'Sofia isn't the only one who's good at making assumptions,' he replied. 'Adam is adept at it too. I don't know where he gets his ideas about me from, but it wouldn't do him any harm to listen every once in a while.'

Blanche nodded, and Henry saw the truth of who she was. She might be thirteen years older than him, but she certainly wasn't the frail or befuddled old lady that Sofia would have him believe. She had more than her fair share of wits about her. And a wicked sense of humour, which for some reason he was only just beginning to discover.

'Of course, the big question,' continued Blanche, 'is why we both put up with it. And why we both come back for more every year. You don't have to answer that, of course, I'm just voicing out loud what you've no doubt thought in your head on countless occasions.'

Henry raised his eyebrows. 'Because we both love our children and worry we'd never get to see them otherwise?' Blanche put down her mug and regarded him steadily. She was right –

there *was* no need for him to have answered her question, but it *did* feel good to say it out loud.

'I do love my daughter,' said Blanche. 'But I don't always like the way she behaves. She never used to be obsessed with *things*. Or impressed by shallow people who have more money than sense. But now those kinds of people seem to account for most of their friends. The ones I've seen anyway. Perhaps that's harsh. Perhaps they only see those people over Christmas, when I'm here, but I suspect not. They used to have such a lovely group of friends where they lived before, but I've no idea what happened to them. They certainly don't seem to be around now. I blame Sofia's career. It's given her fancy ideas.'

'You might be right...' said Henry. 'I mean, look at this house, for one. It looks lovely, but I'm scared to walk around in case I make anything dirty, or touch anything in case I move it out of place.' He frowned. 'I think my son is as much to blame, though. He never used to be so materialistic either, but since his mother and I divorced, he seems hell-bent on ensuring he turns out nothing like me. I can't say anything, because suggesting he should make up his own mind about the way I live my life, instead of believing what she's told him, sounds like sour grapes. Maybe it is.' He shrugged. 'I hate feeling so defensive, too – it's like we're all still in the school playground. Somehow, I thought getting divorced when your child was an adult would be easier, but I'm not sure it is.'

'I think it's called being a parent,' replied Blanche. 'Doesn't matter how old they are, we still worry about them. And it doesn't matter how old *we* are, we're still more than capable of having a difficult relationship with them. My daughter and I used to be very close, once upon a time. Can you believe that?'

'I can. It was the same for me and Adam.' He smiled. 'So tell me about yourself, Blanche. Because I'm ashamed to say I don't know much beyond the fact that you live on your own.'

'Which might as well be on the moon for all the times Sofia

comes to visit. I live in a retirement complex, without which I'm convinced I would have gone doolally a long time ago. I have friends, we go places, we drink wine with our meals and occasionally get drunk on Friday nights playing cards. All things which my daughter has never bothered to find out and would undoubtedly be shocked by. She thinks I sit in my chair all day, watching reruns of soaps while my brain atrophies to the size of a pickled walnut.'

'Yet you don't put her straight?'

'I don't, for precisely the same reason you don't tell your son to stop believing you've failed in some way. And if he could get over his determination to never be guilty of that, he'd see that you're actually pretty happy too, just as I am.'

Henry smiled, picking up his mug. 'Can I tell you a secret, Blanche? It's not really a secret, but it is something I've been keeping to myself because I don't want the thought of it spoiled by the comments I know my son would make if I told him.'

'Oooh, gossip, how naughty. Yes, do please tell me.'

'I met a woman on the drive down here. I hardly know her. But she has long black hair which she wears in plaits, the kindest smile, and makes the most wonderful cheese and beetroot sandwiches. I bumped into her at a petrol station and then again some seventy miles later when we were both caught in the same traffic jam. She saw me and came over to share her lunch with me. We sat and talked, and now I can't get her out of my head. Turns out she only lives fifteen minutes away, which really isn't helping.'

'And presumably, with it being Christmas, she'll be surrounded by family, so even if you did want to see her, you can't just barge in and say hello.'

'Actually, she's on her own. She's a widow. And her children are both away, skiing... She described how she was planning to spend the next few days and it sounded heavenly. Not a golf club do in sight, or an endless stream of people and small talk. No rounds of jolly festivities either...'

Blanche tipped her head to one side. 'You know, now we've established that I'm a sherry-drinking card shark and not a doddery old fool who can't be trusted, I'd be perfectly happy on my own for a few hours. Sofia and Adam won't be back for ages yet. I'll stick on some trashy TV programme and raid Sofia's stash of Baileys while you're gone. And if I wash up my glass, no one will be any the wiser.'

Henry stared at her. He couldn't do that... could he?

'I'd probably need to take her a present...'

'I said *stash* of Baileys. There are three bottles in the pantry, and quite a lot more besides. Take your pick.'

Henry almost turned around several times on the way over, convinced that he was being foolhardy in the extreme. Just because he thought Peg's final words to him might have been 'come over', it didn't mean that they were. She could have said anything. It could also have been something said in the rush of the moment as they were saying goodbye – a polite remark which they both knew was exactly that and no more. He glanced at the bottle of Baileys nestled on the passenger seat and rolled his eyes.

Lower Steeping was a pretty village which didn't seem to have changed at all since Henry was last there. Still the same tree-lined lanes, dotted with warm honeyed stone cottages and neat front gardens. Gardens which, come summer, would be abundant in flower and teeming with bees. The green was at the far end of the main street, a bend in the road meaning that the houses formed a sweeping circle around it, but as Henry drove closer he realised that, although Peg had told him her house was at the far end of it, he couldn't know which one that was. Not unless he knew in which direction she was travelling. Or she knew in which direction *he* would be travelling. And her reference to the church gave him no clue either; it was down a different lane altogether. He pulled into the side of the road and slowed to a stop. This was madness.

He looked first one way and then the other. There were indeed two houses which arguably could be said to be at the end of the green – one, a ramshackle thatched cottage, and the other, set slightly further back from the road, that was painted pink with a bright green front door. Was that the more likely home of a woman who wore her hair in plaits and favoured colourful clothes? He decided that it was and set off towards it, the bottle of liqueur in his hand.

With his heart still pounding in his chest, Henry was almost relieved when there was no answer to his knock on the door. That was until he realised someone was calling to him. Turning around, he spied a woman's face peering at him from over a thick hedge which bordered the property to one side.

'Are you looking for Peg? Only she's not here, you've just missed her... Can I help you?' At least he'd got the right house.

The owner of the voice sounded friendly enough, but she was obviously keeping an eye on things for her neighbour. And he had no idea how to introduce himself.

'Hi, I was just calling on the off-chance that Peg was around, but no problem. I didn't say I was coming, so... Do you think she'll be long?'

The woman's eyes narrowed as she assessed him and Henry wondered whether he'd be considered friend or foe. 'Hard to say, but not for a bit yet. She's gone to visit her aunt in hospital. Is that for her?' She indicated the bottle in Henry's hand. 'I can pass it on for you, if you like.'

Henry thought for a moment. He didn't blame her, but the neighbour was obviously fishing for information. He was pleased that Peg had someone looking out for her, but perhaps it was better to assume that her absence was a sign that he should stop being silly and get on his way. On the other hand, he didn't want the woman to think there was anything suspicious about him. Peg had spoken very fondly about an aunt – the one she'd been to visit – and he wondered if it could be the same one. Now, what was her name...?

'No, it's fine, thanks. I just hate turning up empty-handed, but I can give it to her another time. Is her aunt okay? Didn't she just get back from visiting her?' As soon as the words were out of his mouth, he could see he'd said the right thing. The woman's expression relaxed and she smiled, leaning further forward over the hedge.

'She's had a fall, broken her wrist I think Peg said, so she's gone haring off up there again to look after her, only got back yesterday, too. I'm sure everything will be fine, but you never know, do you? Peg mentioned possible concussion as well, and that can be nasty, especially for someone of Mim's age. And I can't help but feel for Peg if anything were to happen. It's not a great time of year for her as it is.'

Mim, that was it... Henry nodded. 'No, I know. But like you said, hopefully it will all be okay. Just such as shame Mim lives where she does; it's a longish drive.'

'That's what I said. I told her to take it easy, but I can understand her wanting to go, she dotes on Mim. Aside from her kids, she's virtually the only family Peg has now.' She smiled, indicating the bottle again. 'Are you sure you don't want me to take that in for her? It's no bother. I'll be round later to feed the cat.'

Henry shook his head. 'That's kind, but I'll give Peg a ring and pop back another time. Thanks, though. Oh, and Happy Christmas.' He gave a small wave and began to walk back towards his car. He needed to end the conversation before it got any more difficult, or he was forced to tell lies.

He drove off immediately, but as soon as he was out of sight of Peg's house, he pulled back into the kerb and stopped again. If the neighbour was still watching he didn't want it to seem as if he was lingering, but an even more ridiculous idea had popped into his head while they had been talking, and he needed time to think about what had been said, *and* what he should do. Peg was clearly very fond of her aunt, and now he knew that she was one of her only relatives. It was Christmas. Whatever Peg was facing, she would be doing so alone – without the comfort of her children, and only three days away from the anniversary of her husband's death. Might she be grateful for a friendly face? Or someone to talk to? It wasn't difficult to work out which hospital Mim would be in. She lived in Stoke, the same as Henry, and there was only one she would have been taken to. He checked his watch. It was just gone two. If he left now, he could be back by tonight. It would be late, admittedly, but the roads would be quiet by then, he'd make good time. Blanche would be fine, and he still wouldn't miss any of the things which Adam and Sofia had arranged. He pulled out his phone and dialled.

'I've never heard anything so ridiculous,' said Adam, a few minutes later after Henry had explained. The golf club lunch was evidently still in full swing; Henry could hear the sound of some very merry people in the background. He'd probably be the first to admit that it was a ridiculous idea, but the fact that his son had reacted in such a way irritated him enormously. He hadn't shown the slightest concern for Peg, or the situation she was in.

'Who is this woman anyway?'

'She's just a friend.' He was trying not to let his annoyance show. 'This woman' wasn't exactly a complimentary way of describing Peg, but more to the point, completely ignored the fact that Henry was an adult, and perfectly entitled to make friends with whom he chose. And if he had any doubts about the way Adam's mind was working, his next statement made it obvious.

'Oh, I get it... playing the knight in shining armour, are we?'

Henry bristled. 'You could just think of it as showing someone a little kindness, Adam, instead of making stupid comments. Kindness, because she's on her own and it's Christmas – the season of goodwill to all men – the season when we're supposed to be kind and thoughtful and self*less* instead of self*fish*.'

'Yes, but what about Blanche?' said Adam, huffing down the phone. 'You know we probably won't be back for a while yet.'

'I'm not sure why that makes a difference.'

'Because who's going to—' Adam broke off, but it was just as Henry had suspected.

'Who's going to talk to her? Look after her? Is that it? You know I've often wondered why you invite me for Christmas every year, because it certainly doesn't seem as if it's because you enjoy my company. And now I know. It might be a bold statement, but you could try talking to Blanche yourself, you and Sofia. Try talking to her as you would any other adult, instead of assuming she's someone who needs a carer. In fact, even if she did need a carer, wouldn't that be Sofia's responsibility? Or is it more that Blanche is in the way, just like I am? You and Sofia will be fine without me, as will Blanche, and I'll be back in time for all the Christmas festivities anyway. What does it matter?'

'For God's sake, Dad, I should have thought it was obvious. Do you know how much trouble Sofia has gone to to make everything perfect for us? How much time that takes, not to mention the expense?' Henry could almost hear his son wince at the other end of the line, but it was too late; the words were out and Henry knew that Adam's mistake would very quickly be turned around into a problem of Henry's making.

'That's hardly the point though,' continued Adam. 'What Sofia finds so hard, and I admit I understand where she's coming from, is that it often appears as if all her efforts are being thrown back in her face... You never seem to enjoy the food, or any of our other hospitality. You don't like coming out with us, you don't seem to like our friends...'

Henry closed his eyes for a second. *Hospitality?* What was he, a guest at a hotel? And a needy and irritating one at that? It troubled him just how far apart he and Adam had become. He swallowed and inhaled deeply, hoping it would calm him.

'Maybe I don't, Adam. But have you considered that they're not the kind of people I would choose to spend my time with?'

'And what does that mean?'

'Simply that they're your friends, not mine. We don't have a lot in common, that's all.'

'You say that, but perhaps if you gave them a chance instead of dismissing what they have to say out of hand, you might find it broadens your mind.'

'Adam, I'm thirty years older than you. It might be a hard concept to understand, but my mind might even be broader than yours. And, over time, I've learned what makes me happy. I've nothing against your friends, but their views are not mine, which is fine, it happens. *However*, I'm polite to them. I don't argue or take exception to the things they say which aren't to my liking because that would be rude. I also don't want to upset you because I *do* understand the trouble you and Sofia go to.' He paused. 'Look, I don't want to get into an argument about this, and it's not about being ungrateful for all that you do, or throwing it back in your face, but instead, suggesting that maybe you don't need to try so *hard*. I come to see *you*. You and Sofia. I don't care if I'm eating Marks and Spencer's finest or that my napkins match the colours on the Christmas tree. That's not what it's about.'

There was an ominous silence, and Henry could imagine all too well the expression on his son's face.

'Fine. So you're going then, are you?' he said after a moment. 'Driving halfway across the country on a whim.'

'I'd like to, yes,' replied Henry, ignoring his last comment. It was perilously close to what the little voice in his head was saying. 'My friend is all on her own. One of her only relatives, an elderly aunt who she cares about deeply, has just been taken to hospital and this is already a really bad time for her. If I can help in any way, then I'd like to. It's as simple as that.'

'Then I'll tell Sofia she needn't cater for you this evening.'

Henry gritted his teeth. As if one less would make any difference at all, given the feast that she would no doubt be preparing.

'Enjoy the rest of your lunch,' he said. 'I'll phone to let you know when I'm on my way back.'

He paused in case Adam might want to tell him to drive safely or hope that his friend's aunt would be okay, but he wasn't surprised when neither of those things happened. 'See you later,' he added and disconnected the call.

Henry wasn't all that familiar with the hospital, thankfully only having been there once or twice, but it was like many others of its kind – enormous, impersonal, and with a car park that in no way catered for the number of people who wished to use it. Inside the main foyer was a dazzling array of information, all imparted on a number of huge boards inside a concourse made of shiny tiles and glass and steel. There were coffee shops and a newsagent, seating areas and desks, and a row of lifts each with a number above them corresponding to colour-coded areas of the hospital. It made him dizzy just looking at it all.

A quick scout about revealed no one who looked remotely like Peg, and so Henry made his way to the main information board. It listed all the hospital departments, and readily showed him that Peg might, in fact, be anywhere. He knew that her aunt had a suspected broken wrist, but that could place her in any one of several areas – X-ray? Orthopaedics? Henry had no way of knowing. Shaking his head at his own stupidity, he tried to think logically. If Mim had been brought to the hospital with a suspected break, she'd be in an ambulance, which meant that she would have been taken to A&E – perhaps that was the most obvious place for her, and by extension, Peg, to be. Checking the directions on the board, Henry spun around and retraced his steps.

Sadly, even this close to Christmas, the A&E department was full of people. Anxious or pain-filled expressions met his searching looks and Henry dropped his head, embarrassed to be intruding on their space. It only took a matter of seconds to see that Peg wasn't there, and even less to realise that he should never have come. What on earth would he say to Peg if he found her? Meeting up on the motorway had been a happy coincidence that was easy to accept, but seeing one another again here would be a step too far. Tutting to himself, he turned to leave. He'd pay a quick visit to the bathroom, grab something to eat from a vending machine, and be on his way before he made things any worse.

The gents had run out of paper towels and he was still attempting to remove some of the water from his hands by swiping them down his trousers, when he passed a tiny relatives' room opposite the intensive care department. He knew he shouldn't, but it was almost a reflex action to glance through the window in the door as he passed. And there she was – Peg, head bent, with her plaits touching her knees and one hand holding up a tissue to her face. Her handbag was on the chair beside her, clearly dropped there by someone who didn't care where it landed. It gaped open, its contents almost spilling on the floor. It was a picture of such abject grief that Henry felt his breath catch in his throat. He'd been lucky in his life so far; death had stayed away. Both his parents were still alive, siblings too, and close friends. But clearly Peg had not been shown the same consideration, and he had no idea what to do.

All his instincts were to provide comfort, but he hardly

knew her, and given how distressed she was, would she welcome that comfort from a virtual stranger? If he were in her position he would probably question Henry's motives, and the thought brought him up short. *Was* he there to simply offer kindness, or was it something else? The difficulty was that even interrogating his brain didn't reveal the answer. Henry simply didn't know. He was a fool, though, that much was evident.

He crept away, furious with himself, and filled with an emotion he was struggling to put a name to. He was back in his car before he understood what it was. It was pain, but not the physical sort which came from an injury or an upset, but the very particular kind which came from being utterly helpless in the face of someone else's.

Pulling out of the car park, he began the weary drive home. No, not home; to his son's house. He'd give anything to be at home right now.

8

CHRISTMAS EVE

Peg sat down, leaning her back against the solid oak of the pew she was sitting on and willed it to imbue her with its strength. Stone arched high above her, to where, only moments before, their voices had soared, filling the space with joy. She clung onto the thought that, even during times of grief, there were moments of vibrant life to be found. She had discovered this in the years after Julian had died, and it was just as true now.

There was something about this building which always made her feel humble, grateful for all the things she had in her life, even the things she had lost. At this time of year, when the season was all about wanting, it was enormously hard to remember. Maybe that's why she liked coming here on this particular day – as a reminder to herself.

The quiet and peaceful Christmas that she had been so looking forward to would now be turned topsy-turvy by events and, as she stood for the next carol, she thought of her cottage, glowing with light as it had welcomed her home late last night. She had been tired and emotional, but no matter how she felt, it was her one true constant, the centre of herself to which she always returned.

She smiled at a young family across the aisle from her – two primary school age girls and their parents. If past Christmases with her own children were anything to go by, then the next couple of days would be busy and chaotic for them, yet still they had carved out some time to come to the church and sing. Life goes on; she must remember that, even though change had forced its way into hers again.

A little while later, Peg made her way through the churchyard, out of the lych gate and into the lane. Just getting that far had taken a while, as she stopped to chat to neighbours, the vicar and her friends, but now the calls of 'Merry Christmas' had dwindled and the last of the stragglers were making their way home.

The day had been bright and clear. Bitterly cold, but without it, the trees would not be sparkling and the fields would not be crisp underfoot. Dusk had fallen during the service and the sky had turned a deep mauve, a single gilded streak of pink lining the horizon. Although Peg's walk home would take her to the other end of the village, the darkening skies meant her way was now lit by what seemed like a thousand twinkling stars – strings of lights criss-crossed the street, hung in trees, from roofs and windows and woven through bushes. Tiny sparks of joy.

She smiled as she passed a woman posing for a photo beside one of the Christmas trees on the green. There were two, one at either end.

'Peg...?'

She swung around at the sound of the unfamiliar voice. Unfamiliar, and yet...

'Hello!' She laughed. 'What are you doing here?'

The man gave her a gentle smile. 'You remember me then?'

'Of course I do,' Peg replied. 'How are you, Henry?'

'I'm good, thanks.' He paused, looking somewhat awkward. 'Are *you* okay?'

When Peg's neighbour, Judith, had told her about the

mystery man who had arrived at her house yesterday bearing gifts, she had immediately thought of Henry. In truth, she couldn't think of anyone else who might have been to see her, but the thought that it could have been Henry was a nice one. It had made a difference to the turned-upside-down world of the last few hours. She'd also been sad to have missed him, made worse by the fact that she would probably never know the truth for certain. *Had* it been Henry who'd come to her door? And if it was, why had he come? They were questions she had surmised would never receive an answer, but now here he was, and perhaps with him, the opportunity to ask them.

'I'm fine,' she replied. 'Although it only seems five minutes since we were stuck in that traffic jam.'

'It does...' Henry smiled again, warm, but also perhaps a little sadly. 'I'm sorry that—'

He was interrupted by a woman who Peg recognised as the one having her photo taken.

'Hello...' she said, smiling while assessing Peg at the same time – subtly, but it was there nonetheless.

Peg couldn't remember her name, but it had to be Henry's daughter-in-law. She didn't look at all embarrassed to have cut across their conversation. Peg returned the greeting, realising as she did so that two other people were also standing at the periphery of her vision. She turned slightly as Henry took a step to his left. The group looked curious. *Henry* looked distinctly uncomfortable.

He held out his arm to bring them into the conversation. 'Peg, this is my son, Adam, his wife, Sofia and her mother, Blanche. This is Peg, everyone.' He paused. 'We've just been to the carol service.'

Peg nodded, smiling. Sofia, that was it. 'Hello, wasn't it lovely? Have you been before?'

Sofia was the first to shake her head, moving closer. 'No, but we shall definitely be coming again. It's such a pretty village. I don't know why we've never been before given that it's so close.'

Peg wondered how much she should say, conscious that in all probability she knew rather more about Henry's family than they did about her. Sofia's eyes missed nothing as she surreptitiously glanced at Peg's hair and clothing. Let her look, thought Peg. She nodded. 'You should. I can't vouch for any of the other services, but there's something about carols on Christmas Eve, the way it makes you feel...' She was about to say more but something in the woman's blank look told her there was little point.

'It's much busier than I thought it would be,' remarked Sofia.

'I know, isn't it great? Practically the whole village turns out.'

Adam smiled. 'And do you live in the village?'

'I do. I've lived here for thirty-odd years.' They were standing a stone's throw from her cottage but she wasn't about to mention that.

'In the same house?' asked Sofia. 'Goodness... I can't imagine that.'

'Can't say I'd want to be anywhere else,' she replied, smiling at Henry, who was looking even more anxious. She would have liked to invite him in for a cup of tea and a bite to eat, but that would have meant inviting them *all* in, and Henry looked as if he wanted to be anywhere but there.

Sofia looked around her. 'It is very pretty...' She turned so that she could take in the whole of the street. 'There are some lovely houses here. What are the prices like?'

Peg laughed. 'I've absolutely no idea, I'm afraid.'

Now Adam was beginning to look uncomfortable and, given the details of the conversation she'd shared with Henry, she wondered if Adam was worried about the size of his mortgage. Sofia did look as if she was sizing the place up. At first glance though, she'd be far too glamorous for Lower Steeping. Peg had nearly gone to the carol service in her wellies, and had only just thrown them off at the last minute. The freezing temperatures had hardened the surface of the main road today, but with tractors moving up and down it several times a day, for much of the year it was covered in mud.

She smiled again but the conversation had stalled, and Peg worried that if it went on any longer someone would ask the kinds of questions she didn't want to answer. She regretted her opening comment now; wished she hadn't made reference to the traffic jam and revealed how she and Henry had met. His family might not have heard it, but it would be natural for them to ask how she and Henry knew one another, or for how long and, given the look on Sofia's face, she was desperate to find out. Peg wasn't sure why, but she wanted to keep their friendship (was that even the right word?) private. It existed in a little oasis of time and space which Peg was keen to protect.

There were things she wanted to say to Henry, but now couldn't, and wondered if he felt the same. Someone should say something, though; the seconds were ticking by and the silence was becoming a little awkward. She pulled her coat tighter and gave an involuntary shiver.

'We should let you get back to your evening,' said Henry. 'But it was lovely to see you.'

'You too... And have a lovely Christmas, won't you?' The echoes of their very first conversation drifted back to her. *Would* he have a lovely Christmas? Given all that she knew? She wanted to hold onto him for a bit longer but he was already preparing to leave.

He reached out slightly, then thought better of it. 'You too...' The lights were glinting off the curls in his hair.

He hesitated, and she had the distinct impression he wanted to say more. But his family were already moving away, back to their house with the bows on the backs of the chairs and matching napkins, the lavish brunches and trips to the theatre. She stood still for a moment, watching them go, heading towards an enormous car parked by the edge of the green, and then she turned for her own door. She'd only gone a couple of steps, however, when a gentle touch on her arm turned her back.

'It was lovely to meet you,' said Blanche. 'I'm so sorry. Henry told us...' She trailed off as a voice came from behind her.

'Mum...?'

A look of such pained exasperation came over Blanche's face that Peg almost laughed out loud.

'I'd better go,' said Blanche. 'Compliance doesn't always come easy, but it certainly makes life easier. Take care... and Merry Christmas, Peg.'

Peg stared at Blanche's tiny frame in astonishment as she walked slowly towards her daughter, picking her way carefully over the frozen ground.

'You too,' she said.

Sometimes Henry wondered about the universe. Mostly, he thought it to be benevolent but at times it was downright irritating. He'd almost fallen over when Adam had revealed the location of the church they were planning to visit for the carol service, and he had vacillated between a secret excitement that he might see Peg again, and terror that he would. Even though he knew the chances of it were next to non-existent, it could have been the perfect opportunity to 'bump' into her, but not with Sofia, Adam and, to a lesser extent, Blanche in tow. It seemed unfair in the extreme. And, as he climbed into the car, he knew the universe was going to enjoy watching him squirm.

'She seemed nice,' said Adam.

It wasn't a bad opening statement, and one Henry could

deflect relatively easily, but he knew his son was only biding his time. Sofia, however, had no such reticence.

'Obviously quite a character. Not sure I could pull off plaits at that age, but they suited her, didn't they? And I loved her dress... so colourful.'

Henry thought her dress was lovely, too, only he wasn't being disparaging.

'Yes,' said Henry. 'Although I don't know her all that well, just to talk to, say hello, you know.'

'Oh... I wondered if you were old friends,' said Adam. 'As in *very* old friends. Didn't you used to live around here, Dad? When you were little?'

Henry closed his eyes briefly. 'I went to primary school here,' he said. 'But no, she's not someone I knew from school.'

'So where *did* you meet?' asked Sofia.

Henry could see how they would be curious. He only came to visit them twice a year at most, and apart from last night's shocking departure from the norm, he'd never been out of their sight while staying with them. He might as well own up to it though, because the questions wouldn't stop if he didn't.

'It was purely by chance, when I was on my way down to you. I bumped into her at a petrol station before I hit the motorway and then again when we both got caught up in the traffic jam. We got talking, that's all.'

Sofia made a little dubious noise. 'Got talking? How did you manage that in a traffic jam? Come on, Henry, we're not daft, there must be more to it than that.'

'No,' he replied. 'That's really all it was. We'd been sitting there for quite some time, she spotted my car, thought I might be hungry, and tapped on my window to offer me a mince pie.'

'And she just happens to live fifteen minutes away?'

'Yes,' intoned Henry, 'she does. One of life's little coincidences. What can I say?'

From the back seat he could see Adam and Sofia exchange

glances. There wasn't a chance they were about to leave it there. He was waiting for the inevitable next question when Adam suddenly turned around in his seat to face him.

'Hang on a minute... Is this the woman, the "friend" that you rushed off for yesterday? The mercy mission that you drove halfway across the country for? For God's sake, Dad.'

Henry wasn't about to confirm or deny his son's statement. 'For God's sake what?'

'Well, isn't it a bit... I don't know... desperate?'

'Desperate?' Henry frowned. 'That sounds as if I was making some kind of play for her when it wasn't like that at all. Not that it's any of your business, but her husband died four years ago... on Boxing Day. So it's not a great time of year for her and, like I said, I knew she'd be on her own. I also knew how fond she was of her aunt, and I just thought it might be a kind thing to do.'

'Is that what they're calling it these days?' said Sofia, an amused smirk on her face.

'Look, she was nice. We had a really pleasant chat, but that's all it was. And where's the harm in that? It's not like we're going to keep in touch. Not that it would matter if we did. I'm on my own now.'

'Yes, and you never seemed concerned by that before.'

Henry swallowed his irritation at Adam's comment. Was his son ever going to stop going over the same old ground? He was determined to think that Henry hadn't been bothered by the break-up of his marriage, despite his repeated protestations to the contrary.

'I'm not. Besides, I doubt I'll ever see Peg again – not unless we go to the carol service next year, and bump into her a second time.'

'Okay,' said Adam. 'I believe you, although I still think what you did was odd, given that you'd only just met the woman.'

From beside him on the back seat, Blanche cleared her

throat. She was right; this was neither the time nor the place to have this conversation. Henry shot her an exasperated look, knowing that she sympathised with him. Just as she also knew that he would never be allowed to forget his 'transgression'. He sighed.

'Haven't you ever done anything on the spur of the moment?' he asked.

Adam started the engine, catching Henry's eye in the rear-view mirror. 'Plenty of times, Dad... but you haven't.'

9

CHRISTMAS DAY

Henry swung his legs over the side of the bed and groaned. Not at his body's reaction to sleeping on a mattress which was much harder than his own, or his head's reaction to the wine he had drunk the night before, but the fact that there were still two more activity-packed days to be got through, both filled with food and people. And he had little appetite for either. He ran a hand over his face, feeling the lines underneath his eyes, the stubble on his chin and the sag of the skin beneath. He felt tired and old. Merry Christmas, Henry.

Even when he was a child he had mixed feelings about Christmas Day. The day couldn't come soon enough for all his friends – it was all they thought about, talking about the countless hours they lay awake on Christmas Eve, unable to sleep with excitement. But all Henry had longed for was the quiet solitude of Boxing Day. Not that he didn't enjoy Christmas Day, he did, but the day after was always so peaceful. His parents had been happy to let him do his own thing, and for Henry, that mostly meant reading. Of course, as he got older and had a child of his own, he realised that the day after Christmas was also the day to relax, safe in the knowledge that another one had been successfully navigated, expectations had been fulfilled and the stress of the season could take a back seat. So throughout his life, it had always been thoughts of the calm oasis to come which had sustained him through the madness of the big day itself. This year, however, like all the others in his recent past, there would be no quiet interlude to look forward to, and tomorrow would be just as crazy as today. The fact that his son didn't follow the traditions of his youth also grated on him enormously, but there was nothing he could do about it, except comply. He glanced at the clock beside his bed. It was time to get moving.

When he arrived in the kitchen, preparations for the day were already well underway. He desperately wanted a coffee, but one look at Sofia's face convinced him that he could wait. Breakfast would not be served for another hour yet, a lavish affair, and given the quantity of food they would be eating later, in Henry's eyes an unnecessary one. But Sofia would not be deterred and so that was that.

'Morning!' He smiled brightly, nodding at Adam, who was standing in the dining room, peering at their long oak table and another smaller one which now sat beside it. 'Happy Christmas,' he added.

'Happy Christmas, Henry,' replied Sofia, moving past him. Her reply was perfunctory at best, and Henry realised you could cut the atmosphere with a knife.

'This is ridiculous, Adam,' she said. 'Having ten people for brunch is not extravagant these days and yet house builders insist on making dining rooms such poky little places.'

There was nothing poky about Sofia's dining room. Theirs was a modern house, and designed around the type of open-plan living that was so popular at present. Compared to Henry's house, and therefore the house which Adam had grown up in, it was positively palatial.

'I've made the slip covers for the chairs especially for today, so thankfully the fact we have mismatched seats won't be so evident. As long as you don't look too hard, that is. But what is the point of having two tables when the second one is lower than the first and, whatever you do, the join will be incredibly obvious?'

'Will it, though?' asked Adam. 'Once it's decorated and so on, I don't think folks will even notice.'

'Of course they'll notice. Don't be ridiculous.' She gave Adam a look which let him know just how ridiculous he *was* being.

'So what do you suggest I do?' asked Adam. 'Put the second table up on bricks? Cut the legs down on the first?'

Sofia glared at him. 'Now you're just being stupid.'

Henry smiled, trying to catch his son's eye. It was Christmas Day, after all, and as yet Adam hadn't even greeted him. It wasn't hard to see why, however.

'Is everything all right?' he asked, wondering how best he could help.

Finally, Adam smiled. 'Hi, Dad. Yes, fine. We're just trying to work out the seating arrangements for tomorrow's brunch. We've got another six people to accommodate and our original table isn't big enough.'

'The room isn't big enough,' countered Sofia.

Henry imagined that many families were in a similar position come Christmas. With extra people coming to stay, it was a time when spare chairs were gathered from the corners of the house and pressed into service. Similarly, put-you-up beds were dragged down from attics, and spare pillows and duvets were removed from cupboards. It was all absolutely fine and nobody minded having to make do. Nobody except Sofia, that much was clear.

'You know, as soon as you get your new promotion signed off, I'm going to get those builders in I told you about,' added Sofia. 'You know, the ones Amanda and Nick used. Then we can have a proper room – open it up into the conservatory with space for a decent table and have trifold doors which open on to the garden. Can you just imagine how wonderful *next* Christmas will be with all that room?'

'But Amanda and Nick's extension is enormous,' replied Adam. 'It cost them almost a hundred thousand pounds – nearly double what they'd first planned. Nick told me at the gym how ridiculous it was.'

'He's exaggerating,' replied Sofia. 'Because he didn't agree with the specification of fittings Amanda wanted.'

'I don't think he particularly liked them either.'

'Yes, but everyone knows that's not the point. Nick's taste is far too bohemian; most people run a mile at that kind of thing. Keeping everything classic and neutral is absolutely the way to go if you want to get your money back. And you only have to look at their place to know that the increase in the value of their house alone has made the alterations pay for themselves. And the same would be true here. You can't scrimp on quality fittings, not if you want to make a proper investment.'

Henry would have dearly loved to escape to the safety of the living room, but it was too late for that. They were both looking at him for comment.

'It's always struck me as a little odd that people go to such pains to improve the resale value of their houses,' he said. 'Isn't it better to decorate a house the way *you* want it? And then enjoy living there? Not worry about the people who are going to live there *after* you.'

Sofia rolled her eyes. 'But that's so short-sighted. I mean, how long does anyone realistically stay in a house like this, for example? You've always got to have an eye on the value you add to a property. That's the bedrock of my business, so I should know.'

Henry's opinion was evidently not required. He shrugged. 'It was just an observation. And your house is lovely. Surely it's plenty big enough without going through all that added expense?'

'Except that it's not big enough, is it? If it was we wouldn't be faced with this ridiculous situation.'

'I can see what Dad's getting at though, Sofe. Being realistic, how many times a year do we need this room to be any bigger? It's only really at Christmas, and it seems daft to spend a whole heap of money on something we don't need ninety-nine per cent of the time. And the new job doesn't come with much more money, don't forget. I'm not sure it's enough to—'

'Well, maybe it isn't a new job title you need then, but a new school instead.' Irritation flickered across Sofia's face. For one thing, Henry knew she hated being called Sofe, but what was worse was that she hated being thwarted in her plans. He felt a horrible pang of sympathy for his son's situation.

'It isn't all about money though, is it?' said Henry.

As soon as the words were out of his mouth, he knew he'd said the wrong thing. Adam might understand the point he was making, but he'd never admit to it, not in front of Sofia anyway.

'Isn't it?' said Adam. 'We don't all want to settle for mediocre. Some of us want better for our lives.'

Henry clamped his mouth shut. He was very aware that Adam was stressed – the front of his hair looked as agitated as his face did, and Henry wondered if he knew how many times he ran his hand through it. Even so, his words were harsh, completely unfounded, and he was getting tired of his son's disparaging comments.

'There's nothing wrong with having aspirations,' he replied, trying to keep his voice mild. 'But you also seem determined not to understand the point I was trying to make, which is that going after a promotion is great if it's what you truly want, but not if it comes at the expense of your happiness. And from what you've told me about the situation at your school, I can't see how you can possibly be anything other than overworked and stressed.'

'Yes, but sometimes you have to make compromises if you want to get ahead. Put in the effort.'

'Get ahead to where, Adam? What's wrong with what you have now? You have a good job, and a beautiful home, and—'

'And what about children, Henry?' put in Sofia, glaring at him. 'What then?'

'It's always tough, but you'd manage... Yes, you'd have to make changes to your life, sacrifices, too, but they'd be worth it. It doesn't matter if you have to make do for a few years. Being a parent comes first.'

'Hah!'

Maybe he didn't mean it to sound so derogatory, but Adam's derision echoed around the room loud and clear. And it hurt. All Henry had ever done was provide for his son to the best of his ability, both physically and emotionally. And all he was trying to do now was protect him. Maybe he'd overdone it and sounded too preachy, but if Adam found it hard to stand up to his wife's forceful personality then who could blame Henry for wanting to provide a little ballast? The fact that Adam could reject his help, reject *him*, was hard to bear. Henry had held his tongue ever since the divorce, but this was a conversation which was long overdue. And Christmas or not, it was time to have it. He was sick of being made to feel like a failure.

'You might find this hard to believe, but your mother was not right about everything. And over the years she's filled your head with a version of events, a version of me, which you've never thought to question, instead swallowing her opinions wholesale.' He held up his hand. 'I had hoped you'd understand that there are two people in every marriage who share an *equal* responsibility for it. I don't know the ins and outs of yours and Sofia's marriage, neither would I want to, but if it went pear-shaped I'd like to think I'd be supportive, not judgemental.'

'Of course you'd be judgemental,' replied Adam. 'Everyone is. There are always two sides, and inevitably you have to pick one.'

'You can be led down that path, yes, or you can be encouraged to be accepting of a situation without apportioning blame. It's very clear which side you've been encouraged to pick, and I find that odd given that your mother has moved to the other side of the world and you hardly see her.'

'I hardly see *you*.'

It was on the tip of Henry's tongue to say *is it any wonder*, but he held the words back.

'But you *do* see me. And the point still stands – I have never discussed with you the part either of us had to play in the breakup of our marriage, even though your mother clearly hasn't afforded me the same courtesy. And the reason I know this is because I've seen your behaviour towards me change over the last few years. To the point where you reject everything in your life which you believe me to be guilty of, everything she accused me of. Nothing is ever good enough for you now. Everything has to be striven for, in a relentless quest to move even higher and further. She accused me of being complacent, Adam, but this is the part where you need to stop swallowing what you've been told and start thinking about whether you agree with it or not. There *are* two sides to every story, and what your mother saw as complacency, I see as contentment and happiness.

'I also understand the value of the word "enough". And I *had* enough in my life – I still do. I have a house which is comfortable and keeps me safe and warm. I have enough money to live the way I want to, and I have a job which I love. And the reason why I love it is because I'm doing what I'm good at. Your mother wanted me to try for promotion, to earn more money, take on more responsibility. But you know why I didn't? Because it would have taken me out of the classroom, away from everything I loved. I'd be a rubbish manager, so why on earth would I want to swap what made me happy for something which didn't?'

'Yeah, it made you happy, Dad, but it didn't make Mum happy. Some might call what you did selfish.'

'They might. But it's also about being true to yourself. Knowing who you are, and what brings you alive and celebrates your strengths. It's also about knowing what erodes your ability to accept your faults with good grace.

'Your mother no longer liked what she saw when she looked at me, and I can't help that. And I certainly wasn't about to jump through all the hoops she wanted me to in order for her *to* like me. That isn't what love is about. If the only way you can love someone is to change them, then something's not right.' Henry glared at his son, but his expression was inscrutable and it annoyed him more than ever. 'Your problem, Adam, is that you've never worked out what makes you happy. Or rather, you've never given anything a chance to settle for long enough to see if it does. You don't go hunting for happiness, Adam – if you do it will always be out of reach. Happiness comes to you. It comes when you are living in the present, when you are content, when you fully appreciate everything you have and know that it's enough. You're a good teacher. I see a lot of me in you, and you might think that's a bad thing, but I will never see it that way. I learned early on what made me happy and, believe it or not, that's all I ever wanted for you. But you need to stop searching for it, Adam, or you'll never find it.'

Behind him came a furious wail. Sofia flung open the oven door so hard it bounced on its hinges. She dragged a tray from it and practically threw it on top of the hob, where the rows of croissants it contained slid onto its shiny surface leaving a greasy trail behind them.

'For God's sake, Henry, now look what you've made me do! Everything is burned to hell.'

10

Henry was furious. He was furious for being made to feel like an idiot who knew nothing whatsoever about anything. Furious that it was Christmas Day and yet his son and daughter-in-law seemed to have no concept of the joys of the season, and furious that he had let his son's remarks get to him and had bitten back with all the thoughts he'd been harbouring for the last few years. Thoughts which had no place being aired when both parties were angry, and particularly not on a day such as this. If he thought last Christmas was difficult, then this one was turning out to hold all the trump cards, but at least he hadn't stormed out of the house the year before.

He didn't even know where he was going as he gunned the engine before shooting off the drive, but when he reached the end of the road where his son lived, he realised there was only one place he could go. Only one place he *wanted* to go. Even though it might turn out to be an even bigger mistake than the one he'd just made. He turned towards Lower Steeping.

As he might have expected, the roads were quiet and Henry hardly saw another car. Not that he would have paid them much attention if he had; his mind was churning with everything that had just been said. In fact, he was so preoccupied, he scarcely remembered the journey. One minute he was driving and the next he was climbing from his car outside Peg's cottage.

His heart was in his mouth as he knocked on the bright green front door.

'Henry! How lovely to see you.'

He so desperately wanted it to be true, and he was relieved to see that Peg *did* seem to mean what she'd said. Her smile was just as sunny as he remembered.

'Sorry, I...' He felt distinctly uncomfortable. 'I've just had a row with my son and, much to my regret, flounced from the house like a sulky teenager. Trouble was, once I'd closed the door behind me, I wasn't sure where to go. I didn't feel like creeping back in and having to make grovelling apologies, so...'

'You came to *my* door?'

'Which sounds bad, I know. Quite offensive, actually.' He pulled a face. 'Sorry,' he said again.

But to his surprise, Peg simply smiled. 'I shall take it as a compliment. Come in, and I'll make you a coffee. You look as if you could do with one.' She pulled the door open, stepping back from the threshold.

Henry stood on the doormat for a moment, not quite believing his luck as he looked around him much as a child might gaze at sweets in a shop. 'This is lovely,' he said, eyes wide as he took in the details of the cluttered kitchen. It was exactly as he had pictured.

A scrubbed wooden table stood in the middle of the space, above which dangled an array of greenery from a low ceiling criss-crossed with beams. Whitewashed stone walls were either hung with pictures, or filled with an array of shelves housing an assortment of crockery, and flowered curtains hung at the window. A shelf had been fixed across it in order to display a selection of coloured glass, and the whole room glowed with iridescent light. And in one corner stood a dark blue Aga, in front of which a cat was curled into its basket. He could feel his blood pressure lowering by the minute.

'Thank you,' said Peg. 'I like it too. And we don't fuss about the outside coming in,' she added, seeing he was about to remove his shoes. 'Mud is a bit of an occupational hazard living where I do. We don't stand on ceremony either. You can pop your coat on there.' She pointed to a row of hooks on the wall by the door which already held an assortment of jackets, hats and scarves.

Waiting until he had unburdened himself, she led him into her sitting room. 'Have a seat... although in case it bothers you I should warn you that the one by the window will be covered in cat hair.' She smiled. 'Now, coffee, is it, or would you prefer tea?'

Henry sank into one of the two chairs either side of the fireplace, where a log burner danced with flame. The heat was soothing.

'Coffee would be lovely, thank you. Just milk, please.'

With Peg busy in the kitchen, he took the opportunity to study more of his surroundings. Peg's sitting room looked out on to the road with a clear view of the village green and its collection of ducks. They were the only things moving, though – swimming slowly around the pond – the rest of the village was still and silent. All he could hear was the faint ticking of a clock.

He pressed his back further into the chair and took a deep, calming breath. The chair opposite was different from the one he was sitting in, as was the broad sofa, which all but filled the space against one wall. A large bookcase stood against another, a little too small for all the titles which were crammed onto it, so that piles also rested on the floor – a floor which was partially covered in an enormous faded rug. Nothing in this room matched, but Henry didn't think he'd been anywhere so perfect.

Moments later, Peg reappeared with a fully laden tray

which she placed on a wide footstool doing service as her coffee table. 'Look what I found...' she said, lifting a tin from it. The same tin which held the mince pies they'd shared while sitting in the traffic jam. Was that really only three days ago?

Henry shook his head in amusement. 'Sofia doesn't make hers, she gets them from a local bakery.' He took one of the proffered treats. 'It's award-winning, apparently.' He took a bite, nonchalantly transferring fallen flakes of pastry from his lap to his mouth.

'I'm sorry you've had such an awful visit,' said Peg.

Henry chewed for a moment. 'It's not been all bad, it's...' He trailed off, frowning. He'd been about to fill in some of the details from the last couple of days, but it was as if his brain had stuck fast. He couldn't think of a single thing to say. 'I guess this morning's argument has just eclipsed everything.'

'What happened?' asked Peg gently.

Henry sighed. 'Sofia and Adam were arguing about the size of their dining room when I came down to breakfast this morning, which, by the way, is plenty big enough. Something just snapped, and I'm afraid I rather said some things I shouldn't.'

Peg tipped her head to one side. 'Do you want to talk about it?' she asked.

'Not really,' said Henry, disgusted with himself. 'It was stupid... or perhaps not stupid, but ill-timed, certainly. I was daft enough to give my opinion, one thing led to another and becoming thoroughly fed up with the way I was being treated, I delivered a few home truths and then left.'

'Ah...' Peg took a mince pie from the tin. 'It does sound as if you've had a trying morning.'

Peg's face wore such a gentle expression that Henry was suddenly overcome with shame. Barging in on her Christmas wasn't at all fair, and to lumber her with his problems was inexcusable.

'I'm sorry, this really isn't something I should be bringing to your door.' He ran a hand through his hair. 'I should get back.'

'Do you *want* to get back?' Peg was looking at him so earnestly that it made him stop for a moment to think. He'd said the words, but he hadn't meant them. He'd only voiced them because his conscience was shouting abuse at him, calling him all manner of names – cowardly, insensitive, selfish... there was quite a list. But actually, what he wanted to do *was* be cowardly, insensitive and selfish. He didn't think he could bear to return to his son's house and sit through a dinner which would be awkward in the extreme.

Peg was watching him. 'I think you already know that you need to speak to Adam, and Sofia, but perhaps when emotions aren't running so high and expectations of the day are not so great. I think you also know that, if you stay here with me, which you are very welcome to do, then you'll also have to deal with the consequences of missing the family dinner. I'm afraid neither of those things are ones I can help you with.' She smiled. 'So I think we ought to agree that, if you stay, there's to be no more talk about what's happened. Give yourself a break from it and you might find you're better equipped to deal with it later.'

'I know you're a very organised person, but are you always this wise too?'

Peg shook her head. 'I don't think it's wisdom. Just that I know what *I'm* like, and I've learned over time that my brain works best when I don't attack it head-on. If I leave it alone and do something other than quiz it, I find that it gets on and does its own thing in the background. If I later enquire gently if it's come to any conclusions, I invariably find it has.' She swallowed the rest of her coffee. 'Now, I was planning to eat around three, does that suit you?'

'Oh...' Henry hadn't even considered what staying might mean.

'It's Christmas Day, Henry. A dinner of some sort is traditional and I have to eat too.' A gentle smile played around her lips.

'Three sounds perfect.'

'Excellent, you can help me peel the potatoes. But first, I think a trip to the wood is in order. I wasn't going to bother dressing the table when it was just me eating, but seeing as there are now two of us, it would be nice, don't you think?' She paused, glancing at the clock on the wall. 'Come on, or time will run away with us. It's muddy in the woods though, so help yourself to wellies. There are some old ones there which should fit you. Grab those secateurs too, please, the ones on the hook.'

Peg pulled off her pink sheepskin slippers, revealing equally pink thick socks, which poked out from underneath the hem of her dress. The informality of such an unselfconscious action made him smile. Until he took off his own shoes, he had no idea of either the state of his socks or their colour, but he didn't care. Peg wouldn't care either, and it reinforced his decision to stay. For now, he was exactly where he wanted to be.

Moments later, having followed Peg through a gate at the bottom of her garden, Henry found himself in thick woodland, hushed and still.

'You told me about this place when we were stuck in the traffic jam,' he said. 'And I remember thinking how wonderful it sounded. When you said it was behind your house, I didn't realise it was quite so close.'

'I'm incredibly lucky to have it,' replied Peg. 'And although the garden's lovely, there's something special about this place. It is absolutely the perfect spot to think and to breathe... just being here makes a difference to how I feel.'

Henry could understand that. He was already feeling the benefit of the cold, clean air in his lungs. He couldn't remember the last time he'd been for a walk and— He stopped, because that wasn't true; he could remember it exactly. His last ever walk with Meg, after so many years of walking side by side, twice a day, sometimes more. And it was as if she had sensed that something was coming to an end that day, too, only running a few steps ahead before circling back to him, pushing her nose into his hand and nudging his pockets in case any treats had found their way there. He could still feel the soft curls on the top of her head, damp from the rain, and the silky length of her ears. And then the next day she was gone. Just as Linda was. And he'd wondered who would miss him more.

'So tell me about Adam,' said Peg. 'Is he your only child?'

Henry looked up, roused from his reverie, and nodded. 'We'd wanted a large family, three or four at least, but that was back in the days when assumptions about our future were easily made. You never think, do you, that the reality will be so much harder to attain?'

'You couldn't have any more?'

'We didn't know, but Adam was such a gift that Linda and I decided we wouldn't push our luck again by asking for more, and so we stopped trying.'

He'd forgotten that. All the years of heartache. Of waiting, and praying and hoping, for weeks, sometimes longer than at others. But then came the pain of grief, always the pain, sharp and searing, followed by the need to comfort, to quell the feelings of hopelessness, of anger and desolation at something which came so easily to others, yet continued to evade them.

'There were three other babies before Adam,' he continued. 'But none of them lived long enough to be born.'

Peg looked horrified, colour flooding her face. 'I'm so sorry,' she said. 'That was stupid of me, asking like that.'

Henry shook his head. 'It was a long time ago. And once Adam arrived, those early years became a part of our lives we had no need to revisit. You never forget them – our two other boys and a girl – but Adam was so full of life that gradually our feelings about him helped to heal our feelings about them.' He smiled. 'And he was a very curious child, so our days and nights were full. We were happy then, I think.'

'And close? I would imagine you would be.' She held a branch out of his way so that he could follow her.

'We were. For a very long time. We did everything together...' He frowned. 'It seems such a long time ago now.'

Peg stopped, surveying a holly tree burgeoning with berries. 'And then all of a sudden they're grown up, and having lives of their own, without you.'

Henry passed her the secateurs. 'Linda and I weren't ready for that. I think that was our problem. Once Adam was grown up he didn't need us any more and our lives went from being full to being unfulfilled. We should have prepared ourselves for it, but we didn't.'

'Mmm,' acknowledged Peg. 'The empty nest. I know all about that.' Peg snipped at a sprig of holly. 'Although, having two children, that happened more gradually with us. Phoebe went first, ahead of her elder sister by almost two years. Maybe that gave us longer to think about what life would be like after they'd gone, I don't know. All I *do* know is that I didn't have nearly enough time with Julian.'

Henry held her look, hoping his was warm and sympathetic. It was horrible to think of someone like Peg, so vibrant and alive, living with death at such an early age. 'No,' he said quietly. 'That doesn't seem at all fair. I wish Linda and I had made the most of the time we had together but... we didn't.' And it struck Henry that perhaps he *had* been complacent after Adam left home. Had he mistaken happiness for what was actually stagnation? Or had he known it all the while, yet chosen to convince himself he was happy because it was easier than doing something to remedy the situation?

'I think Adam blames me for what happened with his mum,' he said. 'And maybe he's right.'

'*Maybe* you shouldn't be so hard on yourself,' suggested Peg.

'You didn't have sole responsibility for your marriage, after all.' She looked at the boughs of greenery in her hand. 'That ought to do it,' she added. 'We'd better get back.'

The peeling of potatoes turned into carrots as well, and parsnips. Then there were Brussels sprouts to clean up and score, and leeks from the garden to wash and slice, and by the time Henry had done that, Peg had made some stuffing using sausage meat and Bramley apples which she'd picked straight from the tree. Her kitchen was warm, and fragrant with herbs and spices and, despite the mince pie he'd eaten earlier, Henry realised he was ravenous. Not only that, but it was a meal he was actually looking forward to eating.

They had barely spoken for the last hour or so, apart from comments about what to prepare and in what quantities, but the silence had been an easy one, interspersed with Peg humming 'Deck the Halls' at odd intervals. In fact, as he'd surreptitiously watched her from across the room, there were times when she seemed almost as if she were dancing, swaying to some rhythm only she could hear.

'Did you enjoy the carol service?' she asked.

'I did, although...' Henry pulled a face. 'I spent far too many occasions in that church as a small boy wishing I was anywhere else but there. So there was this oddly nostalgic feeling, too, only not in a good way.'

'Oh dear... Do you remember much about the village?'

Henry shook his head. 'Hardly anything. We didn't live here for that long – from when I was about seven for three years or so. I'm the youngest of four, born to very busy parents, both GPs. I think they were relieved to have a child who was so quiet, so I was pretty much left to my own devices and that usually meant head in a book.'

'Hence the love of English...?'

'Mmm, and I didn't venture out much. I remember the green, although I don't think there was a pond on it back then, and I remember the post office because it had a vending machine on the outside wall where you could buy some weird cinnamon-flavoured chewing gum. I can't remember the name of it now, but I loved that stuff.'

'So you were a very quiet and studious child, were you?'

Henry looked at Peg in surprise. 'I guess I was, yes. A quiet, studious child who turned into a quiet, studious adult... I'm an English lecturer so I still have my head in a book most days...' He took in Peg's amused expression. 'Which is possibly not a surprise.'

'I didn't say that,' replied Peg. 'But now that you mention it...' She grinned. 'We talked about stereotypes when we were stuck in the traffic jam, didn't we? Me being a widow and you a divorcee... And I think we both refuted the clichés, but I'm not at all surprised to learn you're a lecturer.'

'Aren't you? What gave me away?'

'Well, perhaps the fact that when we first met you were wearing odd socks and had your jumper on back to front.'

'Was I?' Henry scratched his head, before peering down at his feet. He wriggled his toes. 'I didn't even notice.'

'It probably shouldn't, but it conjured up a vision of a forgetful academic, concerned with far more important things than the triviality of dress.'

'Guilty as charged. And I guess that does make me seem disorganised, but funnily enough, I'm the opposite when it comes to my work. With my students I have everything just so. It's the rest of my life which runs away from me.'

'So you enjoy your job?'

'Oh yes, I think it's the one thing I'm good at.'

'Then you're lucky enough to have discovered what brings you alive – what gives your life meaning.' She pursed her lips as if pondering what she'd just said. 'Everything else is just noise, isn't it?'

Henry stared at her. There was something in what she'd

said. Some distinction maybe between the way in which he lived his life and the way Adam did. Could that be why he and his son didn't understand one another? A thought was trying to make itself understood, but Henry couldn't quite catch hold of it for long enough to make any sense.

He looked around at Peg's kitchen, at the clutter which... no, that wasn't the right word. It wasn't clutter in the sense of being untidy, more that there were simply lots of things in the room. It should feel oppressive, but somehow it didn't. In fact, the opposite was true. Henry found it comfortable, comforting...

'Is everything okay?' asked Peg. 'You seem to be looking for something.'

Henry frowned. 'I was just thinking... When I look at my son's house compared with yours, it isn't just the style which is different, there's something else as well – like nothing there fits properly. Here, everything blends. It doesn't jar your eyes to look at it, it doesn't jar your thoughts either. Does that sound crazy? I'm not sure I can explain it properly.'

'No, I understand,' said Peg. 'When we first moved here the bathroom was downstairs – through the door to the right of the fireplace. Getting to it from upstairs was a bit of a convoluted journey – through the dining room, across the lounge, round the side of the sofa and then...' She paused to look at him. 'Do you see where I'm going with this? We didn't give it a huge amount of thought to start with – it was where the bathroom was and that was the end of it. But after a couple of months, things in the house began to niggle at me. The living room didn't look quite right. Neither did the dining room. The colours were wrong, or a piece of furniture was in the wrong place, and we spent months fiddling with things, but never seeming to fix the problem. And it was sad because this was our dream house in every other respect. We'd so looked forward to moving here and yet... something wasn't working.

'The solution came about quite by chance when we decided to make some alterations to the kitchen and the builder asked if we'd ever thought of moving the bathroom upstairs. Because if we were, with all the changes that would need to be made to the plumbing, that would be the time to do it. It was as if someone had turned a light on. And from the moment the alteration was made, the house righted itself. It flowed, you see... and we were moving *with* the flow instead of against it. I think the same is true with our lives.

'Sometimes, when we think we're unhappy with a particular thing, or want to change it, it's only because we haven't worked out that it's actually something else causing the problems. Does that make sense? And because we don't know what that something is, we go about changing all manner of stuff in the hope that it will make everything feel better, not even realising that we're going about it all wrong.'

Henry was astonished. 'That's it,' he said. 'That's *exactly* what I see when I look at Adam and the way he and Sofia live their lives. All that striving, wanting more, wanting different, and yet none of it will alter the way they're feeling. It's something else which is off, and until they work out what that is, nothing will fundamentally change.'

Peg tipped her head to one side. 'So what's the problem then?'

'That's just it,' said Henry, scratching his head. 'I have absolutely no idea.'

Henry rested his spoon in his bowl. He didn't think he could eat another mouthful, but the chocolate pudding had looked so enticing – oozing with sauce and served with cream so thick you could stand a spoon up in it – that Henry's willpower had entirely deserted him. And that was after he'd laid waste to a plateful of roast chicken with all the trimmings. Not quite the traditional turkey, as Peg had said on more than one occasion, but she preferred chicken and he had to say he agreed with her. The meal had been nothing less than superb.

It had also been relaxed, with conversation that flowed amid laughter and general good humour, and Henry couldn't help but compare it to the one he would have eaten had he stayed at Adam's house. It was the only thing which soured his stomach.

He insisted on doing the washing-up while Peg sat down, something which, much to Henry's surprise, she agreed to, telling him to just stack the dishes on the drainer and leave them to dry. And it was nice, peaceful, pottering in her kitchen among the plants and bunches of herbs dangling from the beams. He dried everything as well – it didn't seem right to leave it – stacking the crockery and pans on the side once he'd finished so that Peg could return them to their rightful places.

By the time he returned to the living room, the house was still, and quiet, just the ticking of a clock somewhere, but even that seemed slow and soothing. Peg had curled herself into the corner of the sofa, one arm propping up her head, with a book open on her lap.

'Is this what you'd be doing if I wasn't here?' he asked.

She looked up, smiling lazily. 'I expect so. Or perhaps doing a jigsaw. Something which wouldn't take me too far away from the fire, in any case.'

'I don't blame you.' The log burner had died down to a bed of glowing ashes, but he could still feel the heat from it, gently radiating into the room. Peg didn't look like she was going anywhere and so he crossed to the bookcase that lined one wall.

'May I?' he asked.

'Be my guest,' replied Peg, waving a nonchalant hand. 'They might not be your cup of tea, but see what you can find.'

There was no order to any of the books on the shelves – gardening books nestled against fiction, a first-aid manual beside a book of poetry – but he rather liked it that way. You had to really look to see what was there, and Henry smiled as some familiar titles appeared. After a few moments, he came to a series of detective novels by an author he admired, titles which he hadn't yet got around to reading. He selected the first, drawing it from the shelf and turning it to read the information on the back.

'Are these any good?' he asked, holding up the book so that Peg could see the cover.

'Wonderful,' she replied. 'And each one seems better than the last.'

Henry carried it to the chair and turned to the dedication. It was something he always did. *For Anne McIntyre*, he read, and he smiled, wondering who Anne was and what she had done to make her worthy of the dedication. Then, turning the page, he settled down to read.

He had barely finished the first chapter, however, when Peg's cat suddenly jumped into his lap. It kneaded his legs gently, turning first one way and then the other, nuzzling its head against him before curling itself into a ball and settling down to sleep.

'I ought to be getting back,' he said, suddenly aware of what he was doing. 'And let you have some of the day in peace.'

Peg smiled. 'Perhaps... But at least let your dinner go down first.'

She didn't seem in any hurry for him to leave, and so Henry dipped his head to the book once more. He *did* need to return, well aware that there was still a situation to resolve, apologies to be made and conversations to be had, but he felt far more able to do so now. Perhaps this *was* all he'd needed, some time away from the situation, some distance in which to order his thoughts and gain a different perspective. His hand lowered to stroke the cat's back, its expanse of fur soft and warm. He would go soon, maybe just another couple of chapters.

The words, however, began to dance on the page, becoming

more and more jumbled as sleep began to soften the edges of his vision. His head dropped forward, and even though he jerked it up again, the same thing happened moments later. This time he let it fall. He was so cosy, so comfortable, relaxed for the first time in what felt like ages. Maybe he'd just rest his eyes for ten minutes or so...

11

CHRISTMAS DAY

Putting her book to one side, Peg got up and wandered through to the kitchen where she stood in a dither of indecision. She wasn't quite sure what she wanted. A cup of tea? Or something to eat? But she'd not long had a couple of those especially chocolatey biscuits and there was still tea in the pot from her last cup. She glanced at her watch. Perhaps she could work on her article for an hour or so, but it was the holidays, and she'd promised herself she wouldn't. Plus, there was plenty of time before it needed to be submitted to her editor. She eyed Rolo, who was curled up in his basket beside the range, a paw over his nose. He was there for the duration.

'See, if you were a dog, you'd drag me out for a walk and that would be that, but...' The cat made no movement at all. Peg sighed. Perhaps she'd read a couple more chapters of her book.

The knock on the door startled her. Odd... Judith was with her daughter and grandchildren today. Besides, it was a hurried knock, purposeful, not perfunctory like Judith's was. And if it *was* her, she'd have opened the door and come in by now. Peg frowned, slightly irritated. It was Christmas Day, for heaven's sake, who would come calling now? It wasn't that she guarded her solitude, Judith often came unannounced, but like a lot of people her age, Peg had become accustomed to routine and found it hard when that altered, yet...

She pulled open the door, causing the woman outside to practically fall through it.

'Oh, thank God you're in,' she said. 'I've had to knock on three doors before I found someone who could tell me where you lived. No one's in, or they aren't answering.'

'Well, it is Christmas Day, people are busy,' replied Peg. She stared at the woman, recognition firing as she overcame her surprise. '*Sofia*? What on earth are you doing here?'

'I'm sorry... this is...' Sofia stopped, her features contorting. 'I don't even know how I'm supposed to say this, for goodness' sake. I mean, I'm not even sure Adam's got it right...'

Peg pulled the door a little wider. 'Would you like to come in?' Something must be wrong, because the perfectly turned out, immaculately dressed woman Peg had met after the carol service looked nothing like the version in front of her now. 'Has something happened?'

'It's Henry,' blurted Sofia, pulling a phone from her coat pocket and jabbing at the screen. She seemed a little relieved by what she saw, or perhaps didn't see. 'There's been an accident and he... are you and he...? Perhaps you just ought to come with me.'

Peg frowned, her mouth working as she tried to fathom what Sofia was struggling to tell her. 'Okay, so you're talking about Henry...' She trailed off, realising she didn't even know his last name. 'Your father-in-law?'

Sofia nodded.

'What's happened?'

Sofia's hand flew to her mouth. 'They had an awful row, and then... It was my fault. I shouldn't have shouted at him, but he flew out the door and we didn't even think anything of it at first. Adam said he was probably just in the front garden, or walking up and down the street and we should leave him to cool off. Adam was furious as well and... It was only when half an hour had gone past that we realised Henry's car wasn't there.' Sofia stared at her, her eyes wide, searching for answers she wasn't sure Peg had. 'He doesn't know anyone else who lives out this way, so he must have been on his way here. And he's been asking for you, too. He was in so much pain, and Adam thought it might help if he saw you. He didn't know if you... well, if you and Henry...'

The penny dropped with a dull clank in the pit of Peg's stomach. 'No, I... we hardly know one another but, where is he?' She could hear the pitch of her own voice begin to rise. Why would Henry be asking for her? Why would he have been coming to see her? Today of all days. It didn't make any sense. 'Tell me what's happened.'

'We don't know,' said Sofia. 'He hit a tree but, other than that, we've no idea. The police didn't think anyone else was involved, but his car's a wreck and—' She broke off, looking as if she were about to cry. 'It's Christmas Day, he can't die today. Adam would never...'

Suddenly aware they were still standing on the doorstep, Peg held out her arms and pulled Sofia into the warmth of her kitchen, hugging her tight. She wanted to tell her it would all be okay, but she couldn't. And she wouldn't. Everyone had told her that about Julian, and she'd said the words to herself like a mantra, over and over – he'll be okay, it'll be okay – but he hadn't and it wasn't.

Her own fear sparked her into action. 'Where is he, Sofia? Which hospital?' She pulled off her slippers and began rooting for her shoes. Why could she never find them when— She thrust her feet into them and snatched up her phone from the table. 'Just give me a minute,' she said. 'I need to sort a couple of things.'

Sofia nodded. 'I'll wait outside.'

Moments later, Peg joined her, looking anxiously at her ashen face and the silent tears sliding down her cheeks.

'My car's this way,' said Sofia. 'I didn't know where you lived.'

Peg took one look at the monstrous size of the vehicle by the kerb and steered them towards her own little hatchback which sat on the gravel to one side of her cottage.

'I'll drive,' she said. 'There's no way you should be behind a wheel, and I'm not getting in that thing. Just tell me where we need to go.'

'He's in Cheltenham, the hospital by the—'

'I know it,' said Peg as she started the engine. She knew it only too well. Seconds later, they were on their way.

Peg didn't know what to say. Clearly, Adam had thought there was more to her relationship with Henry than there was, but what would have given him that idea? Not unless Henry had said... It had been lovely bumping into him again after the carol service yesterday evening and, had he been on his own, it's quite possible she would have invited him in, the thought was certainly there, but... Thankfully, Sofia kept her eyes glued to her phone for most of the journey and Peg didn't need to talk much other than to ask questions about what might be happening at the hospital.

Thankfully time was on their side. Visiting hours didn't start until the afternoon, and with no clinics running today, the car park was mercifully quiet. She had driven round and round it on so many occasions in the past, panic mounting as the minutes ticked by and she was no closer to finding a space. No closer to seeing Julian. She had wanted to shout at people, to accuse them of not understanding. Didn't they realise how critical time was for her? Surely someone would have given her a space if they knew her situation, allowed her to park anywhere under the circumstances. But then she knew, deep down, that so many other people there were just like her, feeling every second slipping away from them, terrified that they would be too late. She prayed for Sofia's sake, for Adam's sake, that today would not be that day.

The accident and emergency department was always busy. It made no difference that a tinselled tree stood in the corner of the waiting room, or that the television hanging on a wall showed a choir singing mute carols, the words running in a stream across the bottom of the picture. It was less busy than when she had last seen it, however, and for that she was grateful. Sofia hurried to speak to a receptionist and, within moments, they were escorted down a long corridor and shown into another. A single figure was sitting in the middle of a row of seats. Adam jumped up as soon as he saw them.

It was awkward. Peg didn't know these people. She knew *of* them, but that wasn't the same thing, and what little she did know wasn't particularly complimentary. But it was Christmas, a time when bad things should never happen, so she hugged Adam as he came towards her and mumbled that she was sorry.

He nodded. 'Thank you for coming. I've been told to wait here,' he said. 'I don't really know what's happening. One of the nurses said something about theatre but there's someone else with Dad just now.' He pointed to a curtained area some distance away. 'He's through there.'

Sofia clutched at his hand and sat down beside him. 'That's good then,' she said. 'If he's got someone with him. It means they're doing something.' She nodded several times, studying her husband's face to see that he agreed with her.

Peg took a seat, smiling a little. 'I'm not sure why I'm here,' she whispered, her stomach tight with anxiety. 'I'm not sure what I can do.'

Adam's face looked pinched and his hair stuck up on one side as if he'd been repeatedly running his hand through it. 'Because Dad was saying your name over and over,' he replied, his voice scratchy. 'He couldn't breathe, and he was in so much pain. Everything has already gone wrong today. If he...' He swallowed. 'If he dies, I didn't want it to be without seeing you first. In case it matters.'

Peg nodded. 'Okay,' she murmured. Adam would expect her to reassure him, to say how certain she was that his dad would pull through, but she'd made a bargain with herself never to promise that again. It wasn't a promise anyone could keep.

The curtain twitched open and two people appeared – a nurse and another man in normal clothes, their heads bent together as they looked at a clipboard the nurse held in his hands. Walking towards them, the nurse looked up and smiled.

'Are you Peg?' he asked.

Heart in her mouth, Peg nodded.

The other person smiled now, his gaze taking in all three of them. He held out his hand. 'I'm Mr Hemmingway, consultant thoracic surgeon. And you are?'

Adam got to his feet. 'I'm his... Henry's son. And this is my wife, Sofia.' They shook hands.

The surgeon sat down, motioning that they should all do the same.

'Okay, so you know that your dad has been in a serious accident.' He cleared his throat and nodded as if he was answering his own question. 'He's badly concussed and has broken a couple of ribs, one of which has punctured his lung. We've got that sorted out for now, but he needs to go to theatre as soon as possible and we'll be taking him down very soon. You can come and see him for a few minutes, though.'

They all stood up again, Peg last, lagging behind so that it wouldn't be her who entered the cubicle first.

The nurse drew back the curtain and Sofia gasped, clutching at Adam's arm. It wasn't good, anyone could see that. There were cuts, bruises, blood... They moved as one to stand beside Henry.

Peg's eyes flew to the machine he was tethered to, the one

which beat out the pulses of his life. Numbers for this, numbers for that, lines and wiggles, each one telling a story, a story which Peg could read like a book. She dropped her eyes, wondering if Adam could understand them too.

The nurse smiled and held out a hand to her. Peg could see his name was Robin. 'Henry's been asking for you, Peg. Why don't you come round this side so he can see you better?'

And for the first time, standing by the side of his bed, Peg allowed herself to look at the man she had shared no more than two hours of her life with. A man she barely knew, but who liked cheese and beetroot sandwiches and mince pies and had joked with her about the colour of paint which may or may not have been spilled all over the M5 motorway. Breakfast Room Green. Would he even remember that?

His hair looked more grey than she recalled, but perhaps the lighting was to blame. And his face more lined, but perhaps that was down to the pain. She forced herself to smile.

'Hello, Henry.'

His eyes turned towards her and recognition flickered, pulling up the corners of his mouth – just a little – not quite a smile, but something... His lips moved, but if he said anything no one could hear it and then they closed again, along with his eyes. His hand lay inches from her own, and she wondered if she should... She slipped her fingers around his and gave a tiny squeeze. It didn't matter that she scarcely knew him, what mattered was that he knew she was there. She shushed the thoughts which were jostling inside her head. They were too much, too painful...

The nurse was making ready. The surgeon was on the move. It was time to say goodbye.

12

The hands on the clock turned. The minutes became an hour and then two. Peg shifted her weight from one haunch to the other, uncrossing her legs and recrossing them in the other direction. There was only so long one could sit on a plastic chair without it becoming deeply uncomfortable, and she was at the point where she needed to stand.

'Can I get anyone anything?' she asked.

It was the third time she'd asked the same question, or some variant of it. First it was drinks, then something to eat, and on both the previous occasions, Adam and Sofia had mutely shaken their heads. Adam's gaze was still fixed on the wall ahead; Peg didn't think he'd moved it in all the time they had been sitting there.

'There's a restaurant here,' she added. 'And I'm going to see what they have. At least get a cup of tea. Are you sure you don't want anything?'

'I'll come with you,' said Sofia, suddenly getting to her feet. 'I'll get some coffees. Adam?' Her husband turned his face, incomprehension the only thing written there. 'Shall I get you a coffee?'

'Yeah, sure...' He turned back to the wall.

Peg shot Sofia a glance before moving to stand directly in front of Adam. She leaned down and touched his arm. 'The restaurant is upstairs if you need us,' she said, waiting a moment until she had his attention before continuing. 'It's right opposite the bank of lifts as you come out.'

Adam nodded. 'Yeah, I know where you mean.'

'Okay then, see you in a bit,' she said before leading Sofia away. She knew Adam's look well; that had been her a few years ago.

'Oh dear...' said Sofia as soon as they had passed through a set of double swing doors and were out of earshot. 'He's blaming himself. I knew he would.'

'It happens,' murmured Peg.

'But Henry was as much to blame. In fact, he started the argument, going on again about Adam's promotion. We were talking about having our dining room extended and he just had to pour cold water on the idea, it's all he ever does when we talk about our plans. And it's Christmas Day,' she added, as if that would convey everything she was feeling.

Peg gave an acknowledgement. Perhaps in Sofia's world that was sacrosanct and still retained its special status, an untouchable oasis of time, but Peg knew that there was no such thing. Things happened whenever they chose – at the right time, a slightly inconvenient time or an inconceivable one, it made no difference.

'I had to turn my oven off,' she said. 'I've got an eighteen-pound turkey in there. Roast potatoes, pigs in blankets... Do you think I can just carry on cooking it?'

Peg stared at her. 'Let's get something to drink,' she said. 'I imagine it's all rather a shock.' The Sofia that Peg knew, even if only by reputation, was returning.

The smell of gravy greeted them as soon as the lift doors opened. It was lunchtime, and whatever else was going on in the world, there was food to be eaten. The restaurant was quiet, more staff than visitors or patients, and she wondered fleetingly if they were able to have a special dinner today. She steered Sofia towards a pile of trays and, picking one up, began to survey what was on offer.

'Do you want anything to eat?' she asked. 'Or will Adam?'

Sofia pulled out her phone and stared at the screen. 'It's gone one o'clock,' she said. 'I'd have been serving Christmas dinner in an hour.'

Peg reached forward to claim a chicken and bacon sandwich. 'Sofia, I hope you don't mind me saying, but I think you need to forget about your turkey, about the fact that it's Christmas. I don't think you're going to be eating your dinner today, and you might not be eating it tomorrow either.'

'But all the food? And the preparation? I've been up since six getting everything ready. And we haven't even opened our presents.'

Peg injected as much warmth as she could into her expression. 'Yes, I know,' she said gently. 'But Henry could be in theatre for quite some time, and it will be a while after that before you're able to see him, depending on how things are. The broken bones are only the start of it. A collapsed lung is serious, particularly if the injury from his rib was bad enough that they have to operate on it.'

'Wait, he has a collapsed lung?'

Peg nodded, softening her expression even further.

'That's what the surgeon meant when he said a rib had punctured it. The chest area where the lungs are located is airtight; it's not meant to have a hole in it. If the air pressure changes it can cause all sorts of problems. Henry wouldn't have been able to breathe, for one thing.'

Sofia nodded. 'It was horrible. He was gasping...' She stared at the tray in front of her but Peg knew that wasn't what she was seeing. Her gaze had turned inward.

'So what will they do?' she asked.

Peg shook her head. 'I don't know exactly, but mend the hole, reinflate his lung and hope it holds.' She paused for a moment. 'I'm not trying to be unkind, but it's better if you know what you're dealing with.'

Sofia's eyes were sharp on hers. 'How do you know all this?'

'I watch a lot of medical dramas,' lied Peg. She added a slice of Bakewell tart to the tray. 'Why don't you have something?' she said. 'You probably haven't eaten, and even if you don't fancy it now, you might in another hour or so. How about a ham sandwich?'

Sofia scrutinised the wrapper of an egg salad roll and reluctantly added it to the collection of food. 'Do they have any turkey?' she asked. 'Poor Adam.'

'Yes, with cranberry sauce and stuffing. Will that be all right?'

A few minutes later they picked their way through the dining room to a table by the window. An empty cup had been left there and Peg moved it to one beside them.

'I made a pavlova, too,' said Sofia. 'With pomegranate seeds. It looked beautiful, like it was covered in tiny jewels. I told Mum to eat it, so I doubt there'll even be much left when we get home.'

Peg drew in a slow breath. 'I'd forgotten that Blanche was staying with you.' It was something else Peg would have to think about. But not just now.

Sofia nodded. 'It was Blanche who worked out where Henry had been going when he crashed his car. He was only half a mile from your village, so she said it made sense, and I guess it does if you think about it. Had you invited him over, was that it? He probably didn't even want to spend the day with us at all.'

'I'm sure he did,' Peg answered, even though she had no idea whether that was true. 'I don't know Henry all that well.

Hardly at all, actually. But I do know that he was very keen to spend time with you. I think he wished he and Adam were closer.'

'Well, he shouldn't go picking fights then, should he? Nothing was ever good enough for him. Nothing I did pleased him.'

Thinking back to their conversation in the traffic jam, Peg didn't think that was the problem at all. 'Perhaps he didn't want you going to so much trouble for him,' she said. 'I can see how that might make it look like he wasn't grateful when, in fact, it's almost the opposite. Perhaps he felt bad about it.'

'Hmm.' Sofia clearly wasn't convinced.

'And I'm sure the argument was one of those heat-of-the-moment situations. People say things they don't really mean, and Christmas can make everyone a bit on edge. Too many hopes pinned on it being a perfect day.' Peg was keen to ensure that if things ended badly, Sofia and Adam's last thoughts about Henry wouldn't be sour ones.

Sofia seemed to come to the same conclusion. 'Perhaps you're right,' she said. 'We shouldn't focus on that now.'

Peg nodded, somewhat relieved that they weren't about to dissect Henry's relationship with his son and daughter-in-law, but she *was* still curious to know why Henry had chosen to visit her. Peg still had no real idea why she was here – that she was needed was indisputable, but the why of it all continued to escape her.

'I think Henry said that you're an interior designer. Is that right?' she asked, changing the subject.

Sofia pulled at the packaging containing her roll. 'I have my own business,' she said. 'You can't believe how busy I've been in the run-up to Christmas, with people wanting everything to be finished. Plus, I've been posting daily, all the tips and hacks I've picked up along the way. My social media has been *insane...*'

'Oh dear,' said Peg. 'I'm afraid I steer well clear of all that. I write for a magazine. Only occasionally now, but back in the day when I was an editor, I looked after all the Christmas features. It got too much though, especially given that the articles were written over the summer. I'm afraid it turned me away from all the hype over the season, and I prefer things to be simpler now.' She smiled. 'I stick with gardening, and nature. It's far less pressured.'

'Oh, it's not pressure...' replied Sofia. 'It's about wanting things to look nice, having fun with it. People like to try new things and follow fashions, they always have.'

'I suppose,' said Peg, suddenly feeling rather conspicuous in her voluminous dress and scruffy shoes. 'But it's made everything so commercial. As if you can't have a good time unless you're wearing matching pyjamas and buy an Advent calendar that costs three hundred pounds.'

'It might seem like an awful lot of money, but did you know that the value of the goods inside the calendar is usually much higher than the price you pay for it?'

Peg smiled, wondering if Sofia really couldn't see what was wrong with that. But, somehow, she didn't think accumulating dozens of unwanted products was going to be an issue for Sofia. She was about to change the subject again when Sofia's phone trilled.

'Where are you, for heaven's sake?' Adam's voice was loud enough for Peg to hear even though he wasn't on speaker. 'You need to get back down here, *now*...'

Sofia shot Peg an anguished look before snatching at her handbag and scrambling to her feet. She dropped one of the handles in her haste and the bag tipped, spilling its contents across the table. A lipstick rolled away and dropped off the edge. A packet of tissues landed on her plate.

'I'll sort this lot,' said Peg. 'Go on, go!'

. . .

It was a bleed on the brain. The nurse who told them didn't know the details, but Henry was on the operating table so he was in the best possible place. Then she told them to prepare for the worst.

Peg swallowed, catching a look from Adam that she couldn't fathom. It was as if he was pleading with her to make everything all right. But she shouldn't be here. It wasn't right that she should sit through whatever was coming next with these people. They were Henry's family. People who, although they might have had their differences, clearly loved him. *She* hardly knew him. But what could she say? *Sorry, but you're on your own?* For whatever reason they had deemed it necessary for her to be there, the longer she stayed the harder it became to leave. She should have gone long before now, when things weren't so in the balance, when she wouldn't feel as if she was walking out and abandoning them.

So she stayed for the two hours it took until the surgeon pushed open the swing doors and walked towards them. *How did he do it?* wondered Peg. How did he arrange his face into such a neutral expression that nothing could be gleaned from it until, in the final moment as he came to stand in front of them, he smiled.

Henry was alive.

The bleed was sudden, but Henry was lucky. If he had been anywhere else when it happened, the prognosis would have been much, much worse. As it was, they were able to quickly stem the bleeding, but although things were stable at present, the brain was unpredictable, and only time would tell what damage had been done. They had, however, repaired the puncture wound to his chest and reinflated his lung, which for the moment was staying that way.

He had been moved to the intensive care unit and would be unconscious for some while. There was a waiting area, a different one, where they would be more comfortable and, in a little while, a nurse would come to fetch them so that they could see him. Wordlessly, they got to their feet.

It was a feeling Peg remembered so well. The feeling that things were being said to you from a great distance. That you could hear them, but you couldn't understand them, and wouldn't, not for a few more minutes at least. You smiled and said thank you and behaved perfectly normally, although if anyone asked you, you wouldn't remember a single thing you'd said.

The new waiting area wasn't far, and the seats were padded. There was a water dispenser in one corner of the room and a low table held a jug of plastic flowers and a box of tissues. A clock on the wall recorded the time in case anyone was interested.

It was Adam who spoke first. 'You just never imagine it, do you?'

And both Peg and Sofia nodded because they knew exactly what he meant.

Peg took the opportunity to put down all the things she had been carrying for the past two hours – her sandwich, the remains of Sofia's egg salad roll. A sandwich for Adam, a piece of Bakewell tart, a Coke, a milkshake and a carton of apple juice. She smiled. And sat down. She had studied the information on each item's packaging over and over again. Ingredients, nutritional details, storage instructions, recycling opportunities, together with the colours and the design and execution of the packaging itself. She was sick of them. She never wanted to look at them again. She took a deep breath.

'Um, I was wondering whether one of us should check in on Blanche?'

It was as if a pressure valve had suddenly been released.

'Oh God, yes, of course,' said Adam.

'I'll give her a ring. Mum will be frantic with worry.' Sofia looked suddenly horrified. 'She won't have had anything to eat.

Or probably drink.' She had obviously forgotten her previous comment about the pavlova. 'She won't, you see, without one of us to... She lives in a home,' she added for Peg's benefit. She pulled her phone from her pocket. 'I should probably go, but...'

Adam's face hollowed. He and Sofia might not have been talking much but it was clear he didn't want to be left on his own, or possibly worse, with Peg.

'Let me,' said Peg. 'My car's here anyway and I... It's probably best if you two go and see Henry on your own. I doubt they'll let me in anyway – too many people.'

She got to her feet, inordinately glad of the excuse to do something. 'I'm happy to go and sit with Blanche, make sure she's okay. I could take her back to my house, if you like. Make her something to eat and drink. Actually, that's a better idea because your car is still at mine, Sofia. So you two can stay here as long as you want and then just come over later when you're ready. Any time, it doesn't matter. Just see how things go...' She trailed off.

'I'll give you my keys,' said Sofia, fishing in her bag. 'We're in Bishop's Coombe, do you know it? The new development by the old post office. Take the first right after you turn in and we're at the end of the cul-de-sac. Number fourteen.'

It was settled. Yes, Peg was fine with the directions. No, she didn't mind. Yes, she would deadbolt the front door behind them. Thank you, she would take the pavlova.

She hurried away, pushing open the main doors to the hospital and finally, only then, was she able to take big, huge breaths of clean, fresh air.

Her eyes turned skyward. *Please, please, don't let him die.*

13

There was no getting away from the fact that Peg was curious. She had no idea what to expect from Adam and Sofia's house, and all she really knew was that Sofia had bows on the backs of her dining room chairs which matched the table napkins. Oh, and that the room itself was too small. Beyond that, Peg had been given various impressions, and she was intrigued to see how reality matched with expectation.

At first glance, it looked no different from most modern houses; neat, square and with few characteristics to distinguish it from its neighbours. However, as Peg drew nearer and swung into a driveway at the side, she could see the property extended to the rear far further than she'd first thought. It wasn't a mansion, but it wasn't of average size either.

Sofia had phoned Blanche to tell her that Peg was on her way, but Peg still rang the doorbell rather than use the keys she'd been given; it didn't seem right to simply walk in.

The door was opened in a matter of seconds, and Peg was surprised anew by how tiny Blanche was. She was slender as a rake and now, in daylight, Peg could see she had bright silver, almost white hair. Importantly, she wore a grateful, welcoming smile. She ushered Peg inside where a wave of stifling heat hit her.

'Come in and sit down,' she said. 'It sounds as if you've had quite a day. Can I get you something to drink? Or eat? I don't suppose you've had anything.'

Admittedly, Peg hadn't been able to form much of an impression about Blanche from the brief occasion when they'd met yesterday, but Blanche was obviously far more sprightly than she'd been led to believe. It was clear that she was quite capable of looking after herself. She cleared her throat. 'A glass of water would be lovely, thank you.'

Blanche nodded. 'It's so damn hot in here, isn't it? I'd turn the heating down but you want to see the gadget that controls it. It looks like a NASA launch pad. One glass of water coming up.'

Peg followed her into the kitchen, awed momentarily by the grandeur of the decoration *and* the decorations – glittering gold and pale pink baubles and bows hung everywhere, with not a shred of tinsel in sight. At first glance it all looked incredible, like something from the pages of the magazine Peg wrote for, but the longer she stood there, the more she realised how sterile it was compared to the cosy comfort of her own cottage. She couldn't get home soon enough.

Blanche handed her a tall glass. 'How is Henry?' she asked, turning to lean up against a vast island unit. 'Sofia wouldn't tell me much.'

'He's very poorly,' Peg replied. 'I'm not sure what your daughter said, but he's just come out of surgery. There were a few problems, which they've fixed, so now it's just a question of waiting.' She gave an apologetic smile, not sure how much information she should give.

Blanche's eyes narrowed. 'What kind of problems?' She was studying Peg's face with gentle concern. 'Is he going to die?'

Peg almost choked. 'No... I'm sure—' She broke off. Blanche

didn't look as if she'd fall over if she told her the truth. 'Actually, we don't know yet. It's possible. And I think the next twenty-four hours or so are going to be the worst. He has some broken ribs and a collapsed lung, which they've corrected with surgery, but he had a bleed on the brain while he was under the anaesthetic and that has obviously eclipsed all else. I'm sorry.'

Blanche nodded, reflecting on Peg's words for a moment. 'I appreciate you being honest with me,' she said. 'Sofia has just told me that everything will be fine, and clearly that's not the case... Poor Henry. He doesn't deserve to die.'

'No,' said Peg quietly, not sure what else to say.

'It's such a shame he never reached you either. Then at least he might have had a nice day. He wasn't going to get one here.'

Now Peg *really* didn't know what to say. 'I gather there was a bit of an argument...'

'There was. I was in the living room and heard every word; very unpleasant.' She gave Peg a sharp look. 'I hope for everyone's sake that Henry pulls through. Having your final words to someone be as unkind as these ones were is not the sort of legacy you want to leave behind. But, just for the record, I don't blame Henry. Yes, he told Adam some very plain truths but, in my opinion, they were long overdue. You only have to look at the man to know how much he loves his son, but Adam almost goes out of his way not to believe it. And Sofia... All she cares about is having her grand occasion ruined. Sorry, but I speak as I find, and there we are.'

Peg wanted to smile. Blanche sounded so like Mim they could almost be twins. Smiling would have felt inappropriate, but she let the corners of her mouth twitch, just a little. And judging by the expression on Blanche's face, she appreciated it.

'Henry's a lovely man,' Blanche added. 'But I'm sure you already know that.'

Peg cleared her throat again. 'Actually... I really don't know him that well at all. But yes, he seemed lovely. Seems lovely.'

Blanche was puzzled. 'How did you know Henry was in hospital?'

'He was asking for me, apparently, so Sofia came and got me. I imagine it was down to the pain he was in. Perhaps he was a bit delirious.'

'Hmm... perhaps.' Blanche gave her a warm smile. 'And so here you are. It's lovely to see you again, even under such horrible circumstances. We didn't have a proper introduction yesterday, did we?'

'No, I...' She gave Blanche a curious look. 'What did you mean by your comment, when you came up to me just as you were all about to leave? You said you were sorry. Why sorry?'

'Yes, that's right. Sorry to hear about your aunt.' Blanche sighed as she looked around the kitchen. 'It's such a bloody awful time of year.'

Peg was slightly taken aback by the cheerful way Blanche swore, but this time she *did* smile; a woman after her own heart.

'Mim gave me quite a shock, that's for sure. But there's not much gets her down.'

Now it was Blanche's turn to look surprised. 'Oh... I think I thought... that you'd lost her.' She shook her head. 'Ignore me, when you're old like me you think everyone dies.'

'No, not Mim. She's made of stern stuff. I had a devil of a job getting her to come home with me, mind. She was determined to stay at her house. If it wasn't for the hospital virtually insisting, I don't think she would have.' She raised her eyebrows at Blanche. 'The more the merrier.'

Blanche was instantly contrite. 'No, that's not right. If your aunt's with you then we mustn't take advantage. Offering to take me home with you is very kind, but you'll have no need of me under your feet. No, I shall stay here. I can look after myself perfectly well.'

Peg eyed her resolute expression. 'I don't doubt it, but you're not staying here by yourself. It's Christmas, that would be horrible. Besides, Sofia's car is still at my house, so she and Adam will have to come back there at some point before going home.'

'You do realise this might go on for some time? With Henry so poorly it could be days before the picture is any clearer. And I imagine that Adam will want to stay at the hospital, at least until he knows his dad is out of danger.'

'I know,' said Peg. 'But that's all right.' She looked around the kitchen, noticing for the first time how neat it was. In fact, it was spotless. 'I was going to say, "right, let's get things sorted", but it appears they already are. Sofia made it sound as if she'd just dropped everything when they heard about Henry. She said she had a turkey in the oven...'

'Mmm, it's still there,' said Blanche. 'But only because I daren't throw it away. It'll be no good now, of course, but I've cleared up everything else. We should take some of it, actually, there's a mountain of food, ridiculous, really.'

Peg nodded. 'Sofia mentioned a pavlova?'

'Ah...' Blanche coloured slightly. 'I'm very partial to those. We can take what's left, anyway.' She flicked an amused glance at Peg. 'But let's leave the trifle behind...' She shook her head. 'I've never liked trifle.'

In the end, Peg had taken responsibility for the turkey and bundled it into a carrier bag, before throwing it in the bin. She reasoned that nobody would want to come home and have to deal with it. She let Blanche decide what else they should take, and after waiting so that she could also pack a few precautionary things for an overnight stay, they set off back to her cottage. The relief was immense.

'Oh, this is lovely,' declared Blanche, walking into Peg's kitchen. 'And don't take this the wrong way, but everything looks so *comfortable*. Not spartan at all.'

Peg laughed. 'It's all very well used, but at least when it's like this it doesn't matter if you make a mess. It is a kitchen, after all.'

'Oh, and you have a Rayburn...' added Blanche, wandering over to look at the cooker. 'Oh, no, it's not, it's an Essie. Goodness, I haven't seen one of these in years. I had one not long after I was married. Good, aren't they?'

'I love it,' replied Peg. 'Makes incredible cakes and roast dinners, so I can forgive it all else. Do you want to sit in here for a minute? I left Mim having a lie-down, so I expect the fire in the living room has gone out. It will be chilly in there if it has, and it will be a while before it warms up.'

'Shall I put the kettle on?' asked Blanche.

'Oh yes, do. Thanks.'

She beetled off to check on Mim, leaving Blanche to make the drinks. It tickled her that Sofia thought Blanche needed someone to look after her. The opportunity to sit down a little more frequently, perhaps, but that was about all.

Ten minutes later, with Mim still sound asleep, they were beside the fire, enjoying a cup of tea while watching the hearth dance with flame. It was almost five in the afternoon. The curtains were drawn against the darkness outside, and the only other light in the room came from the twinkling stars on the Christmas tree.

'I wonder if I ought to check in with Sofia and see how things are,' said Peg. 'When I left, Henry was out of theatre and had just been moved into intensive care. They were still waiting to see him.'

'It wouldn't hurt,' said Blanche. 'And absolutely finish your tea and have a rest first, dear, but if you do want to go back to the hospital, I shall be perfectly all right, and perfectly happy to look after your aunt, too.'

Peg shook her head. 'It's a time for family. I'd only feel in the way.'

'Perhaps later then, once things are a little calmer.' She gave Peg a warm smile. 'Henry mentioned to me that you'd lost your husband at this time of year. I'm sorry, this must be especially difficult for you. I think that was why he was so worried about your aunt, because you'd already suffered such a loss.'

To her horror, Peg felt her eyes begin to well with tears. 'It's just this whole bloody thing about Christmas, isn't it? That everything has to be so perfect and nothing can go wrong. But life's not like that. Sometimes it does what it damn well pleases and there's nothing you can do about it.' She sniffed, blinking furiously. 'And I'm fine, really. Julian died four years ago, but it's just, the hospital, you know. It brought it all back. The waiting... The not knowing whether you should hope or not. Telling yourself you mustn't because it'll only make it worse. Remembering every stupid argument you've ever had and swearing that if he would only make it through, you'd never have a cross word again. And hating yourself because you never told him nearly enough how much you loved him.'

Blanche leaned forward to take her hand. 'You always think you have time,' she said, squeezing her fingers against Peg's. But Time's a thief, and she can steal it from right under your nose when you least expect it. My Daniel has been gone for more years than I care to remember, but there are days, like today, when I rail against how unfair life can be.'

Peg swallowed. 'Yes, I'm sorry, of course you must have lost people too. My grief is no worse than anyone else's.'

'Perhaps not. But you still have a right to feel it, and to express it. Life *can* be unfair. But it can also be wonderful and bring as much joy as it does pain. And people...' She smiled again. 'She can bring people into our lives, too. Sometimes when we least expect it.'

From beside her, Peg's phone began to vibrate. She glanced at the screen. 'It's Sofia,' she said, eyes wide. 'Do you want to take it?'

'Can you put it on speaker?' asked Blanche. 'Then we can both hear it.' She patted Peg's knee gently before withdrawing her hand.

'Hello, Sofia... how are things?' asked Peg. 'How's Henry?'

'Alive,' said Sofia. 'We've just been in to see him, but I don't think he even knew we were there. He didn't move, just lay there. Propped up with wires everywhere. It was horrible.'

'I'm sure he did know you were there,' said Peg. 'He would have been able to hear you, even if he couldn't say anything.' Hearing is the last thing which goes, she thought. She remembered the nurses telling her that.

'They've told us that the next day or so will be critical. Henry's brain is still swollen and until that goes down it will be hard to tell how things will turn out. And then there's his lung, so... That's partly why I'm ringing, because Adam wants to stay. They've a room we can use, apparently.'

'Yes, I thought as much,' said Peg. 'But that's fine. Blanche has brought a few overnight things with her, so she'll be quite all right.'

'Can you put her on, and I'll have a little chat with her.'

'You're on speaker, Sofia. Go ahead, she can hear you.'

'Oh... I see. Well, Henry's fine, Mum, you're not to worry.'

'Sofia, I don't know why you're so keen that I shouldn't know the details of what's going on. I might not be related to Henry, but he's still a part of the family, same as me.'

'Yes, I know but... Anyway. Look, are you sure everything is okay?'

'It's fine. We're worried, of course, about all of you, but I'm perfectly happy here for the time being.'

'Okay... but I was wondering whether you might be better off back at the home.'

Blanche rolled her eyes. 'It's not a home, dear. Haven't you ever read *The Thursday Murder Club*? Admittedly, Athelstone

House is not as swish as Cooper's Chase but it's in a similar vein. It's *my* home, yes, but not *a* home.'

'No, I know that, Mum, but you know what I meant. You get help with things.'

'Only if I ask for them. Although Jordan is *very* obliging.'

She slid Peg a look which Peg was relieved only she could see and she turned away to hide her smile. She was really beginning to like Blanche.

14

BOXING DAY

The call came at a quarter past five in the morning, but Peg was already awake. It was Boxing Day, how could she sleep? She had gone downstairs half an hour ago to make a cup of tea and had taken it back to bed with her, intending to read. But although she had drunk the tea, the book still lay unopened on top of the duvet beside her.

There were another nineteen hours or so left of Boxing Day to be got through, but Henry was still alive. He had come through the night and woken briefly. It was early days but the nurses were pleased with his progress. Peg closed her eyes and offered up a silent thank you to the universe. No one else would be dying today.

From the other end of the phone, Sofia's voice was almost inaudible and Peg realised she had stopped listening, lost in her own thoughts. 'Sofia, can you say that again? I can hardly hear you...'

'Sorry, I know I'm whispering, but Adam has only just dropped off to sleep and I don't want to wake him. Is everything all right? Is Mum okay?'

Peg smiled, thinking about the previous evening. 'She's

fine... In fact, she and Mim would have stayed up half the night if I hadn't sent them to bed. They could talk the hind leg off a donkey.'

'Really? Oh... that doesn't sound like Mum at all.'

Peg frowned. Admittedly, she didn't know Blanche very well, but she certainly didn't seem to be the shy, retiring type. 'It's nice for my aunt, too,' she replied. 'I think she's rather enjoyed having two people fussing over her. Speaking of which, how are you holding up? Have *you* managed to sleep?'

There was a long pause, and Peg wondered whether they'd been cut off. She was about to ask the question again when Sofia replied, even quieter than before. 'Not really, I...' Peg waited for her to finish, but as the seconds ticked by, she realised she wasn't going to.

'It's a very worrying time,' said Peg. 'You're worried about Henry, but you're also worried about Adam. So it wouldn't hurt *you* to get a bit of rest. The next few days are going to be long ones.'

'All I could think of yesterday was that Christmas was never going to be the same again. I think there must be something wrong with me...'

'I imagine it's just the shock,' said Peg, trying to be kind. 'We none of us know how we'd react in situations like these, do we? When we become aware that forever after things might be different. Even without Christmas, that's always a scary thought to process. I'm not going to tell you that everything will be okay, but Henry has done the hard bit. Why don't you get some rest and then see how things are looking in a few more hours?' She winced at what she was about to say. 'And then you must come and have something to eat. A proper meal. You and Adam both need to look after yourselves and I expect making food is the last thing you feel like doing.'

'I'm not sure Adam will want to, but...' There was a pause as Sofia considered her offer. 'Thank you, that's very kind of you.'

'No problem,' said Peg lightly. 'I'll be here whenever you want to come over, just let me know how things go.'

After saying goodbye, Peg ended the call and held the phone against her chest for a moment. She must be mad inviting Sofia and Adam over, but she wasn't sure what else she could do. A little kindness went a long way at times like these.

She turned her phone over again and stared at the screen. It was far too early to call Izzy and Phoebe, but she suddenly longed to hear their voices. Given what she knew about skiing holidays, the après-ski was almost as important as the time on the slopes, and she doubted they would be rising early. She knew they would call her at some point today, but it could be hours yet, and she didn't want to ring them before they were ready. The last thing she wanted to do was spoil their fun. Sighing, she slid her phone onto the bedside table and lay back down, pulling the covers up around her ears. What she wouldn't do for a few more hours' sleep herself...

By seven o'clock, however, she decided it was useless to stay in bed hoping she would drop off. She'd had all night to do that and had hardly managed it; she might as well get out of bed and do something useful. A big breakfast might be just the thing – she hadn't eaten much herself yesterday and the fridge was groaning with food.

To her surprise, Blanche was already up and dressed by the time Peg arrived in the kitchen, and was sitting at the table nursing a cup of tea.

'I've made a pot, I hope you don't mind?'

Peg sank into a chair opposite. 'I don't mind in the slightest. As long as there's some left for me?' She gave Blanche a sympathetic smile. 'Couldn't you sleep either?' she asked.

Blanche's return smile was sheepish. 'I feel bad saying it, but I slept like a baby,' she replied. 'I usually do, but what *is* annoying is waking up so damn early. All those years when I was working and had to get up at the crack of dawn, and then the minute I retired and could stay in bed as long as I wanted, could I heck? Wide awake at dawn.' She shook her head. 'Bloody ridiculous state of affairs.' She got up and collected a mug from the draining board. 'One cup of tea coming up.'

'I've heard from Sofia,' said Peg, watching as Blanche poured her drink. 'And Henry's still with us. He woke briefly, but the nurses seem to think he's doing okay.'

Blanche slid the mug across the table with an audible sigh of relief. 'Thank God. Adam would never have been able to forgive himself. When Henry is back in good health again those two need to have some proper conversations. Sort out whatever's gone wrong between them.'

Peg nodded. 'I think Sofia's feeling it too. She was very quiet on the phone. Adam was asleep, so she was trying to keep her voice down, but I could tell she'd been thinking things over too. There but for the grace of God comes to mind.'

'It does. Families are such horribly complicated things, aren't they? My daughter has something on her mind at the moment that she doesn't want me to know about, and it's been that way for the past couple of years. No matter how hard I try to get to the bottom of it, she just pretends all the harder that everything is fine. She and Adam weren't always the way they are now. This materialistic social climbing is a relatively new thing. Sofia's business doesn't help – pandering to people with more money than sense, or worse, to people with no money but who are desperate for some kind of validation of their worth. I wish they could see it doesn't lead to happiness. It's like they're on a hamster wheel they can't step off.'

'Ah, but it's the stepping off that's the problem, isn't it?' said Peg. 'While you're on it everything is fine – you can keep on keeping on – but try to jump from it while it's still moving and you end up in all kinds of trouble. Perhaps that's what they're trying to avoid.'

Blanche narrowed her eyes. 'You could well be right.

Although I've no idea what could be so bad.' She swallowed a mouthful of tea. 'I'm changing the subject completely, but would it be weird to have pigs in blankets for breakfast?'

Peg leaned towards her, hair spilling over her shoulders as she did so. 'Weird possibly... but very, very good.' She grinned. 'I'll go and see if Mim's awake. She'll need a hand to get dressed.'

'I'll go,' said Blanche, placing her hand over Peg's to still her from getting up. You finish your tea, dear.'

Peg had always loved this kitchen, and she especially loved it at this time of the morning when it was still early, and it was hushed and expectant, waiting for the day to begin. One of the windows faced east and Peg had seen many a sunrise through it, enjoying her first cup of tea of the day, and the opportunity to let her thoughts slide and quietly think things through. And having Blanche take care of Mim was exactly what had brought her current thoughts to mind.

Because Mim lived over two hours away, and if Peg were to look after her, that was something which needed to change. Either Mim needed to move closer to Peg, or Peg needed to move closer to Mim, it was as simple as that. And Peg knew that only one of those options was the right one. What troubled her was that if this was truly going to be her last Christmas in this house, then so far it had been memorable for all the wrong reasons.

'I've had a thought,' she said, when all three women were tucking into their breakfast.

Mim frowned. She was cross at having her food cut up for her. *Like a baby*, she'd scorned. She speared a piece of sausage. 'Well I hope it's not about me,' she said.

Peg ignored her. Given the direction of travel of her recent thoughts, Mim's comment was a little too close for comfort. And it was not a conversation she wanted to get into. She stuck out her tongue instead, her way of teasing her aunt. 'No, it's not about you, Mim. I was just remembering when the girls were little – I think it was the year Phoebe was born, so she would have only been about six months old – Julian and I decided to postpone our Christmas dinner because the day was just running away from us. I don't think I even managed to brush my hair the entire day. Anyway, that's not the point. The point is that we had the dinner on Boxing Day instead, when things were a little calmer. And it was lovely. It didn't really make any difference, and I wondered if we should do the same thing this year. I've invited Sofia and Adam over for some food when they're ready, but perhaps we should make it a definite arrangement. Provided all is well at the hospital, of course.'

'Haven't we just eaten the pigs in blankets?' asked Blanche.

'We've eaten *some* of them,' replied Peg. 'But only a few from the ones Sofia had already prepared yesterday. *I* still have sausages and bacon left. Plus a chicken… and anything else we might want can be easily rustled up.'

A quick phone call to Sofia confirmed that there was no change in Henry's condition, and she seemed grateful for the opportunity of a few hours to escape. The hospital would call if there was a problem, and even if she and Adam didn't stay at Peg's for long, at least they would have had a hot meal and a decent cup of tea.

With dinnertime set for three o'clock, Peg began to think about what to prepare. Henry's accident might have cast a shadow over festivities, but the way she saw it, nothing they did would change the situation, so they might as well try to make the best of it. Besides, the quiet Christmas she had been looking forward to had gone out of the window as soon as she'd had the call about Mim and her wrist. There was, however, one thing Peg wanted to do before preparations got underway. Otherwise the opportunity would slip through her fingers and she would regret it deeply come bedtime.

'I'm just going to take a spin around the woods,' she said.

'I'm not used to eating such a big breakfast, and some fresh air would be good.'

'I could do with some of that myself,' said Blanche. 'Would you mind some company?'

It was the last thing Peg wanted, but she could hardly refuse. Before she could reply, however, Mim chimed in. 'Oh, Blanche, I was about to ask you if wouldn't mind helping me to sort out my hair? If we're having guests for dinner I shall need to put a few rollers in, but this blasted cast on my wrist makes everything impossible.'

Blanche agreed straight away – perhaps as Mim knew she would. Peg was in no doubt that her need for an assistant hairdresser had been invented solely for Peg's benefit. She was, however, very grateful – she and Julian had much to discuss.

The moment Peg was surrounded by trees, she inhaled a deep breath and leaned her back against a stout oak. Its broad beam was solid and comforting, a constant in the ever-changing world in which she found herself.

'Oh Julian,' she murmured. 'What am I going to do?'

Half an hour or so later, she turned for home, conscious that both Mim and Blanche were on their own. Pausing suddenly as she walked, she stopped to listen, her ears detecting something she didn't often hear – footsteps. Someone else was in the woods.

Hearing a rustle which was much closer than before, Peg spun around to see Blanche walking towards her.

'It's okay,' said Blanche, the moment she could see she'd been spotted. 'Don't panic, there's nothing wrong.' She flapped a hand as if she was out of puff.

'Sorry,' said Peg. 'Have you been looking for me?'

'Only because I wanted to let you know that Sofia has called again – your phone rang and I answered it when I saw it was her. I hope that's okay?'

'I should have brought it with me,' Peg replied. 'Only I usually leave it behind when I walk. Force of habit.'

'I don't blame you,' said Blanche. 'This is a little bit of heaven, isn't it? Who'd want the outside world intruding?' She looked around her, smiling at what she saw. 'Sofia only wondered if they might come over a little later than you'd agreed. Not by much, probably just an hour or so. The consultant treating Henry will be on the ward later and they want to catch him for a chat if they can. I said I was sure you wouldn't mind.' She pursed her lips. 'I also want to apologise. I'd forgotten that it's the anniversary of your husband's death today, but I should have realised you wanted some quiet time by yourself. Mim has just reminded me. She didn't need any help with her hair at all.'

Peg smiled. Bless you, Mim. 'Yes, I suspected as much.' She stopped to pick up a skeletal leaf from the ground, every vein and capillary held together by the slightest of threads, like the finest lace. She held it out for Blanche to see.

'It's beautiful,' she replied. 'How lucky you are to have this on your doorstep. It couldn't be any closer.'

'I'm *very* lucky,' replied Peg, nodding. 'The chance to buy the woodland came up some years ago and so my husband bought it for us. Well, for me. He gave it to me for our wedding anniversary.'

'Wow...'

Peg laughed. 'Yes, it did make buying each other presents quite difficult after that. Nothing could ever top this.'

Blanche was studying her face. 'You must have been very much in love.'

'We were. I still am...' she replied. 'Isn't that exactly what grief is? Love with nowhere to go.'

'I've never heard it expressed like that,' said Blanche. 'But how true, and how lovely.'

Peg stared up into the branches of the trees above.

Branches which she had seen through spring, summer, autumn and winter over countless years. Every inch of this woodland was hers, its roots almost a part of her, she felt so *rooted* to them.

'So many of my memories about Julian are tied up in this wood. There's a tree here where we carved our names, and those of the girls. It's going to make leaving here very hard indeed.'

'Leave?' said Blanche. 'But why on earth would you want to do that?' She stared at Peg for a moment, a confused look on her face and, as the silence lengthened, Peg saw the exact moment when understanding reached her. 'Ah... Mim...'

Peg nodded.

'This fall was the second she's had this year. Last time it was just bumps and bruises, and she did that by falling off a crate she was standing on to paint her garden fence. This time she was up a ladder sorting out her cobwebs and now she's broken her wrist. It isn't Mim's balance that's to blame, not fully anyway, but more the problem that she doesn't realise she's not the age to be doing these things, not without help anyway. She had pneumonia last year too, which frightened the life out of her, and me, and I'm worried that, as relatively fit as she is now, that could all change very quickly.'

'But she's staying with you for now. Would that not be an option, longer-term?'

Peg shook her head. 'Much as I'd like that, Mim loves her house as much as I love mine. She only came back with me out of practicality – I have a series of illustrated articles to write and all my notes and sketches are here. Plus, it's Christmas... We usually spend it apart, and this year I just couldn't bear to be away. Possibly because, deep down, I knew it might be my last.' Her eye was caught by a robin bobbing about on a holly bush and she watched it for a moment. 'I don't want to limit Mim's independence but she needs someone to keep a slightly closer eye on her now, and that someone is me. I can't do that when I'm over two hours away.'

'Getting old is a tangled ball of difficult decisions and horrible emotions. I don't recommend it at all.'

'You can't be much older than me,' said Peg. 'But you're absolutely right. I promised Mim she could stay in her own home, right to the end, whenever that is. Hopefully not for years yet, but I will not deny her that chance, not if I can possibly help it. I have a lot more of my life ahead of me than she does, and there can be other houses for me. Mim doesn't have that luxury.'

Blanche laid a gentle arm on Peg's sleeve. 'She's lucky to have you.'

Peg smiled. 'I'm very lucky to have her.' She shivered, suddenly aware of how cold it was. 'We ought to get back,' she said. 'Sofia and Adam will be here before we know it.'

'Put me on potato-peeling duty,' said Blanche. 'I can do that in my sleep.'

Peg turned her thoughts away from both the past and the future. It was time to concentrate on the present. 'You're on,' she said with a grin.

They had hardly been in the house ten minutes when there was a knock at the back door. Sofia and Adam would be ages yet, and Peg threw Blanche a curious look as she crossed the kitchen to open it. The two people standing there were the very last ones she expected to see.

'Surprise!'

Peg stared at her daughters, their faces wreathed in smiles, their hands full of luggage. 'You're meant to be in France!'

Izzy dropped her bag and rushed into Peg's waiting arms. 'I know, but we couldn't bear the thought of you being on your own over Christmas again. We would have been home yesterday but our flight got delayed. Merry Christmas, Mum!'

From behind Peg came an amused voice. 'I'll peel a few more spuds,' said Blanche.

15

Peg still couldn't believe that her girls were home, and her face was beginning to ache from smiling so hard. She gave Phoebe another squeeze, drawing back to look at her.

'But your holiday,' she said. 'Won't you lose all your money?'

'Oh, Mum...' said Phoebe. 'We tried, but the hotel was rubbish, there was barely any snow and the prices were astronomical. We stuck it out for two days, but Iz and I were miserable. However much we pretended otherwise, all we wanted was to be here, with you. We've probably saved ourselves a tonne of money by not staying.'

Izzy pushed at her sister's arm, rolling her eyes. 'We were just supposed to say how much we missed you, Mum, but Pheebes obviously misread that memo.'

Peg laughed, happiness surging inside her. 'I don't care what the reasons are, I'm just very glad to see you.' She turned around, aware that now the crush of greetings was over, the girls were becoming curious about their potato-peeling guest.

'Girls, this is Blanche, she's—' She broke off. How to explain? 'Part of a very long story which I'll tell you about in a minute. And Blanche, as you've probably worked out, these are my girls – Izzy, my eldest, and Phoebe, who came a very close second. There's only just over a year between them.' She paused, listening for sounds of movement from the other room. 'Girls, you'll never guess who else is here?'

And right on cue, Mim came through the door. 'Did I hear voices?' she asked. 'It sounded like...'

'Mim!' The girls rushed over, skidding to a stop when they saw her plaster cast.

'Mum told us you'd hurt your wrist,' said Phoebe, squeezing herself carefully into her great-aunt's good side. 'I hope it doesn't hurt *too* much.'

'No, it's just a blessed nuisance,' came the reply. 'But I've been told off good and proper, so don't you two start. Come here and let me look at you.' She held out a hand to Izzy, pulling her in close beside Phoebe as she smiled. 'Still beautiful,' she declared.

It was Phoebe whose face fell first – always the more serious of the two. 'Is it still all right if we stay? If not, we can find a hotel or—'

'You'll do no such thing,' said Peg. 'Of course you can stay. You'll have to both bunk up in your room though, Pheebes, Mim is in Izzy's room.'

'No problem.' Phoebe's sunny smile filled the room. 'Shall we drop our gear upstairs, and then you can tell us what's been going on in the three whole days we've been away. We only spoke to you on the day before Christmas Eve.'

'Goodness, was it really that long ago?' It seemed to Peg as if an age had passed since she'd gathered holly from the wood in contemplation of a quiet Christmas.

Mim rested herself against the table. 'Well, I don't think any of us were expecting such a lovely surprise,' she said. 'Shall I make us all some tea?'

'The girls will probably have a Coke, Mim, but I'd love one, thank you. Just be careful lifting the kettle.'

Mim waved away her concern. 'Trouble lifting the kettle, my eye,' she muttered as she crossed the room.

Peg caught Blanche's wry smile and nodded before looking away. Her girls were home; nothing bad could possibly happen today.

They were still sitting around the table catching up on the news when, not quite an hour later, there was another knock on the door.

'That'll be the other members of our party,' said Blanche. 'Action stations, everyone.'

Peg was still trying to stifle a snigger as she welcomed Sofia and Adam inside. It felt wrong to be so light-hearted but she couldn't help herself.

'Come in, come in...' she said, pulling them both into the kitchen. They looked exhausted. 'Let's have your coats and then come and sit down.' She rubbed Sofia's arm. 'First things first though, how are things? Did you see the consultant?'

Adam inhaled a deep breath, nodding as he did so. 'Yes, and Henry's okay, we think. There's not really much change but that's a good thing, apparently. The consultant said that the bleed was caught quickly, and it was fortunate it happened where it did otherwise Dad would almost certainly not be with us. I know that's what he told us before but there was more detail this time about some of the possible problems Dad might face. He said he's hopeful, though. All in all, I think it's about as good as it can be at the moment.'

'Excellent.' Peg held out her arm for his coat. 'Let me introduce you to everyone. Numbers have swelled a bit from when we spoke this morning – which is fine, by the way – you're still very welcome, so no nonsense about you being in the way.'

It took a while before everyone was introduced and more

explanations had been given for the situation they all found themselves in, but eventually they arrived at a point where Peg needed to think about the dinner she'd promised everyone.

'So... Adam and Sofia... what would you like to do first? Sit by the fire with a cup of tea? Maybe have a shower? It's entirely up to you.'

Sofia, who still looked distinctly uncomfortable, cleared her throat. 'A shower would be wonderful, if you're sure that's okay.' She sniffed her sleeve. 'I think I smell disgusting... the hospital, it's... I'm sure it's clean, but...'

'They do have a certain smell, I agree,' said Peg. 'Shower it is, then. Izzy, would you mind showing Sofia where everything is while I make a start on the food? How about you, Adam?'

'I wouldn't say no to a shower as well, but some decent tea first would be very welcome.'

Peg wafted her arm in the direction of the living room. 'Go through and make yourself at home and I'll bring you one in.'

'Mum?' said Sofia. 'Why don't you come through as well? Then you won't be in the way. I'm sure Peg has a lot to do.'

'She does,' said Peg, smiling warmly. 'But Blanche is my chief potato peeler so she's needed here, I'm afraid.'

Sofia was about to reply but then changed her mind and smiled tentatively at Izzy who was waiting to show her upstairs.

'I'll come and sit with you, Adam,' said Mim, getting to her feet. 'This blessed wrist is making me next to useless, which I don't like one little bit. Are you cold? I can just about manage to put another log on the fire.'

Blanche and Peg traded smiles as they left. 'Right,' said Peg. 'I've got a chicken, and not a very big one at that, so we'll be lucky if we get more than two slices each, but there are heaps of potatoes. And I can roast come carrots and parsnips. Phoebe, dear, could you pull me up a couple of leeks from the garden, and we'll have those as well in some white sauce. Oh, and broccoli too. There's still one or two heads left. We've got pigs in blankets, and I can make some stuffing, so I don't think we'll starve. Plus, there are mince pies, yule log, a pudding, plenty of cream, cheese biscuits and a very good Stilton from the farm shop.'

Phoebe laughed. 'Good old Mum,' she said. 'No one here ever goes hungry.' She cocked her head to one side. 'Are you still recycling your toilet roll tubes?'

Peg looked perplexed. 'I am... any I've collected will be in the tub in the storeroom outside. Why?'

'And do you have any sweets? Quality Street or something similar? Because I can make some crackers, if you like. I know you'll still have a stash of pretty paper in your study, and some ribbons. They won't have a snap in them but we can always shout *bang!* as we pull them. I'll make some paper hats, too.'

'I think we have ourselves a plan,' said Blanche, reaching for the bag of King Edwards.

Over the last two hours, the kitchen had filled with the most delicious array of smells and Peg inhaled a deep breath, smiling to herself. She had thought she wanted a quiet Christmas, had even told her children to go on holiday and have fun so that she could, but the moment her girls had walked through the door, those thoughts had disappeared in an instant. Yes, she had got used to being on her own. Yes, she had worried about becoming a burden, but she needed her girls just as, she hoped, they still needed her. And Christmas just wasn't Christmas without them. They mattered. People mattered. She'd welcomed three virtual strangers into her home, but she was beginning to think it might have been the best thing she'd ever done... Izzy was playing cards with Mim and Blanche. Phoebe was making some crackers for the table and Adam and Sofia were finally relaxing. Wasn't that worth far more than being alone?

She looked up at the sound of footsteps.

'This is very good of you, Peg,' said Adam, coming into the kitchen. 'Cooking all this without any notice.'

'Well, between us we've got so much food, it's silly not to eat some of it. I know the circumstances aren't ideal but... Actually perhaps they are. It's horrible to think we're all here, about to be merry, when Henry isn't with us to enjoy it, but we're not helping him by sitting around moping, are we? It doesn't change anything. Maybe it's better to drink to his good health and make a pledge to do this again when he's back on his feet.'

Adam nodded. 'I think that's a very good idea.' He smiled sadly. 'I don't think Dad has really enjoyed his last few Christmases, so perhaps we should let him celebrate it the way he would like for a change.'

'From what Henry's said, I think the only requirement would be that he spend it with you,' replied Peg. 'I don't think he cares much about anything else.' She held Adam's look. 'You might not believe that, but it's true. I've not had many conversations with your dad, but I've had that one. What does that tell you?'

'That I probably ought to listen to him more than I have,' Adam replied. He sat down, picking up a stray piece of ribbon which Phoebe had left on the table. He began to twirl it around his fingers. 'I've only ever wanted Dad to think well of me, but he never seems to approve of anything – not my job, our house, even our friends.'

Peg straightened in her chair. 'Then I really hope you get the chance to talk to him about it,' she said. 'But I *can* tell you this. All Henry wants is for you to be happy, so if you think he disapproves of the choices you've made, perhaps it's simply that he doesn't think they *are* making you happy. Maybe all he needs is to see proof.'

'I can see why Dad likes you.'

Peg shook her head in amusement. 'Your dad doesn't know

me. But I can tell you these things because I'm a parent too, and that's the way we think. We'd walk over hot coals for our kids if it would ensure they were happy.' She dipped her head. 'And sometimes kids have to walk over hot coals for their parents, too. That's the way it works; it's a two-way street, the same as in any relationship. I hope with all my heart that Henry comes through this. Losing people you love is the worst kind of agony, but near misses also put the world into perspective pretty damn fast. They help you to understand what really *is* important. If your dad does pull through, then you'll have a long road of recovery ahead of you and I suspect you might find out what those hot coals feel like.' She placed her hand over his. 'But good things can come from this.'

Sofia slipped soundlessly into the seat beside Adam and lay her head on his shoulder. And very quietly Peg got to her feet and left them there. The dinner could wait for a few more moments.

Eventually, though, the smell of the food brought everyone back to the kitchen, with offers of help and gentle enquiries from Izzy and Phoebe into how long it would be before they could eat. It was quite likely several months since her daughters had had a proper roast, and Peg could see the hunger in their eyes – not just for the chicken, but for the opportunity to feast in their mother's kitchen, just as they had on so many other occasions before. How did she ever think it would be better having Christmas on her own? This was their dad's anniversary, too, she mustn't forget that.

'I thought we'd have dinner in here, if that's all right with everyone,' she said. 'It gets a little chilly in the dining room and I'd rather be comfortable than formal. And the table's slightly bigger in here.' She began to clear away the accumulated debris left over from their preparations. 'Izzy, perhaps you could lay the table for me?'

'Sure. Pheebes, you get the glasses and I'll do the plates.'

'I can help,' said Sofia. 'Is there a cloth you'd like to use, or...?'

Peg wrinkled her nose. 'I don't normally bother. Besides, the cat swings on it if I do, so it's not worth the anguish of having everything sliding to the floor. He's done that on more than one occasion. I tell you what would look nice.' She crossed to the dresser on the far side of the room and took down three pottery jugs – all blue, but of different sizes and shapes. 'Would you like to shove some holly in these? I collected a stash a couple of days ago, but I haven't had a chance to string much of it up yet. It's on the side in the pantry.' She pointed. 'Through there.' She handed Sofia the jugs, wondering what she thought about her scrubbed pine table which bore the scars of a lifetime of use. She must be itching to get her hands on Peg's kitchen and work her magic. She'd have the place shiny and perfect in no time.

Peg's chairs didn't match because Julian broke one a long time ago, and she wasn't even sure she owned any napkins. She might have done, once upon a time... yes, a wedding present, she seemed to recall, but if she still had them they would have long ago been relegated to the loft. Which was something else she would have to think about. She had thirty-odd years of belongings accumulated in this house, all of which would have to be sorted through if she moved. It would be a mammoth task. And a painful one. Peg thrust the thought away.

A few minutes later, they were ready to eat. And it might have all been a bit impromptu, but the table looked lovely. She had brought her bright red poinsettia in from the living room and placed it in the middle, and together with the blue jugs of holly and Phoebe's cleverly crafted crackers, it looked very festive.

It wasn't the most perfectly proportioned Christmas dinner Peg had ever produced either, but there was lots of veg to fill up on and, as she ferried dish after dish to the table, the appreciation was audible.

'Don't let it get cold,' she cautioned. 'Please, just get stuck in, no need to stand on ceremony.' She was about to sit down herself when she suddenly remembered something. 'Oh, I haven't opened the wine.'

'Let me,' said Adam, getting to his feet. 'You sit down, Peg.'

It was always the smallest things which caught her unawares. Like that first Sunday dinner without Julian when he had not been there to open their usual bottle. They'd gone without because Peg couldn't bear to open it herself. She glanced at Izzy and Phoebe as she sat down, giving her daughters a warm smile as she waited for her glass to be filled.

She would like to say something, only she had no idea what. Adam had poured himself no more than an inch of wine and she knew this was in case he needed to drive. They might all be here, trying to do their best under difficult circumstances, but the reminders of what had been, and what yet might still come to pass, were all around them.

She picked up a jug of gravy and offered it to Sofia. 'Come on, everyone, let's eat.'

To her relief, the poignancy of the moment passed and the conversation soon resumed. In fact, as the meal progressed, Peg felt more relaxed than she had in days, and it was clear the others felt so too. What could have been a miserable, make-do affair became an opportunity to escape their situations, even if only for a little while, and the smiles became bigger and the faces brighter.

The food was demolished, and Peg was pleased to see both Adam and Sofia tuck in with relish. They couldn't have eaten much over the past day, and if this one small thing made a difference to how they were feeling, then she was glad. She was about to make a start clearing the plates away ready for pudding, when a loud klaxon sounded, cutting through the conversation like a knife.

Adam's phone lay face down on the table beside his plate, the source of the noise, and all eyes fell on it as if it was an unexploded bomb.

Slowly, Adam picked it up and turned it over, the colour draining from his face. 'It's the hospital,' he said.

16

The room fell silent as Adam rushed through the kitchen door to take the call in private. No one wanted to listen to his conversation, but no one wanted to say anything either, and so they sat, rigid, scarcely breathing while the seconds ticked agonisingly by.

A loud 'Oh, thank God,' broke the silence, and the tension, so that by the time Adam returned to the table, all six of them were looking expectantly at him with smiles on their faces.

Adam almost stumbled across the threshold. 'Dad's awake,' he said. 'Properly awake. They've said we can go and see him. He's asking for us, apparently.'

'Oh, Adam... that's the best news.' Blanche drew him into a hug that surprised both of them by its ferocity and for a moment they stayed that way, locked tight in a release of emotion. It was only broken by Sofia's joining them, whereupon two became three as they repeated the action all over again.

'Have they said how things are?' asked Sofia, pulling away. 'I mean, he's okay? Really okay?'

Adam nodded, blinking hard. 'Yes, and that's about as much as I know. The nurse said they could give us more details when we get there, but he's conscious and they're happy with the way things are looking.'

Sofia spun around. 'I'm not sure where I left my bag...' She stopped, looking at the pile of dishes by the sink. 'Oh, but... and we haven't even had pudding.'

Peg unhooked Sofia's bag from the back of her chair and passed it across. 'Don't worry about anything here, just get going. And please, send him my best wishes, won't you?'

'No, Peg, you have to come with us,' said Adam. 'Dad's been asking for all of us, and that includes you.'

Peg got to her feet. 'I shouldn't really, this is a time for family. I can see him soon enough, now that I know he's going to be okay.'

'Don't be silly,' said Sofia. 'We'd like you to come, wouldn't we?' She looked to her husband for confirmation.

'Of course we would,' replied Adam. 'We can't just eat all your food and then leave you here and rush off. Dad would obviously like to see you.'

'We'll wash up,' said Blanche. 'And I'll make sure no one eats the pudding. Yes, Mim, I'm looking at you...' She gave Peg a huge smile. 'Don't *you* worry about anything here.'

'Yeah, Mum,' chimed in Izzy. 'Honestly, we'll be fine. Just go.'

It didn't look as if Peg would be able to refuse, but she still wasn't sure why they were all so keen to include her. Surely this was the perfect time for her to bow out of proceedings? Somewhere along the line they'd all been given the wrong idea about her and Henry, and although she knew it probably wasn't the time to do so, she'd have to explain the situation soon. She had a horrible feeling things would run away from her otherwise.

As it was, Peg insisted that Adam and Sofia go in to see Henry first. A handy sign asking that visitors be restricted to two to a bed added extra weight to her argument, and she was quite happy sitting in the little waiting area opposite the ward.

Besides, Henry would probably be very tired, and having three people claiming his attention would be too much too soon.

Part of her was relieved that he was going to be okay, of course it was. Henry had appeared to be a lovely man, and for everyone's sake, especially his, she was glad that he had pulled through. But one, albeit fairly lengthy conversation, didn't make them anything other than acquaintances, and now that the initial fear that he might die had seemingly passed, she was beginning to feel quite awkward. She liked Blanche, and despite Henry's evident difficulties in his relationship with them, even Sofia and Adam had grown on her. She was pleased that she'd been able to help them, had provided some support and perhaps even a respite from the horrible events of the last day or so, but that probably ought to be where her involvement with the family ended. They'd been thrown together by events, more so because it was Christmas, but very soon they'd get back to their own lives, and so would she.

But she'd scarcely even got settled before Sofia appeared beside her.

'I thought I might give Adam a minute or two on his own,' she said. 'But then you should absolutely go in.'

'How is Henry?' asked Peg, remaining non-committal.

'Tired,' said Sofia. 'And a bit confused, but that's to be expected, apparently. Otherwise, he looks... quite well, all things considered.' She fanned her face. 'Well, that's a Christmas we won't forget in a hurry, isn't it? And I have some serious making up to do with our friends. We've cancelled so many arrangements.' She pulled a face. 'We're supposed to be going out to the theatre this evening.' She checked the time on her phone as if she was considering whether that might still be an option. Peg was astounded that she could even think such a thing.

'I'm sure your friends understand,' replied Peg. 'At least, I would hope they do. It's not as if something like this happens often, is it?'

'No, I guess not.' Sofia stared at the wall opposite, her face suddenly brightening. 'I'll buy Ninette some flowers to say sorry,' she said, as if that settled things.

Peg raised her eyebrows, turning away so that Sofia wouldn't see them. If Sofia needed to apologise for her and Adam's absence from the seasonal social whirl then perhaps it was time to find some different friends. Ninette should be buying Sofia flowers, not the other way around. But there was also something else bothering Peg – the assumption that because it appeared likely that Henry would make a full recovery, everything could go back to normal, instantaneously, almost as if his accident had never happened. Had this whole episode really taught Sofia nothing?

She was still pondering the absurdities of Sofia's statement when Adam appeared at the door.

'Your turn, Peg,' he said, smiling.

Peg got reluctantly to her feet. 'How is he?' she asked. 'I don't want to tire him out.'

'Pretty confused... you'll see what I mean, but I guess that's understandable. It's probably the anaesthetic. He's asking for you, though.'

Peg nodded. 'I won't be long then, he'll need to rest.'

Letting the door close softly behind her, Peg took a deep breath, trying to expel the memories of the last time she had been on this ward – when it had been Julian lying in a bed. She scanned the small unit for Henry, hating the feeling that she was intruding on the other patients' privacy just by looking at them, but as her gaze moved on from one to the next, she realised she was looking for Henry's bright orange scarf. For heaven's sake, he wouldn't still be wearing the navy blue jumper she'd first seen him in, the one he had been wearing inside out.

It was a ridiculous notion, but then, of course, it was the only frame of reference for him she had. So what did that tell you?

And, suddenly, there he was, his face turned towards her, and while his expression was not exactly animated, there was a certain light of welcome there. She hurried towards him, trying to make herself invisible as she walked past the other beds.

'Hello, Henry,' she said, hovering beside the chair which had been thoughtfully placed there for visitors. And she realised that Sofia was right – all things considered, Henry did look surprisingly well. A small dressing had been fixed to his head, the area surrounding it having been shaved first, and it looked odd among the dark curls on the rest of his scalp. It made him look like a small boy, vulnerable and easily damaged. Other than that, his cheeks were pink and he was sitting up in bed. Still trailing wires attached to a monitor, but... Peg smiled. 'How are you feeling?'

'Like I've been hit by a very large truck down a very dark alley.' The corners of Henry's mouth twitched upward in what might have been a smile if he'd had more energy.

'I bet... you gave us all quite a scare.'

'So I gather.' He shifted slightly, wincing as he did so. 'And I'm so sorry I rushed out on you... I...' He frowned. 'I really don't know what happened.'

Peg sat down and leaned forward. 'Don't worry about the details now,' she said gently. 'You had an accident, in your car.'

'Which must be true because otherwise I wouldn't be here, would I? But I can't see how.' His eyes flickered away from her face as if he was trying to revisit his memories.

'There weren't any other cars involved, just a rather large tree...' Peg trailed off. 'But you don't need to think about that. I imagine the police will work out what happened. Maybe you swerved, or... You don't remember anything?'

Henry shook his head, a small movement. 'I wasn't even driving.'

Peg gave him a perplexed look. 'You've had a bad shake-up and it's not surprising it's all a little vague. It'll come back to you, in time.' He obviously couldn't recall the horrible argument he'd had with Adam, or the fact that he'd rushed out of their house yesterday morning. But that had to be for the best right now. It wouldn't do him any good to fret about it.

Henry stretched out a hand towards her. 'But that's just it. It's not that I can't remember, because I can. I can remember everything in exact detail. And I wasn't driving, I'd just settled down to read – *Case Histories*, by Kate Atkinson. You told me how good it was. And you were reading too. We'd not long finished dinner and I said perhaps I ought to be getting back...' Henry lifted his hand and then let it fall again. 'And you said I should at least let my dinner go down, so I sat and... your cat climbed on my lap. I might have fallen asleep, but I was in your chair, sitting beside the fire...'

Peg smiled patiently. 'It's okay, Henry. You don't have to worry about that now, just—'

'No, I do worry about it, because we'd had such a lovely day. The best Christmas I've had for a long time and—' He frowned. 'Don't *you* remember?'

Peg looked around for one of the nurses. Henry was beginning to get agitated and that couldn't be good.

'I've had everyone round at mine for dinner today,' she said, trying to change the subject. 'Did Sofia tell you? And Blanche... she came to stay yesterday when... when things weren't looking so good. She's hysterical once you get to know her, such a cracking sense of humour – she and Mim have been getting on like a house on fire.'

'Mim...?' Henry put a hand to his head as if it was hurting. 'I don't understand...'

Peg backed off. It was evidently far too much for Henry to take in yet. She smiled. 'So you just concentrate on getting better,' she said. 'Because once you're properly back on your feet, I said we should do it again – have dinner, only properly, with everyone there.' She pressed her lips together. She had said that, hadn't she? Why on earth had she done that? 'I know it won't be Christmas, but...'

Henry nodded, but his attention had gone. He was lost inside his head. She patted his hand awkwardly.

'I'll let you see Adam again for a bit now, and then you must get some rest. I'll see you soon.'

She got to her feet, relieved to be leaving. Her heart was pounding in her chest and she was beginning to feel quite panicked. Whether that was down to the current situation with Henry or memories of the last time she'd been in this unit she wasn't sure, but whichever it was, the effect was still the same. She reached the sanctuary of the corridor outside and pressed her back against the wall for a few moments, breathing deeply. Then she plastered on a smile and went to find Adam and Sofia.

'He might be out in a few days, can you believe that?'

They were on their way back to Peg's house and so far Adam had talked non-stop. 'He has a chest drain in at the moment to make sure his lung stays where it should. He'll have another X-ray in the morning to check everything is still okay, and provided it is, the drain can come out in a day or two. He's got to rest as much as possible, although gentle exercise to keep things moving, and he's not to do any lifting – both because of his ribs and also the brain thing, where he had the bleed. Other than that, he'll need to have his dressings checked and changed, but the main thing is that everything is working as it should. He doesn't seem to have any lasting damage to his brain at all, although we have to keep an eye on that; there's a small chance it may deteriorate. He might get headaches to start with, that kind of thing...'

Peg nodded, trying to absorb everything that Adam was

saying when really her thoughts were spinning forward into the uncertainty of the future. Because where was Henry going to be while all this was happening? And who was going to look after him?

'Did they say how long it would be before he's properly better?' said Sofia. Peg couldn't see her expression from the back seat of the car, but she had a horrible suspicion she knew what it looked like.

'Not exactly,' replied Adam. 'But the human body is an incredible thing. I'm sure he'll be back to his old self before we know it. God, I'm just so relieved...'

'Me too.'

There was the expected clamour for information as soon as they arrived back at the house, but Peg excused herself as soon as she could, citing her desire for another cup of tea as the reason.

She stood at the sink, staring out into the garden. Only three days ago everything in her world had been perfect. She had gathered holly from the wood and was looking forward, both to Christmas, and then the expanse of time ahead. Peaceful time. Time during which she could work on her articles, losing herself in both the words and her illustrations as she looked forward to the spring. But just over four years ago she had stood in the exact same spot, knowing that her life would never be the same again. On that occasion her head had been filled with thoughts of all the things she would need to do in order to care for Julian – changes she would need to make to the way in which she did things – changes to her work – changes to the house. She hadn't yet known whether Julian would be able to manage the stairs. Then he had died, and all those thoughts had vanished in an instant. And however much Peg didn't want to think about them, now those same thoughts were back.

Setting the kettle to boil, she wandered through to the living room to see if anyone was ready for pudding yet. She had a sudden urge for sweetness.

There were the remains of Sofia's pavlova, but also the yule log and the ginger and date loaf that she had brought back from Mim's. Plus mince pies and Christmas cake. She laid them all out on the table, encouraging everyone to come and eat. The way she was feeling she wanted a helping of each, but in the end she settled for her favourite – the ginger and date loaf, with a mince pie on the side, served warm and smothered in thick cream.

Full of food and beginning to feel rather sleepy, Peg let her gaze drift idly around the table. The events of the day were beginning to catch up with her, and if the silence from the others was anything to go by, they were feeling it too. It was companionable though, the aftermath of tension released by good food.

'I've got some After Eight mints if anyone has room for them,' she said, more for the girls' benefit than anyone else's. She knew how much they loved them.

From beside her, Izzy laid a hand on her arm.

'I'll get them, Mum. You sit still.'

So Peg did as she was told, realising as the chocolates were placed on the table that rather than retake her seat, Izzy had come to stand behind her. She was talking to Mim, who had asked about their holiday, but also pulling the band from Peg's hair at the same time. Peg leaned back, feeling her shoulders drop even further as Izzy deftly divided her hair into three and began to plait it.

Peg had often wondered whether this was the reason she still wore her hair long, simply because it was a reminder of just this feeling, of her daughter's hands in her hair and the closeness of the bond between them. When they were little, she had plaited the girls' hair straight from the bath when they were warm and cosy, tired from a busy day, and as they grew, she had continued. It was such a simple thing, but they had always found it a soothing balm in times of stress, and so had she. Such was the automatic nature of it now that Peg didn't even think Izzy realised she was doing it. Carrying on with her conversation as she passed each section of hair, one over the other, scarcely looking at her hands.

Idly, Peg smiled at Sofia who was sitting opposite her, and the look on her face was so unexpected that it stopped Peg's reverie in its tracks. At first she thought that Sofia was looking at her, but then she realised that her eyeline was higher. She was looking at Izzy and her expression was... hollow. She seemed transfixed by Izzy's actions.

A moment later, Sofia's chair scraped across the floor as she pushed it backwards, getting up rather awkwardly. 'Excuse me, I just need to pop to the loo.'

No one else seemed to have noticed anything amiss, but Peg narrowed her eyes, thinking. Sofia's expression had been in such contrast to her cheerful mood during dessert, that Peg couldn't help but wonder what had caused such a change. Waiting a few more minutes until Izzy had finished plaiting, she got to her feet, giving her daughter a tight hug before slipping into the living room.

'I'll just check the fire,' she murmured, although no one else seemed bothered by her leaving. They were all in the same soporific state that she had been.

She met Sofia making her way back down the stairs.

'Is everything all right?' she asked. 'You looked a little lost in there.'

Sofia flushed, embarrassed at having been caught out. 'Yes, fine, I...' She was flustered now too, and struggling to find a reply. Her gaze dropped to the floor and, if she could see them, Peg wouldn't have been at all surprised to see tears in her eyes. She'd obviously misjudged quite how badly Henry's accident had affected Sofia.

'I'm sorry. I'm worn out, I think. That must be what it is and...' Her voice caught in her throat. 'I have really bad cramps.' She smiled weakly. 'Horrible timing.'

It might be a good excuse, if it were true, because Peg was certain that's what it was. There was far more to the look on Sofia's face than just discomfort caused by period pains. It was the way she was looking at Izzy, as if...

Peg would give her the benefit of the doubt, but there was an inkling of something beginning to form in her mind. And she wondered whether Blanche had ever noticed it, or Henry...

She gave Sofia a sympathetic smile. 'I've some paracetamol if that would help,' she said.

'Thank you. But I've already taken a couple I had in my bag. I'm sure they'll kick in soon.'

'I think you're also far more stressed than you realise. Apart from what's happened since yesterday, I would imagine you've been busy for weeks, organising everything for Christmas. Henry mentioned before how much you like to entertain. And that's without factoring in your day job. It's a lot to take on, and I know what that pressure can do to you.'

Sofia nodded. 'I know it can't be helped, but all that preparation and planning has been for nothing now. And I hate letting everyone down.'

It might have been the effect of eating pudding in the warm kitchen which had caused Sofia's cheeks to flush, but Peg wasn't convinced that was the real reason. Not at all.

17

27 DECEMBER

'Earth to Mum,' said Phoebe, waving a hand across Peg's face. 'Is everything all right? You're staring into space.'

Peg wasn't. She was looking at the bookcase in her living room, feet rooted to the spot, arrested by a book which had just caught her eye.

'Sorry,' she said, smiling. 'Early morning, and I've not yet had a cup of tea. I was just thinking about something.'

'So I see. Come on, I'll put the kettle on. It will be just like old times.'

Peg had forgotten when both girls still lived at home how often she and Phoebe used to sit in the kitchen, nursing an early morning cuppa. Phoebe always rose so much earlier than her sister.

'So what's the story here, Mum?' she said a few moments later, once they were settled. She leaned into Peg's side with a teasing grin on her face. 'With you and Henry, I mean.'

Peg slid her a sideways glance. 'There is no story with Henry and me, as well you know. You were present, I believe, when I had the exact same conversation with Izzy.'

Phoebe stuck her tongue in her cheek. 'Yeah, and she didn't

believe you either.' She took another sip of her tea. 'You have to admit the way you met was very meet-cute.'

'It may well have been, if this were a Hollywood movie – but here in the real world, I bumped into Henry at a petrol station.'

'And then spent two hours with him, sitting in his car, sharing your mince pies.'

'Yes, but that's all it was.'

Phoebe leaned into her again. 'I know. I'm only teasing.'

Peg smiled, squeezing her daughter's hand. 'I know you are. Getting your own back for all the times I've teased you, no doubt. And I'm not sure how cute it was, but weird it most definitely is. I feel as if I'm on a fast-moving conveyor I can't seem to jump off. Before his accident, I had literally had a total of two conversations with Henry, three if you count the ten or so words we exchanged after the carol service, so why I've ended up in this situation, I don't know.'

'I do,' replied Phoebe. 'It's because you're so kind, perhaps too kind at times. Although, given the position you were in, it's hard to see how you could have done otherwise.'

'Blanche is adamant that Henry was on his way to see me when his car went off the road, and perhaps that's true. It probably *is* true. I can't see where else he might have been going, and I did...' Peg rested her elbow on the table and used her hand to prop up her head. 'I did kind of invite him.' She peeked sideways at Phoebe. 'I felt sorry for him. The way he described his Christmas sounded like some vision of hell, and he clearly wasn't looking forward to it. When the traffic jam suddenly cleared I had to make a quick run for it, back to my car, and I shouted across to him that he should come over. I'm not sure I meant it, or if I did, only in the way that you make an offer to someone because you're certain the person isn't going to take you up on it.'

'And so now you feel guilty and duty-bound to be there for Henry.'

Peg sighed. 'Something like that.' She thought back to the look on his face in the hospital. He was tired and in obvious pain, but he was also very confused. Unable to understand, beyond what people had told him, why he was there in the first place. He seemed to have no memory of the accident at all, although perhaps that was no bad thing. Maybe it was just his body's way of protecting itself, and those memories would return in time.

'Well, one good thing to come out of this is that now Mim has someone new to talk to. She and Blanche don't ever stop, do they?'

'I think Blanche is enjoying feeling useful,' said Peg. 'From what I can make out, Sofia treats her as if she's a ninety-year-old invalid. I'm grateful to her though; she's been a big help.'

Phoebe nodded. 'So what's the plan then? Me and Iz will help out – we're on holiday, remember. Neither of us has to go back to work until after the weekend.'

'I know you will, dear. And actually, there is something I need to discuss with both of you. I hadn't wanted to do it over Christmas, but events have rather forced my hand.' She paused, wondering whether her daughter would think her absolutely mad. Whichever way Peg thought about it, her decision seemed the most obvious solution to the problem, but that still didn't take away the feeling that she'd been boxed into a corner. 'Perhaps I'd better wait until Izzy's up – I really ought to talk to you both together.'

Phoebe tipped her head. 'This sounds serious, Mum.'

Peg was torn. Now seemed like the perfect opportunity, but Izzy had always liked her sleep and... 'Do you think she'll mind if we wake her?'

'Given the amount of Baileys she drank last night, she's

going to have a sore head. She might as well deal with it sooner rather than later.'

'Oi... I had two glasses,' replied Izzy indignantly as she came into the room. 'My head is perfectly fine, thank you.' She scratched her nose. 'But I could do with a coffee. Sit down, Mum, I'll do it,' she added, seeing Peg about to get to her feet.

She plonked herself down opposite Phoebe while she waited for the kettle to boil. 'You've got that look on your face,' she remarked to her sister. 'Like you're up to something. What have I missed?'

'Well, I've been trying to get the lowdown on Henry,' replied Phoebe. 'But nothing doing, I'm afraid.' She grinned at her sister, shrugging. 'I tried...'

Peg shook her head in amusement. 'Honestly, you two... But listen, being serious for a minute, I need to speak to you. Get your coffee first though, Iz. Shall I get us something to go with it? Christmas cake? Mince pie?'

Phoebe groaned. 'Are there any of those chocolate biscuits left?' she asked. 'I don't think I can face another mince pie.'

'I should probably make a proper breakfast,' said Peg, fetching the biscuits from the pantry.

'Don't be ridiculous, Mother, it's Christmas.'

Peg exchanged a complicit smile with her daughter and laid the packet on the table.

When both her daughters were settled, Peg drew in a steadying breath, marshalling her thoughts.

'Was Mim still asleep when you came down, Izzy?'

'Well, she was snoring, so I guess so.' She narrowed her eyes. 'Is it her you want to talk to us about? I can shut the kitchen door, just in case.'

Peg nodded. Given that Izzy had just walked in at the exact moment *her* name was mentioned, it was probably wise. She didn't want to cause any upset.

Phoebe leaned forward. 'Why the skulduggery? I don't get it.'

'I just wondered if you thought Mim was okay, that's all.'

'Aside from the broken wrist, you mean?' Phoebe looked from one to the other, her face blank. 'It's made her more crotchety than usual,' she added. 'But in that lovely Mim way which makes us all smile. But otherwise I think she's okay.'

'I don't,' said Izzy. 'She's scared. She might make out she's cross about the plaster cast and the way it limits what she can do, but only because it lends weight to her argument that she's fit and able. Why do you think she was up a ladder in the first place?'

Phoebe stared at her sister. 'To get the cobwebs down?'

Izzy tutted softly, shaking her head in amusement at her sister's lack of insight. 'That was the outward action, yes, but what she was really doing was proving to herself that she's still capable of such things, that her age isn't catching up with her. It's classic denial.'

Peg winced inwardly at her daughter's astute observation. It made her wonder what Izzy had deduced about *her*...

'Oh...' said Phoebe. 'A bit like what you do, Mum. Pretending you like the peace and quiet when we're not here, yet secretly loving all the chaos we bring with us.'

Peg smiled, found out. 'Something like that, yes. But I am concerned about Mim. She made light of her pneumonia last year, but it knocked her for six. Being made to face your own mortality is horrible. I know how *I* feel, imagine what it must be like if you're in your eighties. And now, with this latest tumble, she's becoming spooked, I know she is.'

'So what are you saying?' asked Phoebe. 'That you think she needs someone to look after her?'

Peg pulled a face. 'Maybe not look after her – I don't think that's necessary just yet – but I do think I need to keep more of an eye on her than I have in the past. And that's not so easy to do from here.'

'She's here now though,' added Izzy, scrutinising Peg's face.

'Yes, and I had a heck of a job getting her to come back with me from the hospital. If it wasn't for the fact that it was almost Christmas, I don't think she would have come. That, and my laying on my work commitments with a trowel.'

'But if she's agreed to stay...' Phoebe reached for a biscuit.

'She's agreed to stay, *for the time being*. And knowing how impatient Mim can be, that gives me a couple of weeks at best. She won't get the cast off her wrist for another four or five weeks yet, and I'll try to persuade her to stay for that length of time, but you know how she is about her house, she'll hate being away from it.'

'But she'll never manage on her own at home,' said Izzy. 'It's her right wrist that's broken.'

'Which might be my only saving grace... So I wondered whether you two girls might encourage her to stay here as well. If we're all saying the same thing, she's much more likely to listen.'

'Of course we will,' said Izzy. 'But that isn't what you want to talk to us about, is it? Or not all of it, I'm guessing.'

Peg took a deep breath. Izzy had always had the ability to read her, even when she was a small child.

'What I want to do is enable Mim's independence, not limit it. But I can't do that when I'm two hours away. So longer-term... I think I need to move closer.'

'Move?' The alarm was stark in Phoebe's voice. 'But you can't do that, Mum, we...' She stared at her sister as if begging her to intercede.

Peg held up her hand.

'Believe me, it's the last thing I want to do,' she said. 'But I've always promised Mim that I would do my damnedest to ensure she could stay in her own house, right to the end. She's not going in a home, and although she's far from needing that level of care at the moment, it's something I need to consider going forward. The last few days in particular have made me realise how life can turn on a sixpence, and the relative good health that Mim enjoys now might all change tomorrow. And I have to be ready when it does. I owe her that much. She's all the family I have aside from you two, and you know how much of a difference she made when your dad died. I don't think we would have coped without her.'

Both girls were quiet for a moment, Phoebe's head bent, the uneaten biscuit still in her hand.

'This is how you feel about us, isn't it?' she said after a moment. 'Why you're always saying that you don't want to be a burden to us when you're older.' There were tears in Phoebe's eyes. 'But you'd never be that, Mum. You don't feel that way about Mim, so why should we feel it about you?'

Peg nodded at the wisdom of her words, and she reached out to take Phoebe's hand. 'I'm beginning to realise that. But sadly, none of it takes away from the situation I'm in now. I'm well aware how much this house means to you. The thought of leaving it is unbearable...' She swallowed. 'But there are times in your life when you have to make some very difficult decisions, and this is one of them.'

'So what do we do now?' asked Izzy, always the more pragmatic of the two.

'Nothing for the time being,' said Peg. 'I just wanted you to be aware what might be ahead of us, that's all. I'm not going to do anything rash, and I promise you that, just as I will do my utmost to do the right thing for Mim, I will also do everything in my power to keep this place. It's always been your home, and whatever happens in the future I'd like it to be yours. Some day. A long way off in the future. A long, long way off in the future.'

She smiled and claimed a chocolate biscuit from the packet. 'So I suggest we work on Mim a little and try to ensure she stays under my roof for a few more weeks yet. And, in the meantime, we enjoy what time *we* still have left together before I lose you again.'

Izzy nodded. 'Okay,' she said. 'I can do that. Pheebes?'

Her sister nodded, slowly, and with sadness still evident in her eyes, but Peg knew she could count on them both. She always had.

Izzy swallowed a mouthful of coffee, eyeing up the biscuits as if she couldn't make up her mind whether to have one or not.

'Just a thought,' she said, 'but I wondered whether perhaps Blanche might be able to help. She and Mim have really hit it off.'

Peg nodded. 'Mmm, kindred spirits, I think. And I had thought of that myself, but with Henry out of danger now I guess she'll want to go home. I haven't heard from Adam or Sofia yet, but I'm assuming they'll be visiting Henry at some point today. He's due to be discharged tomorrow, all being well, although he won't be going home, of course, not for a while yet. Which is something else to think about. There are a lot of arrangements which will need to be made.'

Izzy leaned forward, deciding to take a biscuit after all. She gave Peg a very direct look, her eyebrows arched in perfect symmetry.

'Is this the part where you also tell us you're going to offer for Henry to stay here?'

Peg closed her eyes. A moment to pause, to think about what she was going to say.

'I don't know,' she admitted. 'Part of me thinks I should, because it's the obvious solution, especially given that Mim will already be here. Adam and Sofia will be back at work next week, and I can't see either of them wanting, or being able, to change that. Henry might be convalescing for weeks. They haven't actually floated the suggestion yet, but I can see it coming.'

Izzy nodded, sliding her sister an amused glance. 'And the other part?'

Peg sighed. 'The other part thinks I must be stark raving mad.'

18

28 DECEMBER

The worst thing was the tiredness. Not the pain, or the worry about what might happen to him in the future, but the all-consuming exhaustion which came over him in waves. Even brushing his teeth seemed to require superhuman effort.

And along with the tiredness, right up there near the top of the list, next to his feelings about Adam, and to a lesser extent Sofia, were his feelings about Peg. Despite what he'd been told – that he'd crashed his car on Christmas morning, just outside her village – that sequence of events didn't marry with his recollection of what had happened on that day at all. And yet his car was a wreck and currently residing at a local garage. Trying to resolve that conundrum made his head hurt more than ever.

And now he was on his way to Peg's house, to 'recuperate', and he wasn't sure how he felt about that either. He'd been discharged from the hospital with a long list of things he could and couldn't do – the couldn't do side of things very much longer than the positive one – and an array of outpatient appointments for various checks and follow-ups. Being logical about the situation, he could see that going home to Stoke wasn't an immediate option, but he was sitting in the passenger seat of his son's car with Sofia in the back, and given that they were his family, he had thought he'd be going back to their house. Evidently, this was not to be.

Henry stared out of the window at the passing scenery. There was much to think about, but he closed his eyes briefly before taking in a deep, slow breath. All that could come later. For now he would marvel that the sun was still shining, just as it had been on Christmas morning...

They were only a couple of minutes away from Peg's house now, the road beginning to look increasingly familiar, and he realised he'd been scanning the tree-lined hedges for any signs of where he'd come to such an abrupt halt. He found it, less than a minute later – a straggly end of blue police tape fluttering in the breeze all that was left to mark the spot where his car had veered off the road. He turned his gaze away. That there was proof of what had happened still didn't make it feel real.

Peg must have been waiting by the door, because she opened it seconds after Adam knocked. And then there she was, just as Henry remembered. It seemed as if several months had gone by since he'd last seen her when, in fact, it had only been... He tried to count the number of days in his head but he couldn't. Her hair was still in plaits and he smiled at the memory of her sitting opposite him beside the fire on Christmas Day, one plait hanging down over her shoulder and the other, flung backwards. She had on a different dress today though. Similar style... He wasn't sure what you called them – a smock, maybe? – with a rounded neck, loose waist and a long, wide skirt beneath. Pink fluffy socks poked out of the bottom.

'Henry...' said Peg, holding him lightly by the arms to kiss his cheek. 'I'm so glad you're here.'

Henry nodded.

'Come in, all of you, there's a bitter wind today.'

Henry stepped inside, directly into her kitchen, a warm and welcoming space, although darker than he remembered.

'Is everything okay?'

'Yes, it's just...' He looked around him again. Everything was the same, yet different. There *was* a pine table in the middle of the kitchen, but it was a different-coloured wood than he'd remembered. There *were* beams running in parallel lines across the ceiling but although some holly hung there, there wasn't nearly as much of it as he thought there would be. And the Aga... There was some sort of cooker against one wall, but it was green, not blue. He swallowed. 'You had a shelf across the window there,' he said, pointing. 'Filled with coloured glass.'

'Did I?' Peg smiled. 'Shall I take your coat, Henry?'

Henry laid a hand against the table to steady himself. 'Thank you, I...' But he didn't finish the sentence; he didn't know what to say.

Adam held up the bag he'd been carrying. 'Shall I take this upstairs?' he asked.

'No, just pop it down there,' replied Peg. 'I'll take it up later.'

Adam pulled out a chair and set the bag down. He cleared his throat. 'I'll leave it here, out of the way.'

Everyone smiled again as an awkward silence began to grow. Not that he had any such memories, but Henry felt as he imagined an evacuee might – dropped off at a house in the country with a small bag containing all his worldly goods. He certainly felt like a child. Adam helped him out of his coat and he winced as the movement pulled against his stitches. He wouldn't have been at all surprised to find a label tied around his neck.

'Come and sit down,' said Peg. 'I've made some sandwiches. I wasn't sure whether you would have had lunch yet.'

Sofia wrinkled her nose. 'Plastic ham,' she said. 'That's all they had, wasn't it, Henry?'

He shook his head a little. 'But that was only because I told them not to worry about me,' he said. 'I could have had a proper dinner if I wanted.'

Sofia smiled. 'The consultant was later than expected,' she explained. 'So they found a sandwich for Henry while we were waiting.'

Peg nodded. 'Well, I'll put them on the table and you can help yourselves, or not, whatever you want. The girls will be back soon and they'll make short work of any that get left.'

Henry struggled to remember. 'That's Izzy and... Phoebe, right?'

'Mmm. They've gone for a walk with Blanche and Mim. I thought it might be better if we weren't all, you know... crowding round. It might be a bit much.'

'Good idea,' said Adam. 'We didn't think we'd stay too long ourselves. Not today. Just let you get settled in, Dad, and then we thought we'd come and see you tomorrow. Properly. If that's all right?' He looked to Peg for guidance.

'Come whenever you like,' she said.

'Only there are a few things we ought to talk about.'

'Don't worry your dad with those now, Adam,' said Sofia.

'I wasn't going to,' he replied. 'That's why I said we'd come tomorrow...' He gave a tight smile. 'But we'll wait until Blanche gets back, obviously. Then we can drop her home. She doesn't usually stay with us much beyond Boxing Day, so...'

'Oh,' replied Peg, 'I've made plans for dinner. I kind of assumed she'd be staying today, I don't know why...' She frowned. 'Never mind... I'm happy to drop her home later, if that's better for you?'

Sofia shot Adam a look. 'Well, that's very kind. Um... Shall we see what Blanche wants to do? If you're sure you don't mind?'

Peg shook her head. 'I don't.'

'Well, in that case... I hope Mum's been behaving herself,' said Sofia.

'Oh, she's been the model house guest,' replied Peg. 'I shall miss her, actually. So will Mim. But I've told her to come and visit as often as she likes. I'm not sure how long Mim will be staying with me, but it will be a few weeks at least.'

'And now you have two invalids,' said Henry.

Peg smiled. 'Don't go calling Mim that, she'll have your guts for garters. Besides, you're not an invalid either. I shall be putting you to work on the vegetable patch as soon as you're able. That was a joke,' she added quickly, seeing Sofia's look of alarm.

Henry sat down. He wasn't sure what else to do.

'I'll get the sandwiches,' said Peg, scuttling across to the fridge. 'There are still mince pies left too, if you can bear it.'

Fifteen minutes later, Adam and Sofia left, before the others had even arrived back. Not a drop of tea was drunk, nor a bite of a sandwich taken. Henry wasn't sure what he'd expected, really. Adam and Sofia were tired, he understood that. And he'd totally ruined their Christmas. He imagined they'd be quite glad of some time to themselves.

Peg closed the door and plonked herself down in the seat opposite him.

'Was that the most hideously awkward thing ever, or is it just me?' She smiled, reaching for a sandwich.

A snort exploded from Henry's mouth before he could stop it. 'Oh God, wasn't it?' He grinned. 'I shouldn't find it funny, but...'

'If you don't, you'll cry?' supplied Peg. She pushed the plate of sandwiches nearer. 'And *relax*...'

Henry could feel it. The moment she said it, it was as if all the tension left his body – like a balloon deflating, only without the accompanying high-pitched shriek. Although he knew without a doubt that Peg would have found that funny, too.

God, he was starving. He picked up a sandwich and took a huge bite, savouring the food, which actually tasted of something.

'Not cheese and beetroot today, then?'

'We can have those tomorrow,' said Peg.

A companionable silence lengthened as they both ate, and it was just like he remembered.

'Thank you,' he said, after a few more minutes. 'These are so lovely. After hospital food, this is a veritable feast.'

She pulled a face. 'You missed your Christmas dinner,' she said.

'So did you.'

Peg nodded. 'True... but there'll be others. Which is the most important thing. Two days ago it didn't look as if you'd see another one.' She paused for a moment. 'And can I just say, before the others get back, that if you staying here is going to work, I want you to know that there are no expectations. And I need you to be honest about how you're feeling. If you want to sleep, sleep. Whether that's in a chair beside the fire, or upstairs in your room. Similarly, when you've had enough chat, say so. I know how exhausting that can be when you don't feel well. Basically... just be as you would in your own home. I don't intend to "care" for you while you're here, because I'm not sure that's what's needed, but also because if I did that to Mim, she'd never talk to me again. And I also have things I need to do, and like to do, and while you are absolutely not in the way – please don't ever think that – I want things to be... normal and not in the slightest bit weird.' She finished in a rush, screwing up her face. 'Sorry, is that okay? I wasn't sure how to put it.'

Henry smiled and reached for a mince pie. 'All things considered... I think that's absolutely the best possible thing you could have said.'

The others arrived back just as they were finishing their meal, bursting through the door mid-conversation. Henry got to his feet, suddenly nervous that they would find him lacking.

Blanche was the first to come forward, her smile warm and her hug gentle.

'I'd like to give you a much bigger squish,' she said. 'But I'm scared I'm going to hurt you.'

'I'll take a rain check for now,' Henry replied, patting his side. 'And, as soon as I can, I'll come and claim it.'

Henry turned his attention to Mim, the woman he thought had died. Her wrist was in plaster, but other than that, there was evidently plenty of spark left in her. He could see it shining from her eyes, from her wind-burnished cheeks, and in the mischievous grin she gave him.

'I can't even shake your hand,' she said. 'But I'm pleased to meet you.'

'I'm very pleased to meet you too,' he said, holding back the question he wanted to ask. He offered an elbow. 'Isn't that what we do these days when we can't shake hands?'

Mim offered her elbow in return and they bumped them gently together, laughing.

And finally, there were Peg's daughters – one tall, with dark hair and piercing blue eyes the same as Peg, and one slightly shorter, still with blue eyes, but softer, almost grey in colour and with honey-blonde hair. The two girls were alike facially, but that's where all similarity ended, and he knew instinctively what Peg's husband must have looked like.

The taller of the two gave him a warm smile. 'I'm Izzy,' she said. 'We've heard a lot about you.'

'I'm sure you have,' replied Henry. 'And I'm sorry I've caused your mum so much upset and upheaval. I don't plan on making a habit of it, believe me. But it's nice to finally meet you, Izzy. I've heard a lot about you too. And Phoebe, of course.'

He smiled at Izzy's sister, who returned it, only shyer and not quite as wide.

There were no kisses from these two, or hugs as yet, gentle or otherwise, but that was okay. These were Peg's girls, her protectors. They weren't going to welcome him in wholesale, not until they'd got a better measure of him.

'Sofia's gone then, I see,' said Blanche. 'And Adam?'

Peg cleared her throat. 'Yes, I think... there was some talk about you going back with them so they could drop you home, but I mentioned I'd already asked you to stay for dinner so... I hope that was okay? I'm happy to take you home myself though, if...' She trailed off, seeing, as they all could, the vociferous shaking of Blanche's head.

'I'm certainly not passing up the opportunity to have dinner with you all,' she said. 'And I wouldn't dream of asking you to ferry me about. Sofia can come and fetch me tomorrow. That is, if they plan on coming to see you then, Henry? I do hope so.'

He nodded. 'I believe so,' he replied. 'They're letting me settle in first. Don't want to overwhelm me on my first day out of hospital.'

Blanche narrowed her eyes. 'Good,' she said, although Henry wasn't sure which part she was referring to. 'Well, that's a relief. And I think you staying here is for the best all round. Not being funny, Henry, but could you honestly see yourself staying with Adam? The couple of days before Christmas were enough to drive you over the edge—' She broke off. 'Sorry, that was a bad choice of words. But being serious for a minute, going back home is not an option. At least, not for a few weeks yet – the hospital still needs to monitor you. And you need to be somewhere you can relax and recuperate. Not become so stressed that your head explodes.'

'Blanche, you have such a way with words.'

19

29 DECEMBER

'I feel awful not having you to stay with us, Dad.'

It was the third time this morning that Adam had said these words, or some variation of them.

They were back at Peg's kitchen table. Just him and Adam, with a pot of tea between them and the door to the living room firmly closed. Peg had done this on her way out, retreating into the depths of the house along with everyone else – Peg, to make some notes for the article she was about to start writing, and the girls and Mim watching a Christmas film, a tradition which, thus far, they had missed out on. Sofia was ostensibly helping Blanche to pack, a task which would take them all of thirty seconds, but which they all knew was designed to place them as far away as possible from the conversation about to take place in the kitchen.

'I know you do, Adam, because if you didn't that would make you a bad person and you're certainly not that.'

Adam winced. 'Is that your way of still telling me off?'

Henry smiled. 'No... But if you feel that's what I'm doing, might I suggest that's a guilty conscience talking?' He spread his palms flat on the table. 'Look, whatever the conformist views around children being responsible for looking after their parents when they're old or infirm, the reality is that it makes more sense for me to be here. I also think that Peg's offer, and the simple existence of that offer, meant that you didn't need to consider your options quite as hard as you would otherwise have done.' He smiled. 'But there's nothing wrong with that, and I'm not blaming you.'

'It isn't that Sofia and I don't want you to stay with us, but—'

'You're both busy, I get it,' said Henry. 'And it's fine.' The thought of being at home all day with Sofia while Adam was at work wasn't one he wanted to dwell on. And he was pretty sure Adam was aware of that fact. He would even go so far as to surmise that he and Sofia had talked about that exact point, but he wasn't about to make things difficult. He'd already put them through enough.

'Peg is happy for me to be here,' he added. 'And I'm happy too. That's all we need to say on the matter.'

'Okay...' Adam nodded, clearly relieved. He picked up the teapot and poured its contents into two mugs.

Henry waited until he had finished before speaking again. He didn't want Adam to think that there was nothing to be discussed.

'On the matter of what happened on Christmas morning, however, there are a few things I want to say. I don't remember the accident, but I *do* remember our argument – what was said during it, and why. I don't want there to be any more cross words between us and I *am* very sorry for the way I handled things.' He dropped his head. 'It wasn't appropriate, either in its tone or content. Not least of all because it was Christmas Day.' He paused, wrapping his hands around his mug. 'But those words *were* said, and they were said in response to some things which have been on my mind for a while.'

'Dad, I know, but—'

Henry opened the fingers of one hand in a gesture asking

that he be allowed to continue. 'So I want you to know that whatever I said is because I love you, because you're my son and I only want the best for you. I always have done. And I can't help but be concerned when I heard the way you were talking about your promotion, and what the school was asking of you. I'm also worried by all this talk of extensions and villas and what, frankly, smacks of keeping up with the Joneses. You and Sofia are only young – don't let yourselves get drawn into that game. It will never end, and you will never earn enough money for all the things you think you *ought* to have.'

Adam threw him an irritated look. 'Dad, you don't really know anything about our lives. Have you any idea how much our mortgage alone is?'

'Then tell me,' replied Henry mildly. He bent down to stroke Rolo, who had clambered from his basket and was now winding himself around Henry's legs.

'It's different for you,' said Adam, ignoring his statement, and the cat. 'When you and Mum bought your house, things were a hell of a lot cheaper than they are today. Plus, your generation didn't move around like ours does. You stay in the same house all your lives, pay off your mortgage by the time you're fifty and are quids in. Our mortgage isn't any bigger than anyone else's, it's just what you have to do these days.'

Henry nodded. 'But of course mortgages back in my day were harder to get, and still cost the same proportionally. Salaries weren't as large back then either, don't forget. That aside though, Adam, you have a four-bedroom house. Does it need to be any bigger? That house should see you through your whole lives, even when children come along.'

Adam looked away, staring out of the window. Henry could see his jaw working, as if he was rehearsing what to say, and it worried him. He had wanted this to be an open discussion, but clearly Adam was still holding back on things, and he wasn't sure that the gulf between them would ever narrow.

'Yeah, well, like I said, Dad, you don't know anything about our lives.'

The look on Adam's face was hurt and defensive and all Henry wanted to do was wrap his arms around his son and tell him that everything would be okay. His head was beginning to throb horribly. He took a deep, and hopefully calming, breath.

'So, tell me. We're here now. We have time to talk, and I'd like to know, I really would.'

For a moment it seemed as if Adam might do just that. He opened his mouth to speak, but then his fingers began plucking at his lips and he turned away, swallowing.

'Dad, you've only just come out of hospital. It's not fair to...' He trailed off. 'Another time, perhaps.'

Henry was about to point out that there might not be another time, a fact that he was only too aware of, but under the circumstances that seemed a little harsh. Besides, he could already see that whatever opportunity there might have been, had passed. Adam's expression was closed.

'Okay... as long as we do make the time.' He left a small gap for Adam to jump in if he wanted to, even though he knew he wouldn't. 'So...' He brightened his expression. 'Perhaps I should tell you my news?' He rubbed absently at Rolo's head, who was now standing on the table nudging him gently. 'Peg has very kindly let me borrow her laptop and I've emailed the dean of my university. First, to let him know what's been going on, obviously. But I've also asked him to allow me to take early retirement.'

'Can you do that?' Adam's gaze swung back towards him, his brow furrowed.

'Oh yes. I'm sixty-two. I can take my pension at any point now.'

'But I thought you loved your job?'

'I do. And a week ago I expected to be doing it for as long as I could. But lying in a hospital bed with nothing else to do but think, is quite a revelatory experience. It stops time. And it makes you deal with the present in a way you've never done before, perhaps never felt the need to.' He pushed his chair back slightly to allow Rolo onto his lap.

'I've done a lot of things in my life, Adam. But I haven't done enough *living*. And I don't mean that in a material way, or in the way that your mother would have had me do – chasing every opportunity, shackled to ambition. I still stand by every word I said to you about my life, and who I am, but I've also realised that I haven't been doing nearly enough of what makes me feel alive. I used to write poetry. I used to listen to music, *all* the time. I used to walk outside in whatever conditions the weather could throw at me, because even on the dreariest day, or one full of rain, or wind, there was always something to see which made me feel the truest form of myself.

'I'm no age at all, not really, and I have no idea how long I'll live for. But I know now that if it's a year, it won't be enough. If it's ten years, it won't be enough, and even if it's twenty years, it *still* won't be enough. When I came round in the hospital and realised what had happened to me, how close I came to dying, I thought about what I would miss if my world had ended that day. And it wasn't my job, or my house, but you and Sofia, and everything else in my life I hold dear. And that surprised me. From someone who has made teaching their life's work, I expected to feel some sadness at that thought, but I didn't. So, perhaps it's time for something else, before I get too old to enjoy it.'

Adam nodded, a sudden contrition clear in his expression. 'I can understand that,' he said. 'It must have been terrifying, Dad. I'm sorry...' He rubbed his hands down his thighs. 'I guess we were all so anxious that you wouldn't die, we were thinking about what *our* future might look like, without you. I didn't think about how you must have been feeling about yours.' He dropped his head. 'There's no excuse for that.'

Henry carried on cuffing Rolo's cheek, the cat's purrs loud in the quiet kitchen. 'The thoughts in my head weren't ones I'd ever seen myself having either, so there's no blame here, Adam. It's been a period of time that nothing could have prepared us for. But, seeing as we're where we are, I thought I should at least give things careful consideration.'

'And you won't be bored? Being retired.'

Henry shook his head. 'No. When I think about it, my brain begins to fill with all the things I could do. And it's a nice feeling. It's, if not exactly excitement, then something quite close to it. But I need some time first. To get back to feeling sixty-two, because at the moment it's more like ninety-two.' He smiled. 'I have a feeling I'm not going to be a very patient patient.'

Adam swallowed some tea. 'Ah... patient as a noun... comes from the Latin, *patiens* meaning *I am suffering*...' He pulled a face. 'The adjective referring to someone who is able to *endure* suffering, but I agree, *im*patience as a patient is much more likely. One of life's little ironies.'

'Spoken like a true English teacher,' replied Henry. He lifted his own mug to his lips, using the pause while he drank to consider how to phrase his next question. Clearly discussion around the subject was off limits, but Henry still wanted to know what Adam had decided. 'And speaking of which... Have you and Sofia had a chance to discuss your promotion yet? I know it's been an awful few days for you, but I hope you've found some time to talk.'

'Yes... and we've agreed that I should take it.' Adam lifted his chin as if in challenge.

Henry was disappointed, but not at all surprised. 'I'm not going to try to talk you out of it,' he said. 'Because I'm sure you're taking it for the right reasons.'

'I am. What other reasons would there be?'

Henry smiled in acknowledgement of the truth as Adam saw it. He'd let it go, for now. He leaned forward. 'None at all,' he said. 'But seeing as I've been doing a lot of thinking about the future, perhaps now would be a good time for us *all* to think about what we want from it. You haven't mentioned your writing in a while. How's it going?'

Adam raised his eyebrows. 'It isn't. It hasn't been for some time. There doesn't seem to be much point to it.'

'Does there have to be?' asked Henry. 'Other than to provide enjoyment.' He paused, eyes narrowing. 'Unless you'd like it to have a point, of course. You always did, as I recall.'

'Yes, but those are the kinds of dreams you have when you're younger,' countered Adam. 'They disappear when real life comes along.'

'Maybe they do, but not entirely... If there was a spark there to begin with, the chances are it's still there. And you've had yours a very long time. I remember all the notebooks you used to fill as a child. You were always scribbling something. Don't lose sight of it, Adam.'

Adam's gaze returned to the window as if the answer could be gleaned from staring outside. After a moment, he sighed and his shoulders moved in what might have been a shrug, or perhaps an admission of defeat.

'I'm not sure now's the time,' he said.

Henry watched him for a moment. 'Because of your job?' he asked gently. 'Or something else?'

This time Adam gave a loud sigh. 'There is no job, Dad. I lied. No promotion, nothing. I've been made redundant.'

20

Henry stared at his son, feeling the ripples of his words flowing outward into ever-increasing circles, as if they were a stone dropped in a pond. The ramifications of what he'd just said were... But Henry couldn't begin to think about that now.

'I don't understand,' he said, shaking his head.

'Yeah, you and me both,' replied Adam, his voice laced with bitterness. 'I get offered a promotion one minute and then I go into school on the last day of term expecting to meet with the head to discuss it, and then... boom...' He motioned a bomb exploding with his hands. 'I get called into a meeting where I'm told my services are no longer required. Can you believe that? Right before Christmas. Bastards...'

Henry licked his lips, trying to work some moisture back into his mouth. 'I'm struggling to, that's for sure. But I still don't see how they can threaten redundancy when they've only just offered you a promotion.'

'They're not threatening, Dad, it's happening, there's no doubt about that.' He flicked a glance towards the kitchen door as if worried that one of the others might burst through it at any moment. 'Now I know the truth of what's been going on, it makes perfect sense. I told you that the promotion was being offered because the school was doing away with some head of department roles in an effort to save money. Well, the reality is that they're bankrupt, so it was a case of too little, too late. And being an academy, it means that their funding comes directly from the government rather than the local authority. They've been bailed out on a couple of occasions already and so now it seems that the funding agency has had enough. They've brought in another, much larger academy group to run the school, a group which already has heads of department and pretty much every other managerial role you can think of. And, as we're the ones in the shit, we lose all our people in place of theirs.'

Henry frowned. 'But surely you must have known how bad the school's finances were?'

'Above my pay grade,' said Adam harshly. 'I knew some of it – they've been banging on enough about budgets and cuts to this, that and the other, but no one had bothered to tell those lower down the food chain what the reality was, never mind what the consequences might be. The head's a spineless—' Adam broke off, his face stony. 'Insert whatever derogatory term you like.'

'So when will all this happen?'

'It's a done deal. Emergency order, or whatever you call it. The governors had an extraordinary meeting during the last week of term and were all booted off the board. Term starts in January under the new regime. Not that they'll bother to show their faces for a while yet, I don't suppose. They'll let all the dirty work be done first before they swan in and save us.' He rubbed a hand across his mouth. 'Not sure I want to be saved.'

'No, quite.' Henry regarded his son's expression. Anger, disgust, *fear*... 'Jesus, Adam, I don't know what to say. It's a crap way to behave, but you already know that.' He scratched his head. 'Have they said what happens now?' he asked. 'What the timescale is for the redundancies?'

'They're working with the unions, but I doubt anything above and beyond the statutory requirement will be achieved. So that's a term's notice and the usual redundancy pay. The head said we should get our calculations shortly, whatever that means in terms of time. I'd kind of stopped listening by then, it's all bullshit and none of it—'

But Henry had stopped listening too, the last of Adam's words heard but not making it any further than his ears – his brain was preoccupied with other thoughts. Conversations which had taken place previously...

'You haven't told Sofia, have you?' he asked, although the question was rhetorical. 'She still doesn't know...'

Adam looked distraught. 'How could I tell her?' he replied, his voice a hoarse whisper. 'It's Christmas...' He raised his hands in a helpless gesture. 'And I'd only just told her about the promotion. You saw how she reacted. She already has every last penny of my supposed pay rise spent. Making videos about our Instagram-perfect life...'

'She's your *wife*,' said Henry.

Adam rubbed a hand across his forehead. 'I was going to tell her. Straight away when I got home, but then it was this arrangement and that arrangement... You were arriving the next day and—'

'Then before you knew it, it was Christmas and I crashed my car,' supplied Henry. 'I know, I've made things very difficult for you.'

'It's not your fault,' replied Adam. 'The truth is that I bottled it. Christmas is bad enough without adding something like this into the mix and I just thought... It doesn't change anything, does it? When she knows makes no difference. I thought that if I go into school as normal after the holidays I could pretend that's when I found out.' He lowered his head, hardly able to hold Henry's look. 'I know, I'm a coward.'

Henry closed his eyes, sinking his hand deeper into Rolo's soft fur. Agreeing with his son wouldn't help and, wrong though it was, part of him understood Adam's actions all too well. He wouldn't want to break news like that to Sofia either. He patted Adam's hand awkwardly.

'Like everything in life, you're going to have to live with the consequences of that decision, so I'll say no more about it. You know what you have to do.' He paused. 'So you will have until Easter before you lose your job, which I know is not that long, but if you're lucky, long enough to find another position. Unless you decide to fight the decision, that is.'

Adam sat back in his chair and stretched out his legs. 'The school can…' He made a wry grimace. 'Again, insert the expletive of your choice. But there's no point arguing the toss, or fighting, I've seen this happen to enough colleagues to know how fruitless that is. It's the lack of loyalty which is most galling – that I've given my all over the past few years and in the end it counts for absolutely nothing. The head made a show of telling me what a difficult time it's been, and thanked me for my hard work, blah blah blah, but it's pretty meaningless when you know that he doesn't really care because he'll do whatever it takes to save his own arse, and stuff the rest of us – I'm not the only one being made redundant.'

Henry nodded. 'Sadly, I think that's probably true. People my age are notorious for viewing the past through rose-tinted glasses, but I'm not sure organisations were ever any different. Some hide it better than others, but essentially they promise loyalty and respect until it no longer serves them. Then, you're on your own.' He took another swallow of tea, trying to order his thoughts. His head was pounding.

'So I'm guessing what's worrying you the most about this is the financial aspect?'

Adam shook his head, almost in disgust. 'Yeah, the mortgage. It's crippling, and yes, before you say it, I know it's my own fault.'

'But you have a beautiful home to show for it, and that's your choice,' said Henry, giving his son a soft smile. 'But I don't think your dining room needs to be any bigger.'

Adam rolled his eyes. 'No, it doesn't.'

'Okay... so I think the likelihood is that you'll find another job quite easily, but I guess the real question is whether or not that's something you want to do – find another job, fund your enormous mortgage, carry on arguing over the size of the dining room, and have everything go back to being exactly as it was. And if that's what you decide, then I'll help you in any way I can. Financially too, if it's necessary.'

'Dad, I can't ask you to do that.'

'Possibly not. But I'd like to, if I can. It *is* the kind of thing parents do for their children, after all.'

'The ones who deserve it, perhaps.'

Henry let Adam's words hang in the air for a moment. He wasn't about to refute Adam's comment, not when it held grains of truth, but this wasn't the time to be harsh about lessons which needed to be learned either. It was time to be kind – to Adam *and* himself. He was equally to blame for the state of their relationship.

'You've been an idiot in keeping this from Sofia, but under the circumstances I understand why. You also said earlier that I know nothing about your lives, and that's something *I* need to fix. Parents can't expect to be a part of their children's lives unless they *are* a part of their lives.' He smiled. 'So, I would like you to know, if only to calm the terror you're feeling about your future, that this is something I will support you with if I can. But I would also like to throw something else into the mix... which is that getting another job and having everything the way it was is absolutely fine, if that's what you *really* want to do, but you *could* also decide to take the fork in the road which is being offered to you.'

Adam's eyes were curious. 'And do what?'

Henry raised his eyebrows. 'You tell me... But I think you might already know.'

'You mean get back to writing, don't you?'

'Do I?' He held his son's look with a slight challenge of his own.

Adam sighed. 'Would that it were that easy... There's no way I could pay our mortgage by writing for a living.'

'Not immediately, no. And probably not one of the size you have now. But if you had a smaller house, and a job which didn't demand so much of you, which didn't necessitate working of an evening, or trying to catch up on the weekend. Perhaps then you might have a little writing-shaped space in your life.'

Adam held his look, but he wasn't convinced.

'It wouldn't be the life you have now,' added Henry. 'I'm well aware of that, but that's kind of the point. And if it's not a stupid question, why *do* you have such a big house?' He expected to see Adam bristle, ready with his defence, but to his surprise, his head dropped. Along with his shoulders. In fact, he looked like a soft toy someone had pulled the stuffing from.

'Adam...?' Henry leaned forward, concern making his heart beat faster, the thudding sound in his ears loud in the near-silent room.

'The reason...' Adam lifted his head, seeking out his father's eyes before glancing away again. He swallowed. 'The reason we have such a large house is because we thought we'd have children to fill it by now.'

Hot shame flushed Henry's cheeks. How did he not know something so fundamental? Something so pivotal to Adam's dreams for his life? His life *and* Sofia's.

'I'm so sorry, Adam, I... Why didn't you ever tell me?'

'Because having kids is one of those things which everyone

just takes for granted. That no one talks about because it's awkward. Because I didn't want to look like a failure.' He held up his hands in an appropriately helpless gesture. 'All of the above.'

Henry closed his eyes, expelling a long breath. 'You will never be a failure, Adam. Nothing could be further from the truth, and although you might not believe it right now, would it help you to know just how special you are?' He took a moment to compose himself. 'I should have told you this before. *We* should have told you, your mother and I, but...' He shook his head. 'But we didn't, and what's done is done. I regret it, though. All children are special, Adam, but we considered ourselves so lucky to have had you in the first place, that we decided not to try for any more children after you came along. It seemed like tempting fate, and she hadn't been all that kind to us up until then.'

Adam's eyes widened, anger sparking deep inside. Belatedly, Henry realised why and held up his hand. 'It wasn't because of any problems we had conceiving, you mustn't worry on that score. It was because none of the other babies lived long enough to be born.'

Adam stared at him, silence stretching out in the still room. 'How many were there?' he asked after a moment, his voice barely above a whisper.

'Three...'

'But there must have been a reason why.'

Henry shook his head. 'There wasn't. And believe me, we had every test going – turned ourselves inside out trying to work out what was wrong. But, in the end, we just had to accept that it wasn't meant to be. And then, almost when we'd given up hope, like a star lighting up the night sky, you arrived, and decided you'd like to stay. We didn't dare question it, we just thanked whatever had changed and tried to live our lives making it clear how grateful we were.'

'I can't believe I didn't know any of that.'

Henry was very aware of the distance which separated him from his son. Both physically and emotionally.

'No, and I can see now that you should have,' he replied. 'I think – hindsight is a wonderful thing – but I think it was because we were scared.'

'Scared?'

'That if we told you, it would make you feel less special. That if we did...'

'A fairy would die?' Adam's smile was warm. 'If it helps... I always did feel special.'

'Although maybe not so much in the last few years?'

'Maybe...' But there was a softer look in Adam's eyes now.

'And the reason why I'm telling you all this is because I *do* understand how you must be feeling. How sometimes the thought of what you can't have grows so large in your mind that nothing else gets a look-in. But the one thing you are not, is a failure.'

'I don't know, Dad. I mean, the job, the writing, the money, the ridiculous way we live our life, none of it's exactly a success, is it?'

Henry smiled. 'Someone wise once said that failure is not the opposite of success, it's a part of it. And I think that's true.'

'You sound like one of those motivational posters which are all over the internet.'

'Doesn't make them untrue,' said Henry, catching Adam's look and pulling a face. 'Clichéd, yes, but in essence... Failure isn't a weakness at all. In fact, it can be one of our biggest strengths, as long as we see it that way. As long as we own up to it and embrace the opportunity it gives us to change something for the better. '

'I don't think Mum saw it that way. At least not where you were concerned.'

Henry shrugged. 'No, I don't think she did. But I guess the

difference between us is that I understand it's okay to not know what you want from life. Just as it's okay to change your mind. Sometimes, the universe deals us a card which forces that change, and sometimes we change because we know it's what's needed. And either way is fine. Right now, I think you're in the wonderful position where *both* of those things are true. Just in case the message wasn't clear enough.'

'You're making it sound as if it's a done deal. That everything has to change. That's a very scary prospect.'

Henry shook his head. 'It needn't be. But I'll ask again, why do you need such a big house? Babies don't take up much room, for a while anyway, and all they need is you... and somewhere you can stick a cot. And even when they're older, and bigger, and have more toys, and then get joined by brothers or sisters, that all happens over a period of years... you can start off quite small.' He drew in a deep breath. 'A month ago I thought *I* was settled. But what I've realised now is that those things I thought were important just aren't any more. I could have died on Christmas Day, and the thought which keeps running through my head on a loop is whether I've been a good person, whether I've lived a good life. And the truth is that if I *had* died that day, I'm pretty sure I know what the answer would be. I got lucky, Adam. I've been given a chance to change, and I think the way I do that is by filling my life with the things that truly mean something to me. Because, when my time does come, it won't be money or a nice house that made my life good, but the way in which I lived it.'

'Yes, I get that, but what about everything Sofia and I have both worked for over the last few years?'

'Adam, I've been teaching for over thirty-five years, and a month ago if you'd asked me how I'd feel to give it all up – almost a lifetime's work – I'd have said it didn't bear thinking about. But now, it isn't that I don't care, but that I've realised none of it really matters. Yes, the university might think I did a good job, the students might miss me, possibly even prefer me to whichever tutor comes in my stead, but they'll still graduate. They'll still get their degrees and go off and live the rest of their lives. And in a year's time, they probably won't even remember me. And that's fine. It's something I've done, but it doesn't fit with how I feel now, with what I want for my future. And the same can be true for you.' Henry reached across to lay his hand on Adam's, giving it a light squeeze. 'At the moment all you can see is something ending. But what if it were just beginning, Adam? What then?'

Adam and Sofia left shortly after that. There didn't seem to be much else to say, and although the conversation began to falter, the silences now were comfortable. And for the first time, in quite some while, the hug the two men exchanged on parting was warm. Henry was exhausted, but it was a small price to pay.

He had promised to keep Adam's revelations to himself until his son had had a chance to speak to Sofia, but he hoped it would be the start of more open communication between them all, Blanche included. He was only too aware that secrets were being kept from her too, and as she gave him another gentle hug before leaving, Henry realised how much he would miss her being around. He'd grown to like her acerbic wit.

He sat quietly at the kitchen table for a few minutes after they'd gone, trying to muster the strength to move. His head was throbbing badly and he felt vaguely nauseous – all symptoms which the hospital had warned were likely, but which were still worrying. He had meant what he'd said to Adam about the span of his life not being enough, and given where he was currently, the thought that that life might still end was harrowing.

Lifting his head from where it had been cradled in his hands, he realised that Peg was watching him from the doorway. How long she'd been there, he had no idea, but she smiled once she realised she'd been spotted.

'Can I get you anything, Henry?' she asked, concern creasing her forehead.

He didn't want her seeing this pathetic version of himself and he shook his head. 'I'm fine, thanks.'

'Then might I suggest you come and sit by the fire? The girls are going out shopping and Mim is reading, but between you and me, will be asleep in minutes. It wouldn't hurt you to join her.'

'I heard that...' came a shouted voice from the other room.

Peg grinned. 'Regardless of that, it's true,' she whispered.

Henry didn't have the strength to argue, and even if he had, he probably wouldn't. The thought of falling asleep by the fire was most appealing. Even so, he didn't want to give in straight away.

'The last time I did that, I woke up in hospital,' he said with a smile. 'I'm not sure it's a good idea.'

Peg was watching him again, a curious look on her face. 'Is that what happened in your dream?' she asked. 'You were very confused after your surgery.'

'It didn't feel like I was dreaming,' said Henry. 'I spent Christmas Day here. We went for a walk. We had dinner. I washed up and afterwards we sat by the fire, reading. I can describe everything I saw, and everything that happened, right down to the leeks we had with our dinner which came from your garden. You also told me a story about your bathroom, which was originally downstairs – off your living room – and, when you first moved in, made the flow of the house all wrong. You couldn't work it out to begin with and tried all manner of things to make the room feel better, but nothing did until you moved the bathroom. Then you realised that there had never been a problem with the living room at all. You just hadn't realised what the *real* problem was.' He stopped, frowning as he recalled the point of the story. 'You said that was probably the reason why Adam and Sofia have been behaving the way they have – that they're fixating on the wrong thing, too.' He stared at her in surprise as the memory came back to him. It had made sense before, and now, suddenly, it made even more sense.

Peg blushed. 'I like the sound of the dream me,' she said. 'I sound very wise, but I'm not sure that's me at all. And the bathroom has never been downstairs.' Her smile was tinged with sadness. No, it wasn't sadness, it was something like it, but more... poignant, more... more a commiseration. 'I'm sorry, Henry.'

21

30 DECEMBER

Peg put down her pencil and frowned. Something wasn't right, but for the life of her she couldn't work out what was wrong. Perhaps the perspective, or... She pushed her sketch pad away. She didn't usually have this much trouble with her illustrations – bringing her articles to life in this way was usually the part of the process she enjoyed most.

She sat back in her chair, staring through the window at the garden beyond. Sometimes, when she found her inspiration wasn't flowing, it was because her thoughts were drawing her outside, but it wasn't sunny today, or warm, and the squally rain which had been falling since dawn certainly didn't incline her to visit the woods, or tend to any number of the jobs in the garden which needed doing.

Perhaps, then, it was the quietness of the house which was disturbing her concentration. The holiday was over and the girls had gone back home, taking with them the lively chatter which had been such a feature of the house over the last few days. It was always the same after a visit, when the first few days without them became almost overwhelmingly silent, but Peg ought to be used to it by now.

She tutted, cross with herself. She'd been cross with herself for days, ever since Henry had told her the details of his dream, because she knew perfectly well what the problem was, and trying to kid herself that it was anything different was just silly. Worse, the preoccupations of someone half her age. Henry had got lucky, that was all. She might have picked leeks from the garden for Christmas dinner but that was logical – she was a gardener, and they were a seasonal vegetable. The book, which he'd told her about in the hospital, was harder to explain but... She shook her head and got up.

The worst thing was that she had lied to him. And if not lied, then misled him, at best. She had denied being any of the things which Henry had attributed to her, when the simple fact of the matter was that his descriptions had been unerringly close. His accuracy had surprised her, made her a little uncomfortable, and just because she couldn't explain it, it gave her no right to be so dismissive. Henry had looked bereft at her response, and she was angry that when she could have been kind, she had chosen instead to protect her own feelings and tramp all over his. Glancing at her watch, she picked up her sketchbook and headed downstairs. Perhaps a look at some source material would help her in her work.

She was surprised to find Mim standing in the kitchen with her coat on.

'Ah... I was just coming to find you,' she said. 'Blanche is calling for me in her car. She's invited me to afternoon tea – with scones – and you know how fond I am of a naughty treat.'

'Blanche is? Oh...' Peg frowned. 'Somehow I didn't think she drove. I don't know why.'

'Probably because her daughter always insists that they pick her up whenever she visits them. Blanche reckons it's so she can't run away.'

'*Mim...*'

'What? I'm only repeating what Blanche said,' she replied, an innocent expression on her face.

'Well, okay, but are you sure you're feeling up to it? You said your wrist was hurting this morning.' She paused, taking in the expression on her aunt's face. 'Sorry, you go. Of course you're up to it.'

'Don't write me off just yet,' cautioned Mim, but she was smiling.

'No, I won't. Go and stuff your face with jam and cream, I'm only envious.'

'You could come with us. I'm sure Blanche wouldn't mind.'

But Peg shook her head. 'No, I'm having enough trouble buckling down to work as it is. I don't need any more distractions. Besides, you two won't want me tagging along. I'll cramp your style.' A car tooted from the lane outside. 'Just don't eat too much or you won't want your dinner.' She shook her head, amused. 'God, I sound like my mother.' She kissed Mim on the cheek and opened the door for her. 'Have a lovely time.'

Still smiling, she went through to the living room, to the bookcase where her collection of wildflower books lived. There was one in particular whose style of illustrations she loved, and she was sure that if she found the right flower for her piece, the rest would follow. Her gaze travelled the titles, finding the one she needed before alighting, unbidden, on the shelves which held her fiction collection. Henry had been very interested in these since his arrival, but he wouldn't find what he was looking for, she had made sure of that.

Selecting the book she needed, she carried it to the sofa, where she perched on the arm to leaf through it. She was about to take it back upstairs when Henry appeared in the doorway. He'd been sitting at the dining room table helping Mim do a jigsaw, something which, much to his amusement, he'd found himself enjoying.

'You didn't feel up to afternoon tea then?' she asked. Henry was still getting headaches, although the severity of them seemed to be easing.

'I wasn't invited,' he replied, pretending to be hurt. 'I think it's a "girls only" thing,' he added, grinning.

'Or a "pensioners only" thing?'

'And either way I don't qualify, although I'm very much closer to one than the other. Closer than I thought.' He cocked his head back towards the dining room.

First it's jigsaws, next it will be crochet,' said Peg. 'It's a slippery slope.'

'So the jigsaws aren't yours then?' he asked. 'Mim brought them with her, did she? From her house?'

Peg smiled. 'Busted... But, as you're just discovering, they're actually rather addictive.'

Henry rubbed at his neck. 'I'm trying to pace myself,' he said. 'My head feels as if it's about to drop off. I thought I might check if there's anything on the TV worth watching. Would that be all right?'

'Of course, you won't disturb me. I'm away upstairs again anyway – I only came down for a book to help wrestle something I'm drawing into submission.'

Henry pointed to the sketch pad under her arm. 'May I have a look?'

'It's not finished yet, just some working sketches.' They were a lot more than that, but Peg hesitated. She wasn't sure if she wanted to hand them over just yet.

Henry was immediately contrite. 'Sorry. It's none of my business.'

'No, it's not that...' Peg blushed. 'I'm just being self-conscious about some drawings which are not all that good. It's silly really.' She didn't want to admit that his opinion mattered. That she worried he might think her a poor artist.

Henry's smile was warm. 'I have the artistic equivalent of two left feet... two left hands, is that it...?' The smile widened.

'So I won't be judgemental, I'm not at all qualified. But I understand if you don't want me to see them.'

Peg considered his reply. What did it matter if he looked at her stuff? They were just drawings. She needed to stop being so precious. But the little voice in her head was telling her it had nothing to do with being precious, and everything to do with not letting Henry into her world. She smiled and plucked her sketchbook from under her arm, holding it out for him to see.

'I'm writing a piece about wildflower gardening, and I want some dreamy watercolour washes to illustrate it. The kind which might make you think you were sitting in a meadow at the height of summer – soft sun, warm breezes, that kind of thing. What I've got at the moment are more like botanical drawings, and that's not the same thing at all.'

Henry nodded. 'And the book?'

'Illustrated by an artist whose style I admire. I thought it might help me find the right...' She trailed off, unable to find the word she was looking for.

'Vibe?' offered Henry. 'I can imagine that might be difficult on a day like today. When you're aiming for dreamy summer meadow, and outside we've got freezing squally rain.' He took the sketch pad. 'I'm not sure I can help with that, although I do have a bright yellow tee shirt with "The Bees are Coming" written across it. You're welcome to borrow it, if you think it might help.' His smile was teasing.

He began to turn the pages of the book, silently, rotating the sketches this way and that as he studied them. Peering closer at a detail before holding them further away. And all the while, Peg watched him, seeing his eyes grow rounder. Eventually, he reached the most recent page she'd been working on.

'I can see what you mean,' he said. 'In that the style might not be what you're looking for... but these are still stunning, Peg.' He looked up at her, his brown-eyed gaze searching her face for several seconds. 'And they remind me of...' He waggled his fingers. 'No, never mind, but there's a couple of sketches here...' He turned back several pages. 'What will you do with these?'

Peg shrugged. 'Nothing. They were just preliminaries... Me stretching out muscles which hadn't been used in a while.'

'Might I borrow one?' asked Henry. 'But it would mean removing the page from the pad, would that be okay?'

'I don't see why not. What are you going to do with it?'

Henry was about to reply when he changed his mind. 'Now it's my turn to be self-conscious. Can we just say I'll show you when it's done?'

'Okay... Sounds mysterious, but sure, take what you need.'

She waited while Henry carefully peeled one of the sheets from the pad before handing it back to her.

'Sorry,' he said. 'I'm aware I haven't helped with your problem.'

But Peg smiled at the thought which had already come to her, one which was beginning to take a delightful shape in her head. 'You might have,' she replied. 'You actually might.'

Henry scratched his head. 'One last thing before I let you get back to work,' he said. 'But would you have any kind of drawing pen? Like a fountain pen, or even just a nib and some ink? And maybe a pencil, too.'

Henry's expression was inscrutable, but he couldn't hide the tiny light which had come into his eyes. One that certainly hadn't been there before. Well, if that's all it took to make him feel better, how could Peg possibly refuse?

'Coming right up,' she said.

She worked steadily all afternoon, the artist's collection of illustrations she'd taken from the bookcase earlier unopened at the side of her desk. Another idea had taken centre stage, and the moment she sat down and picked up her brushes, she knew exactly what she needed to do in order to realise it. What, only half an hour before, had seemed so arduous, now flowed with ease, and she lost herself completely to her art.

When, finally, her hand stilled on the page, she realised she'd been sitting at her desk for over two hours, scarcely moving, and she had the stiff muscles to prove it. She was also desperate for a drink.

She sat back, studying her work once again, looking for where she could make improvements, but as her eyes moved from detail to detail, she realised it was finished. There was nothing she didn't like, and she was astonished at how quickly the piece had been completed. She would usually have many more hours' work ahead of her before she would be satisfied.

Getting to her feet, she also realised that the house was silent. Had, in fact, been silent for a while. She checked her watch. Mim would probably not be back for another hour or so yet, but whatever Henry had been up to, he'd done it quietly.

The answer was apparent the moment she descended the stairs. Henry's long body was stretched out on the sofa, and, being longer than its length, his feet were propped up on one arm, while his head rested on a pile of cushions. His right hand lay upon his chest, while the other curled around Rolo who had snuggled up beside him. He looked as a mummy might. Except, *his* chest rose and fell gently, slowly, and without a sound.

Peg stood there for a moment, rooted to the spot. He looked so peaceful, and so comfortable, that her first inclination was to find something to cover him. The fire had burned low, and while the room was still reasonably warm, the afternoon was dwindling, as was the daylight; it would be bitter again soon. But the longer Peg stood there, the more apparent it became that Henry wasn't just peaceful or comfortable, he looked at home. In her home. And Rolo obviously thought so too. The niceness of that feeling brought her up sharply.

Tiptoeing past the sofa, she made for the sanctuary of the

kitchen, somewhere she could take a deep breath and gather her thoughts, which felt scattered to the four corners of the earth. Her cheeks were burning and she pressed her palms against them. The last thing she wanted to do was compare Henry to her husband, but her head had other ideas. Because it wasn't the sight of seeing another man lying on her sofa which had disturbed her, but the fact that Henry did so so peaceably. He didn't snore, or grunt, his breathing was so soft as to be undetectable, whereas Julian was such a big man, he didn't do anything quietly. When he died, it had made the silence in the house feel so much worse, simply because life with Julian was never without noise.

Once her own breathing had returned to normal, Peg remembered the reason she had come downstairs in the first place. Yes, her work was finished, but she was also in need of a cup of tea. She had no desire to wake Henry, but perhaps if she gently moved about the kitchen as normal, he might come to of his own accord. And if he didn't, well, that would be fine too.

It wasn't until she had filled the kettle and set it to boil that she noticed the rectangle of paper on the kitchen table. Centred. Presented. Waiting to be found. And what she saw there nearly took her breath away for the second time. Her hand trembled as she lifted it, her mouth moving as she read the words written there, words she already knew by heart.

> *The way a crow*
> *Shook down on me*
> *The dust of snow*
> *From a hemlock tree*
>
> *Has given my heart*
> *A change of mood*
> *And saved some part*
> *Of a day I had rued.*

Henry had taken her sketch of winter greenery, the page she had filled with images of bright-berried holly, branches of yew and curls of flowering ivy, mistletoe, jasmine and cotoneaster, and filled the spaces in between with the words from one of her favourite Robert Frost poems. A favourite because it exactly described the way she felt whenever some small miracle of nature bestowed its gift on her. And she couldn't help but wonder what it was that had saved some part of a day for Henry.

It was several seconds before she realised her cheeks were wet with tears.

22

NEW YEAR'S EVE

'What are you two huddled up about?' asked Peg coming down the stairs. 'You're thick as thieves, the pair of you.'

She had meant it as a joke, but Mim's sudden start was a guilty one for sure.

'I don't think I should tell you,' replied Henry. 'You already think I'm mad, and this will only cement that opinion.'

'Want to try me?' she said, smiling benignly, although in truth she was intrigued. This wasn't the first time she had come across Henry and Mim having a whispered conversation.

Henry shot Mim a look before raising his hands in a gesture of submission.

'If you must know, Blanche is picking us up shortly,' said Mim, butting in. 'I'm going for a gossip and Henry is going to look at Athelstone House.'

Peg frowned. 'The place where she lives?'

'One and the same.'

Peg turned her attention back to Henry. 'So when you say look at... I'm guessing this is not a trip to study its architectural features, or muse on its history.' She suppressed a smile. 'Not being funny, Henry, but aren't you a little young for all that? I know you're worried about your health, but this is only a temporary setback, I'm sure of it.'

'They cater for people over fifty-five,' said Mim. 'Even *you* could go there, Peg.' Mim's tongue was firmly in her cheek.

Peg was about to say 'over my dead body' when she thought better of it. 'Thank you, Mim, but I'm not sure I'm ready for that *quite* yet.'

'No, it's not my cup of tea either,' said Mim. I mean, it's very nice – Blanche's flat is lovely, but...' She shuddered. 'Talk about one foot in the grave. All those old people.'

Peg smiled, wondering whether Mim had ever said anything to that effect to Blanche. She could easily imagine the response if she had.

'Yes, thank you,' muttered Henry. 'And you're absolutely right, I am too young for the type of accommodation Blanche has, but the main house is set in several acres of parkland, and within its boundaries are also several bungalows and chalets. There's a health club there, too. And although they are for people of *early* retirement age, it's the setting that appeals. It's very private and, well, altogether rather lovely...'

Peg nodded. 'Yes, I've seen it advertised,' she said. 'But you haven't even been out of the house yet, Henry. Are you sure a visit like that isn't going to be too much?'

He raised his eyebrows. 'Point proven, I think.'

'Yes, but it's not, is it? The way you feel now isn't going to be the way you feel in a couple of months' time, maybe even a couple of weeks.'

Peg didn't really know why she was trying to put obstacles in his way – perhaps it was simply that she was surprised by his decision – and although she'd promised Adam she would keep a careful watch on Henry, she wasn't his keeper, he *could* actually do what he liked. She had sounded a note of caution anyway; it was up to Henry what he did now.

'True...' Henry smiled. 'But it doesn't hurt to look. And I've probably made it sound more formal than it is. I don't even know whether there are any properties for sale. So, in truth, what we'll be doing is having a cuppa with Blanche, and I promise I won't overtax myself.'

'Adam would never forgive me if you did.'

'No, I know.' Henry's expression was warm. He was obviously grateful for her concern, even if he didn't say it.

'Will you be back in time for lunch?'

Henry exchanged a look with Mim. 'Possibly not... Perhaps it would be better to assume we won't be.'

'Okay,' said Peg lightly. 'I'm just popping into the garden to get some of the leaves up. The lawn is clogged with them and it would be good to let it breathe a little, it's such a lovely day. Let me know when you're going.'

She walked straight through to the kitchen and quickly shrugged on her welly boots and coat. The conversation had disturbed her, and she needed some time alone to get a grip on her thoughts. For heaven's sake, she'd thought her hormonal days were long behind her.

Raking the leaves was one of those jobs which, on the one hand, was irritating because it seemed never-ending during several months of the year, but on the other, one she was grateful for at times like this. Times when the physical exercise was just the thing to help her vent her frustrations. There were plenty of occasions when Julian had driven her out here and... She turned the thought away. She'd gone over and over all that in her head countless times, and she was done with it. Nothing she did, or didn't do, would have changed the outcome, that much was abundantly clear.

She hadn't even got the first load of leaves corralled into a pile when she saw a shadow stretching out across the lawn, bobbing up and down as its owner walked. She turned around to see Henry coming down the path towards her.

'It's lovely out here,' he remarked. 'But crikey, is it cold.'

She smiled. 'Hence the leaf raking. It certainly keeps you warm. At least you've had the good sense to put on a coat.' She dropped her head. 'Sorry, I'm fussing. It's what I do.' She was well aware that she wasn't just referring to her last statement. 'And probably made worse by having Mim live so far away that when I do get to see her, or something untoward happens like a broken wrist, I go into smothering mode. It's become something of a habit.'

Henry squinted against the sun. 'I don't see concern as smothering. And, actually, it's nice to have someone show it at all, I've lived a long time without it. Plus, you were right to temper my enthusiasms, it *is* early days and I do need to learn to walk before I can run.' He pulled a face. 'So I'm sorry too. I didn't mean to be defensive.'

'Even if you had been, I wouldn't blame you.'

Henry smiled, looking around. 'This is quite some space you've got here. The garden is beautiful. You must put in a lot of hours to keep it looking this good.'

'I do.' Peg nodded. 'It's something I very much enjoy but... it's been my saviour, too. I feel different when I'm out here.' She dipped her head. *'The dust of snow from a hemlock tree, has given my heart a change of mood, and saved some part of a day I had rued.* So you see why I've always loved that poem. What you did... I didn't get a chance to say much about it the other day. You were asleep, and then Mim arrived home and there was dinner to make, and... it got a bit lost in all of that, but it was beautiful, truly beautiful. And a beautiful thing to do.' The sun was turning the grey strands in Henry's hair into silver threads.

'If I'd got my act together I'd have written some words of my own, but...' He tapped his head gently. 'The old bonce isn't quite what it was just yet. And besides, Robert said it far better than I could.'

Peg smiled at his deflection of her compliment. 'I didn't know you wrote poetry.'

'I don't. Or rather, I haven't, not for a long while. But I'm hoping it's something I might find my way back into. Now that I'm going to have a lot more time on my hands.'

'Have you heard back from your dean?' she asked. 'Will they let you go, do you think?'

'I don't see that they have any choice, but yes, I'm to go with their blessing, which means a lot. The dean is a very articulate man, so it's no surprise that his reply to my email was everything I could have hoped for but, even so, he didn't have to write it that way.'

'No, I'm sure.'

'There are some administrative procedures to put into place, but I shall officially retire at Easter. I'm on sick leave until then anyway, so the reality is that I have given my last lecture.'

Peg hoped her expression was sympathetic. 'That must be hard.'

Henry thought for a moment. 'You know, I thought it would be. But surprisingly, it doesn't seem to feel that way. I'm taking that to mean the timing is right.'

'Things happen for a reason. Isn't that what they say?'

'It's something I've always believed in, certainly.' Henry was studying her face. 'And recent events have definitely given me a great deal to think about.' He smiled. 'How about you? Are you a mistress of fate? Or a proponent of free will?'

Peg glanced away. The conversation was edging into territory she was keen to avoid. 'The latter,' she said, looking down at the pile of leaves at her feet. 'We make our own fortune. Which brings me neatly around to what we were discussing earlier. Are you really thinking of moving?'

Henry ran a hand through his hair, frowning when he encountered the dressing that was still there.

'I don't know what I'm doing, not really. But I guess I'm

exploring all the possibilities,' he said. 'I'm not used to having all this time on my hands for thinking about stuff, and one topic which is sorely in need of it is my relationship with Adam. It hasn't been good for a while, and there's nothing like looking death square in the face to make you consider what's important in your life. I don't want to go through whatever time I have left being alienated from my son, or from Sofia, for that matter. He told me some things the other day and...' He broke off and stared into the distance for a moment, as if thinking. 'Anyway, one of the things he said is that I know nothing about their lives, and he's right. The truth hurts, but I can see that I've used the rift in our relationship as an excuse to further withdraw from it, when what I should have done is the opposite. I need to be a much bigger part of their lives going forward, and it's going to be an awful lot easier if I'm based here, rather than nearly three hours away.'

Peg had to admit that made considerable sense. 'Don't say anything, because I don't want Mim to fret, and she will if she finds out, but I'm having the same discussions with myself,' she said. 'I've been thinking about how Mim's future is going to look, and in order to ensure it stays as it is, I think I'll need to move closer to *her*. So I can keep my watchful eye.'

Henry looked horrified. 'But this house?' His head swivelled, taking in all the areas of the garden. 'All this...? You wouldn't want to give this up, would you?'

Peg eyed the kitchen window, making absolutely sure that there would be no way for Mim to hear her. 'It'll break my heart,' she said. 'But I don't know what else I can do.'

'No... But you've a while yet to think about things.'

'I haven't, not really. Mim's wrist isn't causing her much pain now, and although the cast is hampering her ability to do things, knowing Mim, I think she'd much rather struggle than have me wait on her hand and foot. If anything, having you here is helping, because otherwise I think she'd be clamouring to go home. I'm amazed she's stayed as long as she has.'

Henry dipped his head. 'And there was me thinking my being here was a right pain in the arse. I'm glad I'm useful for something.'

Peg met his look. He didn't seem to be fishing for compliments, so was his expression something else? She glanced away, embarrassed. Henry being here was rapidly beginning to feel timeless, as if it had always been.

'Is everything okay?' She was wondering what had brought him into the garden.

'Yes, fine. I was thinking about what you said – about the fact that I haven't been out of the house yet. So I thought I'd come and take a look at your garden and test the water, so to speak.'

'And how's the water feeling?'

Henry faltered. 'Like jelly,' he admitted. 'But I've got to start somewhere and arrangements have been made now. I'll be okay. I'm sure I can manage to get out of the car and walk to Blanche's flat. We don't have to go on a tour of the place. I'll think of it as more of a fact-finding mission than a field exercise.'

Peg smiled. 'Make sure you do.'

Henry had turned to go when a sudden thought came to her.

'Actually, Henry? I've been meaning to ask you something for ages. About Mim.'

He raised his eyebrows. 'Oh…?'

'Just that my neighbour told me that on the day I got the call about Mim breaking her wrist, someone came here to see me while I was away. That was you, wasn't it?'

For a moment, Henry looked completely blank, but then his face lifted. 'That feels like it was years ago,' he said. 'But yes, I did. I just popped over to say hello.'

Peg nodded. 'I thought as much. But what was odd is that

when you first came to stay you seemed very surprised to see Mim, and Blanche even told me she thought Mim had *died*.'

'Died?'

'Yes. She came up to me after the carol service and told me how sorry she was. It seemed a really odd thing to say, so I asked her later what she'd meant by it. And her reply was that she'd been sorry to hear about my aunt.'

'Okay...'

'Yes, I know *that's* not odd. But when I went on to say how Mim was as tough as old boots and nothing much gets her down, Blanche looked most surprised. Which was when she admitted thinking that Mim had passed away. That's what's odd. Why would she think that?'

Henry's brow wrinkled. 'Yes, that is odd...' he said slowly. 'Have you asked her why?'

'Yes, she just said that because she was old she usually assumed the worst. But that's an awfully big leap – to go from someone having a broken wrist, to them dying. And I thought Judith told you what had happened.'

'Yes, she did... so, I'm not sure why the confusion, but... perhaps I didn't tell Blanche the details...' He rubbed at his head. 'I'm sorry, Peg, I can't remember what I did or didn't say. Like I said, it feels as if that happened ages ago.'

'Okay,' said Peg lightly. 'Probably just a misunderstanding then.'

'Mmm... and thankfully Mim *is* okay. That's the main thing.' Henry smiled, pulling his coat a little tighter around him.

Peg nodded, suddenly ashamed not to have noticed how uncomfortable Henry was becoming. 'Sorry, go on back inside or you won't be in a fit state to go anywhere. I'll just finish this up and then I'll be in myself.'

Henry nodded and headed back up the path, but it was some moments before Peg felt able to return to her task. Her head was such a jumble of thoughts.

. . .

Dishcloth in hand, Peg sighed as she looked around the kitchen. The last of the crumbs from underneath the toaster had been wiped away, and the plates from breakfast had been dried and returned to their home on the dresser. There was nothing else she needed to do. Yet the prospect of a quiet day wasn't quite as welcome as she had thought it would be. In fact, it had come at completely the wrong time. What she needed was activity, not a long stretch of hours to fill with nothing to do but wrestle with her thoughts, and as it was both Mim and Henry who were occupying those thoughts, their very absence ensured they were *all* she would think about. Perhaps if she did some drawing, lost herself in its colour and form; but she shook her head. She wasn't in the mood, and the activity would become irritating, not soothing.

She was still dithering over what to do when a knock at the back door sounded, and she rushed to open it. Any kind of distraction would be welcome, especially if it was Judith; they could talk about nothing for hours. But she already knew it wouldn't be her neighbour. Judith never waited for the door to be answered, simply marched right in with a jolly, 'Only me!'

'Oh, hello...' Finding Henry's daughter-in-law on her doorstep was a surprise. Seeing she was on her own, an even greater one. 'It's lovely to see you, come on in.'

'I'm not interrupting, am I? I've just been to drop off an order and was passing, so...'

Peg smiled. 'Not at all. I was feeling a bit at a loose end, actually.' She peered past Sofia's shoulder, just to make sure. 'Are you on your own? Adam not with you?'

'No, he's... gone into school. He had a few things to sort out.'

'I bet it's nice and quiet at the moment without the children there. When does term start?'

Sofia fiddled with a button on her coat. 'I'm not sure... it's usually a couple of days into the new year, but there are training days sometimes.' She smiled, a little awkwardly it seemed.

Peg held out her arms, wrapping her best welcoming smile across her face. 'Let me take your coat.' Judging by the look of it, it was cashmere – an elegant long length in a traditional camel colour. It would make Peg's pink anorak look even more vibrant than usual.

'How's Henry?' asked Sofia, sliding her arms out of her sleeves.

'He's getting there,' replied Peg, taking the coat from her. 'The headaches are lessening, and he's beginning to feel stronger, but I think it'll be a while until he's back to his old self. That's if it happens at all.'

Sofia nodded. 'I hope it does.' She glanced towards the living room door, leaning slightly closer to Peg and lowering her voice. 'It's been horrible thinking he might not be around. And Adam's been really upset. I have too, but... I don't think I've ever told Henry how I feel, let alone shown it. I find it difficult... I'm not sure he likes me very much.'

'I don't think that's true at all,' said Peg. 'But he perhaps doesn't know you as well as he'd like,' she added gently. 'I'm afraid he isn't here, though.' She wasn't sure how much she should say about where he had gone, *or* the reason for his visit.

'Blanche invited Mim and Henry over for afternoon tea. I think she thought the change of scene might do him good – he hasn't been out of the house yet, and a gentle excursion might be just what he needs.' She folded Sofia's coat over her arm, running her hand across the smooth fabric. 'But you're welcome to stay. Would you like a drink?'

'No, I probably...' She trailed off, looking suddenly anxious, and Peg realised belatedly how tired she looked. Her usually flawless complexion was blotchy and puffy. Peg studied her a little more closely – had she been *crying*?

'I'll put the kettle on anyway,' she said, making the decision for her. 'I'm going to have one, so if you change your mind...' She hung up Sofia's coat, turning her back on her for a moment. She desperately needed to think of something to make a conversation from. Sofia must have been nervous about coming here on her own, and she was clearly still reeling from the shock of everything that had happened over recent days. Peg couldn't just let her leave, but she had no idea what they would talk about.

'There was something I wanted your opinion on, actually,' she said, crossing to the sink. Her eyes alighted on the kitchen window, the one where Henry had seen shelves filled with coloured glass. 'I, um... I've been thinking about making some changes to this place. It's been years since I decorated, but I have no clue where to begin. Do you have some ideas I could look at? Or maybe if you had a proper look around...' She turned back to face Sofia, smiling at her suddenly eager expression.

'I keep a lot of my sample books in the car when I'm out visiting a client,' said Sofia. 'Why don't I go and fetch them and we can have a chat?' She looked suddenly relieved. 'I won't be a sec.'

She bustled back out through the door and Peg almost groaned aloud. She was doing the right thing, she was convinced of that, but she was also going to get herself into a right pickle if she wasn't careful. She set the kettle to boil and waited for Sofia to return.

Moments later, Sofia had covered Peg's kitchen table with pattern books, so many that she'd had to make more than one trip to bring them in, piling them up one on top of the other – wallpapers, fabrics, paint charts, too; a dizzying array. She looked at Peg expectantly.

'Perhaps you should show me which areas you want to change, and why. Then I can get a feel for what you want to achieve. Which rooms are we talking about?'

'Well, the bathroom... and the bedrooms certainly, so that's five rooms altogether.'

Sofia nodded. 'And how do you want them to look?'

'Look?'

'Yes. What style? Like, opulent or luxurious, industrial or botanical... Think of what words you'd use to describe them.'

Peg stared at her. 'Um... I don't know, I just want them to look nice.'

'I see...' Sofia glanced down at the table. 'Well, what about colours then? Dark palettes are enormously popular at the moment, and—' She broke off suddenly as the kettle began to whistle. 'Why don't we have that drink, and then we can sit down and have a look through the books? If you see something you particularly like, we can start from there.'

'Okay,' said Peg, sliding the kettle from the Essie's hotplate. 'That sounds good. What would you like? Tea or coffee?'

Sofia was about to answer when her eyes suddenly narrowed. 'You don't want to change anything in your house at all, do you?'

Peg pulled a face, giving what she hoped was an apologetic smile. 'Not really, no. But then I suspect you didn't come here to see Henry either, not by yourself...'

To her horror, Sofia's face crumpled and her eyes filled with tears. 'Adam's been made redundant,' she blurted. 'What on earth are we going to do?'

23

Carrying both mugs of tea in one hand, Peg pushed aside a pile of books and carefully lowered their drinks to the table. She placed one in front of Sofia who was now sitting, sniffing intermittently.

'Here,' said Peg gently. 'I found a packet of brandy snaps no one has discovered yet.' She took the packet out from where she'd tucked it under her arm. 'One end is dipped in chocolate, too.'

'The worst thing is that he never told me,' said Sofia, staring at her mug. 'He's known since before Christmas. I can't believe he kept it from me.'

'Can't you?' said Peg, sitting down. 'In my experience, that's just the sort of thing men do. Not all men,' she added hastily. 'But some certainly do. Julian would have, without a doubt. He didn't like difficult subjects and usually went out of his way to avoid discussing them. It used to drive me up the wall. And then if I got cross about it, he'd say he didn't want to upset me and was only trying to protect me – which was even more irritating because I knew it was true. But, eventually, I got to read the signs and was able to winkle things out of him. Perhaps Adam's just the same.'

'He said it was because of Christmas.'

Peg winced. 'It doesn't make it right,' she replied. 'But I can understand that. Christmas is such an emotive time of year, there couldn't be a worse time to announce news like that. And then... well, I guess events just snowballed, didn't they? I don't imagine there was much of an opportunity to talk after Henry crashed his car. Adam must be furious though. Especially after his school had offered him a promotion. That makes no sense at all.'

'He didn't tell me all that has gone on, just that the school is in financial trouble and they're being taken over by another academy.' Sofia's eyes no longer shone with tears, but her head was bowed, her voice quiet.

Peg nodded, but she had no idea how education worked. 'It's scary, I know. It must feel like the rug has been pulled out from beneath you. But try not to be too hard on Adam. Yes, he should have told you, but admitting what he probably sees as failure must have been hard. Not to mention the fact that he must be feeling guilty, too.'

'I know, but that still doesn't change the fact that we need his salary, we can't possibly manage without it. And to think I was wondering about the possibility of extending our dining room...'

Peg let her comment pass. Sofia was angry and upset, and pointing out how extravagant it was to make an already big house even bigger wouldn't help matters. 'Right now, I'm sure it seems as if everything is about to come crashing down around you, but don't forget that you and Adam both have really valuable skills. I have it on good authority that he's a fantastic teacher, and English as a subject is always going to be in demand. Plus, you have your own successful business, and working for yourself gives you so much flexibility in terms of where you work *from*. All those things will stand you in good stead, moving forward.'

'I suppose so,' replied Sofia, but she didn't sound at all convinced. Her hands were balled in her lap, her uppermost thumb rubbing across one knuckle, over and over again.

Sensing there was more to come, Peg let the silence stretch out. When it was clear she wasn't going to say anything further, Peg opened the packet of biscuits and took one, pushing the rest towards Sofia in the hope she might do the same.

'There are always solutions to a problem, and in many ways you're lucky. You own your home and yes, I know you have a huge mortgage, like a lot of people your age, but at least it gives you options. Hopefully the bank will be understanding if you need to take a payment break or something, but I'm sure it won't come to that. I bet you Adam will get another job in no time at all. You just might need to put your ideas for the house on hold for a little while.'

Sofia ran a hand over the cover of one of the pattern books, pulling it towards her slightly, before lifting the pages and then letting them fall in a desultory manner.

'I don't even like our house,' she said. 'So I'm not sure why I want to extend it.' She looked up, her eyes focused over Peg's shoulder. 'Don't ever change your cottage, will you? It's perfect just the way it is.' She examined a fingernail. 'And I don't suppose you believe me – why would you? But it's true. I'd love a home like this. With some character, and a kitchen garden... you've made it all so beautiful.'

Peg couldn't be more surprised. 'I'm not sure I ever really thought about how to decorate the cottage, it just kind of evolved over the years. I do love it though.'

'It suits you,' replied Sofia. 'Or you suit it. I don't think our house does that.'

'It's very different to mine, admittedly, but it's still very nice.' She bit her lip, hoping that Sofia wouldn't notice her little white lie. 'Why don't you like it?' Peg wasn't sure why the conversation had changed direction, but at least Sofia was talking again.

'Because I try to make it one thing, and then I change it and make it something else, but no matter what I do, it never looks right. Maybe because it's a house and not a *home*...'

'Perhaps you haven't worked out yet who you want to be,' replied Peg. 'And that can take a long time – some people never manage it. You're still young. You're experimenting with life, trying on different hats, but eventually you'll find one which not only looks good, but is comfortable too.'

Sofia sat silently, staring at the table, and Peg wondered whether she had gone too far. Perhaps she sounded critical; she hadn't intended to be.

'I think we all go through a stage like that,' she added. 'And it wasn't something I realised about myself until the girls were at school. Before that, life was so busy I never really thought about who I was, or what I wanted, I just went with the flow. I wasn't unhappy, but, looking back, I certainly wasn't settled either. I think half the battle is having the headspace to figure all that out.' She tipped her head to one side, studying Sofia's expression. 'So what is it about my cottage that appeals to you?'

'All of it.'

'What, the draughty windows and the dodgy plumbing? And the mud which tracks in endlessly no matter what I do to keep it out?'

Sofia smiled, but it was tinged with sadness. 'Maybe it's not the cottage itself, but the person I could be if I lived here.'

'And who would that be?'

'Someone who doesn't care if the walls are plastered in children's drawings, or the kitchen table has crayon on it. Someone who walks around barefoot, wearing jeans and a tee shirt. Someone who hangs washing on the line every day just to hear it flapping in the wind, or who brings in flowers from the garden to stick in a jam jar. Someone who bakes wonky cakes and doesn't care that she fishes honey out of the pot with a knife and not a spoon...'

Peg swallowed, alarmed to see tears welling again in Sofia's eyes. The person Sofia described couldn't be more different from the one sitting opposite her, and Peg's heart ached at the young woman's sadness. Did Adam know that she felt this way? Did Blanche? Did anyone? Surely Sofia must have friends to talk to. And as Peg sat there wondering how on earth she could respond, what on earth she could say to make Sofia feel better, she also thought about the words she'd actually used. Sofia wasn't just unhappy with who she was, she knew *exactly* who she wanted to be. And top of the list was someone whose walls were plastered in children's drawings. Suddenly, a lot of things began to make sense.

'How long have you been trying?' she asked quietly.

'Three years...' The first tear tipped from the corner of Sofia's eye and made its way down her cheek.

'And when it didn't happen, you threw yourself into making your home bigger and better than it needed to be. You threw yourself into making your business such a success that you'd never be able to take a break from it, even if you wanted to. You threw yourself into finding anything and everything which might make you happy. And Adam... threw himself into his career, chasing management roles which would take him away from the children he had gone into teaching for in the first place. Oh Sofia...' Peg placed her hand over Sofia's, feeling the tremble in her thin arm. 'There's nothing I can say to make any of it better. Nothing I can do either, except give you a hug, if you think one might help?'

Wordlessly, but with a minute nod, Sofia rose and allowed Peg to come around the table to comfort her, and as she did so, her arms around Sofia's shaking shoulders, Peg could suddenly see a tiny glimmer of hope. If life had taught her anything it was that there was always one to be found, and that they often appeared right when you least expected them.

Gently, she drew away and let Sofia sink back into her chair. 'You know, if you're worried that Adam's redundancy might mean things will have to change, maybe that's not such a bad thing. Sometimes, all we feel is the loss when something is taken away from us, when really it's an opportunity for something else to arrive.' And the thought which filled Peg's head was that she couldn't be sure she was still talking about Sofia.

'Does Henry know about any of this? Or Blanche?'

Sofia nodded. 'Henry does. Adam told him yesterday.' She swallowed. 'That's why I thought I'd come over. I just wanted to talk to someone who *knew*... I can't tell Mum stuff like this – she thinks our life is ludicrous, I know she does. Well, she thinks I'm ludicrous, for doing what I do, for wanting things to be better.'

'She might...' conceded Peg, knowing full well this was true. 'But I'm also certain that if she knew any of what you've just told me, she'd understand the reasons for your behaviour. She's your mum, she knows you better than anyone, and she'll already know that something hasn't been right for a while. Trust me, she will. You just need to find a way to open up to her, same with Henry.'

'But how do I do that when he doesn't even like me?'

Peg shook her head sadly. 'You know, he'd hate the fact that you've never shared any of this with him before. He probably doesn't feel he knows you all that well, and that's because, by holding it back from him, you've held yourself back too. Sometimes you have to let a person see who you really are, and that bond of trust – allowing someone to see the real you, with all your faults and failures as well as your strengths and successes – that's how you become close. I think if you share how you're feeling with Henry, he'll be a lot more understanding than you give him credit for. Same with your mum.' She smiled.

'And if you think about it, Henry is in a very similar situation to you and Adam. He's having to take stock of a few things and put some changes into place. He might be moving towards living a different kind of life, but that doesn't mean it will be a bad one. It might even turn out to be much better.' She studied Sofia's face, at least the small part of it she could see. 'You know, this is an opportunity for all of you to think about what you really want from your lives. If all the balls are being thrown up in the air then you need to make sure you know which ones to catch.'

Sofia lifted her head from her hands, staring at Peg. And almost immediately her eyes began to well up. 'I don't think you understand,' she said, a flash of anger crossing her face. 'I make cushion covers,' she added. 'Cushion covers and curtains, and that's pretty much it.'

It was Peg's turn to stare. 'I'm sorry?'

'The rest of my business doesn't really exist. It's just me trying to pretend that I'm a successful interior designer. Throwing loads of money at it in an attempt to gain some high-profile clients which, by the way, includes broadcasting every detail about our Instagram-perfect lives in an effort to convince people that's what they want too. And what they can have, if they would only give me full rein over their bank balance. But it doesn't work, so in the end I make cushion covers. And curtains.' She swallowed, the tilt to her chin a little defiant.

Peg glanced up at her window. 'Did you make the curtains in your house?' she asked. 'The incredible set in your big bay window which I remember thinking must have cost you a fortune?'

Sofia nodded. 'I've made all the curtains in our house. Plus the blinds, the covers for the sofa and the drapes in our bedroom, too. Although, of course, you haven't seen those.'

'Then sorry, maybe I'm missing something here, but isn't that a successful business? What you've made is beautiful.'

'Maybe... but anyone could do that.'

'I couldn't,' said Peg.

'Okay, but it's not being an interior designer, is it? That's the point. Only a handful of really successful designers get to work with the kind of clients who have the money to do something different, to fundamentally change their houses instead of just fiddling with the soft furnishings, or swapping the colour of paint on the walls.'

Peg thought about Farrow & Ball's Breakfast Room Green and smiled. 'There's nothing wrong with that though, surely? We don't all have money to burn.'

'No, I realise that, it's just...' Sofia sighed, frowning as if she was trying to catch a thought. 'Maybe it's not that at all, maybe it's the fact that the few clients I *do* manage to get just want the same as everyone else does – which is whatever's trending on Instagram. Because, in reality, no one wants to stand out from the crowd, do they? We all want to belong. Only it's to a club that has no name, and no organisation, and the rules of it change almost every day. Yet we still want to be a part of it. It's baffling when you think about it.'

'And that club is full of people with picture-perfect lives,' agreed Peg, nodding. 'With beautiful houses, beautiful bodies and in beautiful relationships... things that most of us struggle over and never feel we attain. And yet we keep on striving, because we keep on believing. But what if we tell ourselves those lives are fake, Sofia? What then? Doesn't it change the pressure we put ourselves under? Doesn't it make us kinder to ourselves? More accepting?' She paused to give Sofia a warm smile. 'Doesn't it make us realise that being ordinary is okay? That, in fact, being ordinary is *extraordinary*, because that's what each and every one of us is – unique and utterly extraordinary.'

Sofia's gaze dropped to her hands, still clutched in her lap. 'That might sound good in theory, but it's not that simple, is it? We're all expected to be something these days, be some*one*.'

'Can I ask you another question then? Going off on a tangent here, but what made you want to be an interior designer in the first place?'

'Because I have a degree in textiles, and I thought...' She gave Peg a perplexed look. 'I didn't know what I wanted to do. I thought I'd give fashion a go, but that's such a competitive area and I knew I didn't have the stamina for it, nor the skill either, not really. But I'd started making a few things for myself when I was at university, mainly to save money, and it started from there. I ended up working in a fabric shop...' She pulled a face. 'Which was fine. I enjoyed it, actually. I learned a lot, too, and once Adam and I got married, it was all right for a bit, but then it didn't seem... enough, maybe, I don't know.'

'And that was when you decided to throw a lot of money at your business, and do all the social media stuff to try to attract clients?'

Sofia nodded, looking miserable.

'So why wasn't what you were doing before enough, if you enjoyed it?'

'Because I thought when we got married that children would come along and I'd be a mother. I never really wanted to be anything else. I certainly didn't want a career.'

'So why go chasing one?'

'Because the few friends I told about how I felt thought I was odd. None of them want kids. Or not for ages, anyway. Not until they've got where they want to be.'

'What, none of them?' Peg frowned, thinking of her own children. Is that really what young people wanted these days?

Sofia's glance flickered away. 'Not all of them, no. Quite a lot of our friends already have children. Our old friends that is – but we don't see them much any more.'

And suddenly Peg understood. She remembered how it was

when she was Sofia's age, how all the friends in her circle gradually paired off, got married, started families, and she'd wondered when it would be her turn. But then she'd met Julian and suddenly it *was* her turn. But how would she have felt if that hadn't happened for her? Quite probably the same as Sofia did now – choosing to move in a different circle where the differences between them were no longer so obvious. Where she wasn't made to feel left behind and yet she still felt it anyway.

'My mother used to call it having your cake and eating it,' she said. 'Describing women who didn't just want to be a stay-at-home mum. Didn't want to be *just* a wife and mother. She made it sound as if there was something wrong with women wanting to run a global company at the same time as having children. But the point is that it's a choice, and each decision has its merits. It's whatever is right for the individual concerned. Though, admittedly, it's often financial pressures which make those choices for us. Both my husband and I needed to work when our children came along.'

'Yes, but it isn't just that. It's the pressure to be *something*, be some*one*... Which is exactly my point. *I* have to be something, someone...'

'Why?'

'Because...' Sofia looked up, her eyes suddenly wide. 'Because I don't have anything else...' She trailed off, a surprised look on her face. Surprise at having finally given voice to the thought which had been in her head for such a long time, the hurt she had held inside of her for so long. A hurt that coloured everything.

Peg let Sofia's words hang in the air for a moment, giving them space to breathe, to swell and fill the room and hopefully take root in Sofia's head so that she fully acknowledged them. She leaned forward.

'I can't take away your pain, Sofia, but I can remind you to never lose hope. Because if you have hope, you usher in possibility. And where there's possibility, anything can happen, and often does. Don't live your life putting distance between yourself and the thing you want the most. Make a home for it instead, here in your head.' She tapped two fingers lightly against her crown. 'You have to make it welcome or it will never arrive. It takes a lot of courage to break from the crowd. To do things differently... But you know, if you did, I think you'd find that people would admire you for it. Perhaps even be a little bit envious, even a lot envious. Maybe you should try it. Maybe this is the perfect time to break the mould, Sofia.'

24

Peg had been watching the clock for almost an hour before Mim and Henry finally arrived back, much, much later than she'd thought they'd be. And Henry was exhausted.

'I know, I know... I've overdone it,' he said, in reaction to her expression. 'But I didn't realise how knackered I was until we got in the car to come home and my head started spinning.'

He rubbed at his chest and Peg wondered whether that was hurting as well. For goodness' sake, why were men all the same? Determined not to listen. Well, she was damned if she'd let history repeat itself. Mim was looking sheepish as well, and were it not for that fact, Peg would have said something far stronger than she was going to.

'You're both as bad as one another,' she said. 'But I shall have to have words with Blanche if she's going to have you gallivanting about.'

'No, don't do that,' said Henry. 'It's not her fault at all. And to be fair, she did ask repeatedly if I was okay.'

'And you told her you were?'

'I thought I was.' Henry dropped his head. 'I underestimated how much even conversation tires me.'

He looked so disgusted with himself that Peg immediately felt contrite, mentally pushing back the conversation she needed to have with him about Sofia and Adam. It would keep for another day. She was, however, still keen to know what had happened while he and Mim had been with Blanche, but maybe it wasn't the time for that either. She gave him a softer look.

'Have you eaten?' she asked.

'A fat slab of Christmas cake this time,' said Mim, replying on his behalf. It was clear she felt as bad as Peg did. 'But she made it herself and it was very nice.'

'Well, that's something,' said Peg. 'Dinner won't be for a while yet, so hopefully that will give you two time enough to have a rest.'

'I'll make some tea,' said Mim, even though she would struggle to do so with only her left hand.

Henry wearily took off his coat, and even that seemed an effort.

'Would you like a bath?' offered Peg. 'Perhaps a long soak will make you feel better. Then I would have a nap, if I were you.'

Henry looked like a small boy who'd just admitted to scrumping apples. It tugged at Peg's heart more than ever.

'Actually, that would be heavenly. Would you mind?'

'Of course not. I wouldn't have offered if I did. Sit down a minute and I'll go and run one for you.'

By the time Peg returned, Mim had joined Henry at the table, and a pot of tea stood between them. *If* Mim had managed it by herself, then it only lent weight to the argument that she would soon want to be home, and Peg wasn't sure she was ready to think about that yet. All the talk of Henry moving had been unsettling enough; she didn't want to contemplate her own relocation. Then again, taking Mim home would make the logistics of looking after Henry very difficult, and Mim must know that. So perhaps the longer he stayed, the longer Mim would stay too... Time was fast slipping through Peg's fingers, but if she couldn't stop the flow entirely, then she at least might be able to slow it down.

'He's not like Julian, you know,' said Mim as Peg returned to the kitchen again after checking that Henry had a clean towel.

'I should hope not,' she said. 'They're different people.'

'You know what I mean,' Mim replied, patting the chair beside her so that Peg would sit down. 'He's very conscious of what you think, and the last thing he wants is to be difficult.'

'Julian wasn't difficult. He was frustrated by his illness, Mim. I understood that.'

'But he still took it out on you when he shouldn't have. And he was a belligerent so-and-so before he got ill. Don't pretend he wasn't.'

'And we all have our faults,' Peg replied. 'You're a stubborn mule at times, Mim, and you know it.'

Mim gave her a stern look. 'We weren't talking about me.'

'No, and we're not talking about Julian either.'

'All I'm saying is that you turned your life inside out caring for Julian, at times. And did he thank you for it? Did he change his ways? No, he didn't, and even though you never stopped doing everything you could, he still went and died on you. But this is not going to happen with Henry. He's doing okay, honestly.'

'*Mim...*' For heaven's sake, was she a mind-reader now? 'I'm well aware of that. It's a completely different set of circumstances.'

'Perhaps... Some of it is, anyway.'

Peg looked at her aunt, exasperated. What was that supposed to mean? Sometimes she was next to impossible.

'I can see how anxious you are about Henry,' Mim added. 'But he's a really nice man. Not that Julian wasn't,' she added quickly.

'I'm glad you think so because otherwise you and I might have a falling-out.'

Mim patted her hand. 'That came out wrong, you know what I'm like. What I mean is that I understand how strange it must feel having Henry here, but that you're not to worry. I think it's a good thing.' She gave Peg a bright smile.

Peg gave *her* a sideways glance. 'Good, I'm glad we've cleared that up.' She returned the smile though, just to show Mim there were no hard feelings. Peg found it very difficult to stay cross with her aunt for long.

'Tell you what, I quite fancy a bath myself after Henry's finished. Do you think we could rig up that cover we used last time so I don't get my cast wet?'

Peg almost laughed. 'I'll go and find a carrier bag,' she said.

Henry really ought to get up. He'd slept for far longer than he had intended, but his body was warm and relaxed; another five minutes wouldn't hurt.

He traced the series of fine lines on the ceiling, letting his eyes move from one to the other. He hated lying to Peg, but he wasn't sure what else to do. Explaining about Mim would only complicate things, and he was having enough of a problem getting his feelings straight in his head as it was.

He wasn't well yet, he knew that. It was a constant source of frustration that tasks which had come so easily to him before now felt utterly beyond his reach. And the truth was that he might never recover the good health he had enjoyed before; the doctors had warned him about that. But he'd been lucky. His lung seemed fine, and although his chest was still painful, if he moved slowly and breathed shallowly, it was tolerable. His ribs would heal in time, as would all the other cuts and bruises, and even the bleed in his brain hadn't left him with the kind of damage it might have. But something was different, it must be. It was the only way he could explain how he was feeling.

He should be longing for everything to be as it was before his accident – missing his home, his belongings, his work, and yet, even though he felt as if he'd been lifted bodily from his old life and set down somewhere else entirely, he was far happier with this new situation than he should have been. His house and everything which made up the day-to-day living of his previous life seemed further and further away each day. And he didn't miss them at all. He should feel uprooted. And restless. But he didn't. He felt comfortable and at peace.

And there were things he wanted to talk to Peg about. Because he wanted to know how she was feeling. She was endlessly kind, and compassionate, and seemingly quite happy having him in her midst, but he still couldn't work out how she truly felt. About him. Every time he mentioned the way they had met, or how lovely Christmas Day had been, even if he hadn't actually spent it with her, she turned his comments gently away and held herself back from him. They could sit for hours of an evening, listening to the comforting tick of the clock, with a glass of mulled wine in their hands, watching the logs on the fire settle, the lamplight low, and barely speak. It felt... right... he could think of no other word for it. The silences were peaceful, companionable, just as he had remembered. Just as he *thought* he remembered.

With an audible groan, not of pain, but regret at having to move at all, Henry swung his legs over the side of the bed and sat up. He didn't want to be considered lazy, or even rude. He picked up the book he'd been reading before sleep claimed him, and carried it downstairs to the kitchen.

There was no sign of Mim, but Peg was still there, and now hard at work, scrubbing furiously at a metal shelf which looked as if it had come from the oven. The Essie door was open so his assumption was probably right.

'You look as if you're doing penance for something,' he remarked, putting the book down on the table.

Peg startled on hearing his voice, but swung around with a smile on her face. 'I am,' she said. 'I'm doing penance for not having cleaned the oven sooner. It's a mess.' She swiped at a stray hair which had fallen across her face.

'Can I help?'

'Not with this,' she replied. 'I think you've done enough today.' She visibly checked herself. 'Sorry, I didn't mean to tick you off like a small child. You look better for having had a sleep though.'

Henry passed a hand over his face, rubbing away the last of his tiredness. 'I feel better. And thank you... for looking after me.'

Peg smiled, and turned back for a moment, rubbing at the tray. 'You could peel some potatoes for dinner if you really want to do something. Or just sit and keep me company. There's probably something I should tell you.'

'Oh?' said Henry, taking a seat.

'Yes, I've been thinking. About quite a few things. And I also keep meaning to ask you whether you need to get anything from home. You haven't got very much with you.'

Henry shrugged. 'I probably should, but for the life of me I don't know what.'

'Well, clothes, or... maybe check for post? Or water your plants, that kind of thing?'

Henry thought for a moment, mentally walking through his house, checking everything the rooms contained. And although he could remember what was there, it was as if none of it belonged to him any longer. 'Curiously, I seem to have everything I need,' he replied. 'Life seems a lot simpler at the moment.'

Peg stared at him. 'Does it?' She frowned and scrubbed

some more at the oven shelf. 'Oh well, let me know if you change your mind.'

'Okay.' Henry waited, but Peg didn't seem in a rush to say anything else. 'What was it you wanted to talk to me about?' he prompted.

'Oh... something you said in the garden this morning, which now suddenly makes more sense. About you wanting to move closer to Adam and Sofia. She came to see you today...'

'Sofia did?' He gave a wry smile. 'Why would she want to see me?'

'She made out at first that she was just checking how you were, but, as it turned out, what she really wanted was someone to talk to. She told me about Adam's redundancy...' She paused, staring at the dirty cloth in her hand. 'And then... I kind of worked it out, but she told me how much she and Adam want a family. How her business isn't what we think it is at all, and how so much of their life has evolved to hide the truth they don't want to admit to. Both to themselves and everyone else.' Peg looked distinctly uncomfortable. 'I'm sorry, none of it is my business, but I was here and...' She licked her lips. 'If Sofia were my daughter, I'd be devastated to know she'd been feeling the way she has. I couldn't ignore what she told me, but it probably wasn't my place to say anything.'

'Peg, I'm *glad* you know,' said Henry, his eyes seeking out hers. 'I didn't say anything yesterday because I promised Adam I wouldn't – not until he'd spoken to Sofia, but I can't think of anyone I'd want to give advice more than you. More than me, even. I'm ashamed I didn't know what had been going on in their lives. Not the redundancy, that's come out of the blue, but everything else...' He scratched at his chin, touched by the humbleness of Peg's words. 'Adam and I had a good talk. Better than we have in a long while. But it made me realise how remiss I've been. I've taken a back seat in their lives because I was fearful of having difficult conversations, but they were important conversations and we should have had them. I intend to put that right.'

Peg smiled. 'Don't be too hard on yourself,' she said. 'From what I've seen, neither Adam nor Sofia have made that easy in the past, but perhaps now there's a chance for things to be different. For them to see that the redundancy is not the ending they think it is, but instead an opportunity to start over, to make their future one they really want.'

'You're very good at this, aren't you?'

Peg dipped her head. 'Positive reframing,' she said. 'And I'm a master of it.' She put down the oven tray, peering at it in disgust. 'So I quite understand why you want to move. How did you get on this morning?'

Henry could feel his neck growing hot. 'Okay, but...'

Peg raised her eyebrows. 'Yes...?'

'I was just thinking how Life likes to keep us on our toes, doesn't she? She's full of little ironies, having jokes at our expense.'

Peg frowned. 'Sorry, I'm not sure what you mean.'

'Simply that, given the chance way we met, which, let's face it, must have taxed the odds of chance severely, Life is now determined to be contrary by having you planning on moving further up north, and me planning on moving down here. It doesn't seem right, does it? That Life should deny us the universe's shenanigans.'

Peg looked down at her hands, clearing her throat. 'Well, I've been thinking about that... and I've had an idea... possibly.'

Henry was disappointed. He didn't want Peg to be practical. He wanted her to agree with him, to take delight in the direction that fate seemed to be leading them in.

'And it's probably not something we'd want to look at long-term,' Peg added. 'But it might provide a temporary solution for us before we commit ourselves to anything definite.'

Henry got up and crossed to the other side of the kitchen,

taking out a loaf from the bread bin. 'Would you mind?' he asked. 'Blanche's cake was lovely, but it didn't go very far.'

She shook her head. 'Not at all, just take what you want.'

Henry quickly cut a couple of slices before adding them to the toaster. 'Go on, I'm listening.'

'It's just that moving isn't a quick process. And I can't give up this place and swap it for a house I don't truly love, so I'd want to take my time in finding somewhere just as nice. But I don't want to be driving back and forth for ages either, so I wondered if we should swap houses? That way, I'd be close enough to Mim to keep an eye on her, and you'd be nearer to Adam and Sofia and would be able to suss out property around here, too.' She gave him a quizzical look. 'It's not a perfect solution, and the timing of things might be tricky, but...' She trailed off, looking less sure of herself than she had to start with. No doubt she'd clocked his dismay at the thought of them being so far apart again.

She screwed up her face. 'Or is that a really stupid idea?'

'No... it's...' Henry didn't know what to say, and he was struggling to keep his expression under control. 'I mean, in principle it sounds like a good idea, but you've never seen my house, Peg. It's nothing like this. It's very ordinary and... tired. A bit rough around the edges.'

'Oh, that wouldn't bother me. Besides, I'm sure it isn't. I'm sure it's perfectly lovely.' She smiled, before turning back to her task. 'Anyway, we don't have to think about it now. Or at all... I just thought I'd float the idea out there seeing as it had popped into my head. It's the manual labour – my brain goes off at tangents all the time when I'm doing stuff like this.'

'Yes, it was... a good float,' finished Henry lamely. 'And we should definitely think about it.' What else was he supposed to say?

Neither of them spoke for a moment, while Peg sloshed

water around. 'Have you heard any more about your pension?' she asked eventually.

Henry nodded, the change of subject hitting hard. 'I've had an email from the Teachers' Pension Scheme, so it looks as if the wheels have already been set in motion. Actually, would you mind if I borrowed your laptop again? Only when it's convenient. I need to reply to the email, but it's not so easy on my phone.'

'Sure. You can have it any time. As you can see, I'm set on other things. It's upstairs on my desk. I'd get it for you, only...' She held up her hands, which were clad in a pair of plastic gloves and covered in gunk.

'Thanks,' said Henry. 'I'll just eat my toast.'

Twenty minutes later, he headed up the stairs, feeling every one of his sixty-two years, plus about thirty more. How on earth could he explain to Peg how he was feeling when she clearly didn't harbour the same emotions? And as for explaining about Mim, it was far too soon for revelations yet. Still, there were one or two other things he could do while he had the benefit of Peg's laptop.

Henry had only been in her study briefly – to bring her a cup of tea one afternoon – and on that occasion he'd got no further than a couple of feet inside the door. It wasn't a large room, but it overlooked the garden and he could see why Peg had chosen it. Given the work she did, it must provide the perfect inspiration. He crossed to the window to look outside. Staying in this house was some kind of dream. Perhaps it was all a dream...

Peg's laptop was right where she said it would be, and he lifted it from the desk, pausing as he did so to peek at some of her paintings which lay beside it. He picked up a watercolour of some spring flowers – snowdrops, crocuses, hellebores and snake's head fritillary – no more than a few brushstrokes depicting each, but each still instantly recognisable. It made his head itch to find the right words to go with them.

He reached down gingerly to unplug the charger from the wall, and was about to straighten again when he caught sight of something on the floor – something tucked behind a wastepaper basket – in fact, a whole stack of somethings. Laying the laptop down for a moment, he lifted the pile of paperbacks from the floor and placed them on the desk. They were out of order, but the whole series was there, and his heart began to beat uncomfortably in his chest. He rubbed at his breastbone, easing his shoulders back gently to open out his ribcage, the source of the pain. He should never have bent over like that, but it wasn't the pain which was causing his heart to leap about.

Taking one of the titles from the stack, he picked up the laptop and charger and carried all three back to the kitchen.

Peg was rinsing one of the oven trays under the tap, her back to him.

'Did you find it okay?' she asked.

When Henry didn't speak, she turned around, her gaze immediately flying to the book he was holding.

'I didn't know you had these,' he said, rotating the cover towards her just in case there was any doubt which title it was. '*Case Histories*, by Kate Atkinson – the book I was reading on Christmas Day.'

Peg's smile was frozen on her face. It was almost a grimace.

'What were they doing in your study? Face down behind the bin.'

She lifted her chin a little. 'If you must know, I hid them there.'

'Why?'

'Because I didn't want you to find them. Isn't that obvious?' She dropped her head. 'I'm sorry. I shouldn't snap at you, but Henry...' She sighed. 'This whole thing about the dream you had, with me, here on Christmas Day. You've been clinging onto it, as if you believe it's real, when surely you must know it wasn't. It was lovely – a lovely thing to dream about and a lovely thing to have happened, but none of it was true…'

'But I saw everything so clearly. The details… How could I have known stuff like that?'

'You saw what you wanted to, Henry. It wasn't my house, or my belongings, and it wasn't me living there. Just a version of me your mind had created.'

'So how do you explain the copy of this then?' he said, holding up the book. 'I was looking for something to read on your bookcase and I saw these, asked you what they were like, and you told me they were good. That each one seemed better than the last. I carried it to your sofa and I started to read it, and I—' He broke off as a sudden memory came to him. 'It had a dedication in it, to Anne McIntyre, it…' He turned the pages, swallowing as the exact same words leaped out at him. 'How could I possibly have known that?'

Peg looked distraught. 'I don't know, Henry, but… it's a popular book. I imagine loads of people have the same titles on their bookcases, and maybe you'd seen it somewhere before. In fact, I think you must have, for you to be able to remember it in that way.'

'What about the leeks we had for dinner then? Ones which were gathered from your garden? Just like the ones you actually grow.'

'But you knew I was a gardener, and leeks are a seasonal vegetable. A lot of people have them at this time of year. It was an educated guess, that's all.'

'So you don't think that any of this means something? Even when coupled with the way we met?'

Peg was clearly thinking about his words. But she was also taking her time to reply. 'I think perhaps you'd like it to,' she said gently. 'Which is perfectly understandable. You were in a bad accident. You nearly died, Henry, and I think your brain was trying to protect you from the horror of it all by showing you something you wanted to see. Even now you can't remember what happened when you crashed. Surely that must tell you something?'

'It does, which is exactly the point I'm trying to make. Because I think it tells you something, too, otherwise why hide the books?'

Peg was struggling to respond, that much was obvious. She looked upset and awkward, but the expression on her face conveyed more than that, and the more Henry studied her, the more he realised what it was. She looked sad. Unbelievably sad. Despite her outwardly sunny nature, and her smiles and her kindness, the sadness ran deeper than it all. She carried it with her everywhere she went, all day, and every day.

'I'm sorry,' he said. 'I didn't mean to put you on the spot.'

'Oh, I think you did,' said Peg. 'And I'm sorry I—' She stopped abruptly as the back door opened.

'Izzy! What are you doing here?' She held up her filthy hands, laughing as she did so.

'I just thought I'd pop down to see my favourite people and check on how you're all doing.' She gave a cheeky smile. 'You've forgotten, haven't you? It's New Year's Eve, Mum, remember? Alice's wedding? We agreed I could bum a bed for the night...'

Peg was struggling to free her hands from the rubber gloves, pinging flecks of soapy scum everywhere in an effort to pull them off quickly. 'Is that really the date?' she said, finally free of them. 'How on earth did that happen?' She wrapped her arms around her daughter. 'You're right, I had completely forgotten, but it's so lovely to see you!'

Izzy returned her mum's fierce hug before pulling away and turning to Henry. 'And *you* look very much better than you did the last time I saw you.'

Henry dipped his head. 'I'm being well looked after,' he

said. 'So, yes, I'm much improved, thank you. He smiled as Izzy came forward and, to his surprise, lightly kissed his cheek. He didn't even get that kind of welcome from his son. Or, at least, he hadn't in the past. He was hopeful that might change now.

'And how's Mim? Where is she?'

'Having a nap. Despite what she says, I think she's rather enjoying being looked after. Gone are the days when she's up at the crack of dawn.' Peg checked her watch. 'You're just in time for dinner.'

'Oh...' Izzy dropped her head, cheeks flushing. 'I probably should have reminded you I was coming,' she said. 'I didn't think, sorry. But I'll have to get up at the crack of dawn myself if I don't stay over.' She rolled her eyes at Henry. 'Alice is a friend of mine who's getting married tomorrow... of all days. I mean, who does that? But she lives in Somerset. Are you sure it's okay for me to stay, Mum?'

Peg nodded, shaking her head in amusement. 'Of course it is, but don't expect wild celebrations tonight. You know I've never been big on the whole New Year's Eve thing.'

Izzy pulled a face. 'Oh, don't worry, I'm planning on an early night – tomorrow is going to be *craaazy*. And then the day after I promised Pheebes I'd go round hers on my way home. She's got some new furniture for her living room, but it's flat-packed and you know what she's like. I said I'd give her a hand... and by that I mean build it completely. Because who doesn't spend their bank holiday doing DIY?' She grinned at Henry. 'Phoebe missed out on inheriting Mum's practical genes – she got saddled with Dad's complete inability to read instructions of any kind.'

She looked between the two of them, smiling happily.

Henry cleared his throat before the silence could lengthen. 'I was just about to borrow your mum's laptop,' he said, tucking the copy of *Case Histories* underneath it and lifting them both as proof. 'I'll take it into the other room – leave you two to have some time together.'

He smiled and walked from the room, well aware that both women were staring after him.

25

Peg brightened her smile. 'Let me just get rid of this lot and I'll make us a drink.' She turned to rinse her gloves under the tap and stack the shelves on the draining board ready to go back in the oven.

She bustled about for a moment, fetching mugs, filling the kettle and taking milk from the fridge. She even fetched some biscuits from the pantry which she knew Izzy would never be able to refuse. And all of it giving her a little more time to get her face straight and her head back where it needed to be.

'I know you've told me what time the wedding is, but remind me,' she said, turning back around and holding out the cookies.

'Two o'clock,' said Izzy. 'But I said I'd get there mid-morning to help her get ready. I can't wait to see what she looks like – her dress is *insane...*'

'In a good way? Or a bad way?'

Izzy grimaced. 'Depends on your point of view. It's insanely beautiful – covered in tiny seed pearls, all hand-sewn by virgins who live in a remote village in Tibet – it's not, obviously, but you get my drift – and is therefore insanely expensive. If I ever get married, don't let me go mad like that, will you? I think I'd rather keep the thirty grand and do something slightly more lasting with it. I don't mean the marriage,' she added hastily. 'I hope that lasts and lasts, but all that money... just for one day.'

'Thirty grand?' asked Peg, horrified. 'Is that how much it costs these days?'

'Yep... although that includes the engagement ring and the honeymoon. The wedding itself is only twenty grand.'

Peg laughed. 'Oh well, that's all right then. Although, if I'm going to need that kind of money to pay for you and Phoebe to get married, perhaps moving will be a good thing. I was thinking it might be an ideal time to downsize.'

'Mum!' exclaimed Izzy, her forehead furrowed with concern. 'There's no way you're going to be paying for us; Phoebe and I have agreed. Besides, that's not how it's done nowadays. Couples pay for themselves. The whole father of the bride thing – or even mother of the bride thing – it's kind of considered old-fashioned now.'

'Thank heavens for that.' Peg wafted a hand at her face as if she were having an attack of the vapours.

Izzy frowned. 'You're not still thinking of moving though, are you, Mum?' she asked quietly. 'I hoped once Mim was feeling better that would all fizzle out.'

Peg drew in a breath. 'Well... she is feeling better, but longer-term, the situation isn't going to change, Iz. I'm not sure what else I can do.'

'But you can't move from here, Mum, it—' She broke off, looking rattled. 'I just can't imagine you being anywhere else.'

'I'm having a hard time with that myself, but irrespective... I made a promise to Mim, and I'm not going back on it. I couldn't live with myself if I did. I'm not going to make any rash decisions, though. I want to take my time and make sure I find somewhere equally as nice as this place.' She directed a look through the kitchen door and lowered her voice. 'I've no idea how long that might take, so I've come up with a way which would allow me to be close to Mim at the same time as having a look around.'

Izzy followed the direction of her eyes. 'Go on...'

'Henry is thinking he might move down this way. He wants to be closer to his son and daughter-in-law, which, given what's just happened to him, I can understand.' She cleared her throat; his name seemed to get stuck in it. 'So I've suggested we swap houses for a bit. We haven't properly discussed it yet, but it would buy us both some time before we commit to anything.'

Izzy was studying her face. 'I thought something was up,' she whispered. 'Not being funny, but you could cut the atmosphere in here with a knife when I walked in. Is it not working out with Henry staying here?'

'No, it's not that, just...' Peg tilted her head in the direction of the living room.

Iz nodded in understanding. 'Garden?' she said.

Peg nodded. It had always been their go-to place whenever they needed a private chat. Wordlessly, they donned boots and a coat each from the stash which Peg kept by the door and headed outside. The times she and Izzy had retreated into the garden over the years... during Julian's last few months, it had seemed almost a daily occurrence, and the memory of the reasons why was stark in her mind.

'So what's up?' asked Izzy, hands thrust in her pockets. 'I thought you were enjoying having Henry here?'

Peg looked helplessly at her daughter, wondering how on earth to begin. 'I am, Izzy, I... It's just that I think Henry's impression of our relationship is somewhat different from mine. I know I told you that on the day of his accident he'd been on his way to see me, but what I haven't said is that Henry doesn't remember a thing about the crash. He thinks he drove over here and spent the rest of the day with me – a day he can "remember" down to the last tiny details. Needless to say, it was perfect in every regard.'

Izzy frowned. 'So, what... he was dreaming then?'

'He must have been. He described falling asleep after we'd eaten dinner, and I think his brain was trying to protect him from the trauma of the crash by manufacturing something pleasant. Except that he seems to have it in his head that this is a sign – of something between us.' She sighed. 'It's hard to know what to say to him, particularly given what he's been through, but I don't want to encourage him. I've tried to let him down gently but I think I might have sounded a bit rude... not rude, exactly, but dismissive certainly.'

Izzy was staring at her wellies, wriggling her toes inside them. 'So you don't want there to be anything between you then?' She peered up through her lashes, something she always did as a child when she was trying to get away with being cheeky.

Peg stared at her, lips pursed. 'No, Izzy, I don't. We met by chance. And yes, when I saw his car ahead of me in the traffic jam I did feel compelled to talk to him, even though I knew it was an odd thing to do. I can't explain it, and I'm having trouble rationalising this myself, but that's all it was, a chance meeting. I like him. I'd even go so far as to say it's been nice having him here, but... anything else is just ridiculous.'

'Not that ridiculous,' replied Izzy. 'I mean, he's gorgeous. All studious and bookish.'

'Is he?'

'Yes. Haven't you noticed the way his hair falls over his forehead when he talks? He reminds me of a young Hugh Grant.'

Peg, who had, said nothing.

'Have you even looked at him properly?' asked Izzy, becoming exasperated. 'And I don't mean compared him to Dad.'

'Izzy, I don't have anyone else to compare him *with*. I was with your father a very long time.'

'Yes, you were. But there are more men in the world than

just him. All I'm suggesting is that something a little more than just friendship wouldn't be a completely dreadful thing, would it?'

'Oh, Izzy, it's not that simple.'

'Why? Why is it not as simple as two people falling in love?'

'Love...? Peg frowned. 'We're a long way from that, Izzy. I'm not a teenager any more, hankering after some romantic dream. Trust me, it's different when you're older.'

Izzy shook her head. 'No, I don't believe that. You always told us that love was love. Why does your age change the situation?'

'Because there are more things to consider. You, for example. And Phoebe. I have a house, a life. I've *had* a life, with someone else. When you're young, it's an adventure, it's exciting thinking about your future and all the things it might hold, a future you might create with someone. When you're older, you've done all that. Things are more settled... You know your own mind, for one, and yes, hard though it's been without your father, I've got used to being on my own. Used to doing things how I want them, and when I want to. I'm not sure I want any of that to change.'

'So you're going to throw away a chance of happiness because Henry might not like curry? Or watches ITV instead of BBC?'

'That isn't what I said.'

'But it's what you meant. You're so determined not to fall in love, you won't ever give yourself a chance. And I get it, Mum, we all get it. It's scary. You didn't think you'd ever have to think about this again. But you've faced fears many people haven't and you've got through them. You're tough, and brave, and well, just lovely, Mum. You *deserve* to be happy. I mean really happy. And Henry isn't scary at all. At least give him a chance.'

Peg tutted, although she smiled too. 'Okay, okay, you've made your point.'

'But you're still not going to listen, are you? You've already made up your mind how your future is going to look. But it was Dad who died, Mum, not you.'

'Izzy!'

'Well, it's true. You've holed yourself up here, with your garden and your drawing and never given yourself any reason to go out again.'

'Maybe because I don't need to. I like my life.'

'Do you, though? Or do you just pretend to? We all saw you at Christmas – how much you enjoyed having us all here.'

'Yes, I did, but that doesn't mean—'

'It was the worst circumstances imaginable and yet you welcomed Henry's family in like they were our own.'

'Well, of course I did, what else could I do? It was Christmas and, for a time, we were all convinced Henry was going to die. I couldn't just leave his family in the hospital and ignore them. Don't forget I know exactly how it feels to lose someone at this time of year.'

Izzy dropped her head. 'I know, Mum, but loving Dad doesn't mean that you can't ever love anyone else. Dad was no angel, but the more the years go by, the more he's become one. Don't confuse your grief with the truth. You told us never to think how we *ought* to feel, but to be gentle with ourselves because whatever we *were* feeling was okay. You don't need to feel guilty about anything, Mum.'

Peg looked away, staring down the garden path at the woodland beyond. She could remember so clearly when her girls were little, and on the bad days when life was fraught, with too many demands, how she would remind herself that whatever her children got up to, whatever anguish they caused her, that it *would* get easier. And it did, except that now they were adults themselves, they no longer simply did as they were told. She was no longer just a mother to them, she was a thinking, feeling equal, who they could figure out in a heartbeat. And how many times had she stood in this garden, grateful that this was the case because she so desperately needed them to understand what she was going through? Too many times to count. And they had, just as Izzy did now.

She gave a rueful smile. 'You're too clever for your own good, did you know that?'

'And I wonder who I get that from?' Izzy smiled and held out her arms. 'I just want you to be happy, Mum,' she said, pulling Peg into a hug. 'And I'm not saying it has to be with Henry, not at all, but don't you remember how you always told us that you knew you were going to marry Dad the minute you met him?'

'Did I?' said Peg, pretending not to remember. 'Well, that's rubbish. It doesn't happen like that.'

'And yet... you meet a guy in a petrol station and then bump into him again seventy miles down the road. I mean, what are the chances of that? I don't know, maybe it's like *fate* or something.' Izzy rolled her eyes in dramatic fashion and then grinned. 'Love you, Mum. But can we please go in now, it's freezing. And I'm starving...'

26

NEW YEAR'S DAY

Izzy was gone by eight the next morning, leaving an empty space at the breakfast table and an awkward silence in the kitchen. Peg was only too aware that her conversation with Henry of the previous day hadn't been finished, and although she was mindful that it needed to be, Peg couldn't think of a way back into it.

Izzy was good company, and so they'd spent a pleasant evening, all four of them sitting around the fire, drinking a bottle of wine and chatting about anything and everything, except of course about Henry and Peg – the Henry and Peg which occupied one sentence, that is. They could talk about Peg and they could talk about Henry, that was fine, but what they mustn't do was talk about them together.

Now, though, it was New Year's Day, a day which came with a weight all of its own – the weight of tradition. New starts, and changes and plans, and all the things which Peg, when newly widowed, couldn't bear to think about. Back then it had seemed the cruellest of days, and even now there was a poignancy to it which was hard to evade. Even Mim seemed unusually quiet this morning.

And to make matters worse, Peg had snapped at Henry when he'd risen from the table to wash up the breakfast things, telling him she would sort them herself. Not surprisingly, he had slunk from the room, and moments later, Mim followed him, leaving Peg staring out of the window, disgusted with herself.

She was still sitting at the table some fifteen minutes later when Henry poked his head back around the door. He waved his phone tentatively, almost as if it was a peace offering.

'That was Adam,' he said, still standing on the threshold. 'He just called to wish us a Happy New Year. All of us, that is.'

Peg nodded, noting the *all of us*, as opposed to the simple *us*, which would clearly have meant just her and Henry.

'How are they?' she asked. 'I hope they found a little time to talk things through. Or were they out partying last night?'

'That's just it,' said Henry, finally coming into the room. 'On every other New Year's Eve that would have been the case, but they stayed at home last night. And they've asked if we'd like to have lunch with them. Nothing fancy, Adam was keen to stress that.'

Henry was making light of it, but Peg could see how happy he was with the suggestion. It was the type of spur-of-the-moment arrangement he'd been hoping for for years.

'Are there still matching bows on the backs of the chairs?' she asked, but then she checked herself. 'Sorry, that was rude.' She could still remember the shake of Sofia's shoulders as she held her.

'I said I'd ring Adam back to let him know,' added Henry. 'Because I wasn't sure if you had anything planned for today.'

Peg smiled. 'No, nothing planned.' In fact, she had no idea what she was going to do with the expanse of time in front of her; her head was all over the place. She felt as if she was fighting an unseen opponent – one whose intentions were not yet clear. And the thought of being alone with Henry had gone from something she scarcely noticed, like wearing her softest jumper, to something which felt horribly scratchy.

'Tell him that would be lovely,' she said. Because what else could she do?

Given all that Adam and Sofia were going through, it would be churlish to refuse. No, worse than churlish – it would be a rejection of the very thing which Peg had offered in advice. She'd never turned her back on anyone who'd needed help in the past, and she wasn't about to start now just because of her own stupid emotions.

Henry's face lit up at her reply and her traitorous heart swelled at the sight of it. Clearly it wasn't done making its point.

The drive to Adam's house was virtually silent, and Peg had no idea what was running through Henry's head. He was worried, though. Throughout the journey his hands lay in his lap, twisting around themselves repeatedly. It was something he often did, probably without even being aware of it. And she had to admit, she was more than a little apprehensive herself. Adam and Sofia had obviously found some time to talk, but Sofia had still been angry with her husband for keeping things from her, and Peg had no idea what the repercussions of that might be.

She was struck by how different Adam looked as soon as he opened the door, finally able to see the resemblance between father and son. Gone was the Adam in charge, the confident achiever, and in his place was someone a little more humble and uncertain. But he was also smiling.

'Happy New Year! Dad... Peg, come on in.' He pulled the door wider, urging them over the threshold so he could give Henry a quick hug. 'Go on through, Sofia's in the living room.'

The last time she had seen this room had been on Christmas Day when it was festooned with decorations, but now it was totally devoid of its seasonal dressing. All Peg could see were acres of pale paint, glossy surfaces and curated uniformity. She supposed some people would find this kind of style calming, but it made her feel awkward. Just like Sofia had remarked, Peg fitted into her cottage at home, whereas here she felt out of place – too colourful, too unpolished and too lumpy. Sofia, on the other hand, with her slender figure, wearing beautifully tailored light trousers and a white linen shirt, could stand against a wall and look like an elegant decoration herself. Not today, though. Today Sofia was wearing jeans and an old, worn sweatshirt, and was curled into the corner of a sofa with a book in her hand. *She* looked out of place now – relaxed, but no longer a part of her surroundings. And it *was* just as Sofia had said – the woman she wanted to be would look far more at home in Peg's cosy cottage.

Sofia immediately uncurled her legs and got to her feet, crossing the room to meet Peg's hug – a warm and heartfelt hug. Peg could see now that the shallow, materialistic woman Peg thought she knew had never really existed. She was no more than a painted shield, behind which the real Sofia had been hiding. And Peg was suddenly very aware how many shields were worn during the course of an average lifetime. How many shields *she'd* worn. Perhaps it was time to lower hers, too.

Sofia held onto Peg's hands as they pulled apart, her eyes bright with excitement. 'Will you come upstairs? I've got something I want to show you.'

Unsure of what to do, Peg swung around to look at Henry and Adam, who were still standing behind her. Adam waved a hand. 'You go,' he said. 'Dad, you can give me a hand with lunch, if that's all right?' Henry didn't reply, but then he didn't need to; his face revealed that he was more than happy with the suggestion.

Peg had no idea what Sofia wanted to show her, but it soon became evident that whatever it was lay in a room which had at some point been her workroom. Now it wasn't sure what it was. What must have originally looked like the foyer of a plush hotel, with its coffee-coloured tub chairs and fitted shelves and cupboards in complementary shades, now looked like somewhere a tornado had blown through. The doors to the cupboards had been flung wide and the drawers pulled open, their contents disgorged onto the floor, the table – in fact, anywhere they landed. Papers, sample books, fabric, paint charts – all of it lay abandoned.

'I'm having a bit of a sort-out,' said Sofia.

'So I see...' replied Peg, her eyebrows raised in amusement. 'Are you sure you aren't just making a mess?'

Sofia looked around the room, the smile on her face growing wider. 'I can't remember the last time I made a mess. I'm really enjoying myself.' She bent down to pick up a sample book which lay on top of one of the stacks, very much like the ones she had brought to Peg's house. 'Some of the wallpapers in this book are over two hundred pounds a roll, can you believe it?'

Peg could, and she smiled. 'Do your customers really buy that kind of thing?'

Sofia tossed the book back on the pile. 'No,' she said. 'That's exactly the point. They don't, and I can't believe I ever thought they would.'

'So, what...? You're getting rid of them?' asked Peg.

'Yep...' Sofia grinned. 'The customers I make curtains for aren't ever going to be interested in what's in those books, so I'm just going to keep the ones which are for normal people.' She rolled her eyes as if she couldn't believe how ridiculous a notion it had been doing otherwise.

'I'm sorry I didn't want you to redesign my house,' said Peg, staring at the chaos around her.

'I'm not,' said Sofia, her voice resolute. She looked tired, but perhaps for the first time in a long while, at peace. 'It's ironic, isn't it?' she added. 'I should know more than most that papering over cracks never works out in the long run – it only delays the inevitable – but that's exactly what I've done.' She pushed her foot into one of the piles of books, causing it to topple. 'So no more wallpaper,' she said. 'I'm going to stick with what I do best, stop pretending and start being honest – with other people, but more importantly, with myself.' She paused, giving Peg a shy smile. 'I just wanted you to know.'

'It's certainly a good way to live,' said Peg, touched by the expression on Sofia's face. 'And that kind of truth takes courage – not everyone can handle honesty, but those who respond to it with grace are the ones to keep close.'

Sofia dipped her head. 'I think Adam and I have talked more in the last day than we have our entire lives. And yet if you'd have asked me a week ago, I'd have told you we talk all the time.'

'I'm glad you've forgiven him,' said Peg. 'For not telling you about the redundancy.'

'He was *terrified*...' answered Sofia, whispering the final word. 'How could I be angry with someone so scared? And I never knew, that's the worst of it. Not about the job thing, but the fact that he's been putting on a brave face for such a long time.'

'I don't doubt he has,' she replied. 'Ordinary everyday life is scary, without all the extra things you two have had to deal with. And Henry being so poorly must have really hit home. It's been a horrible, confusing time for you both, *but*, if you want them to be, those things are behind you now.'

Sofia smiled. 'Shall we go and see what Adam and Henry are up to?'

'I think that's a fine idea,' said Peg, smiling.

She stood back to let Sofia lead the way, and together they walked down the stairs, leaving the books exactly where they had fallen.

The living room was silent. Not even so much as a murmur of voices could be heard as they walked through the kitchen and into the dining room, the source of such irritation in the past. But Peg could sense immediately that the silence wasn't awkward, or angry, and, as they reached the conservatory and the two men came into view, it was clear that they were simply sitting, drinking coffee and looking out into the garden. A slanting ray of sunlight had found a gap between the trees at the far end and was working its way up the lawn towards them.

Henry was the first to rise, getting to his feet as Sofia crossed the room to walk into his open arms. Their hug was quite possibly the nicest thing Peg had seen. She blinked rapidly, feeling a surge of happiness – happiness of the kind which often heralded tears. It *was* a beginning, not an end, of that she was certain.

'I've just been telling Dad what we've decided to do,' said Adam, gesturing to the spare chairs. 'Come and sit down, lunch is ready.'

'I hadn't got much in,' said Sofia. 'So I just made a few sandwiches and opened a bag of crisps. Is that okay?'

Peg exchanged a look with Henry. 'Absolutely perfect,' she said, taking a seat.

Adam cleared his throat. 'I wanted to thank you, Peg, before we eat. Not only for what you've done for Dad, but for us too, welcoming us into your home and looking after us so well. It must have seemed as if an unexploded bomb had landed in your life.'

Peg laughed. 'Horribly accurate,' she said. 'But you're welcome. And, thankfully, the bomb never exploded. Besides, next year will be better. The best Christmas ever.' She rolled her eyes, catching Sofia's look and matching her grin. 'Although it's New Year's Day, so I guess it's already this year's Christmas.'

Henry groaned. 'I don't know where the time goes,' he said. 'But I have a feeling that a lot of things will change over the next twelve months.'

'They better had,' said Adam, looking at Peg. 'Sofia and I have decided to move. A house has come up for sale only ten minutes away from where we used to live. It's one of those lovely nineteen-thirties semi-detached places – solid, with big bay windows, open fireplaces and a huge south-facing garden. We haven't seen it yet, and it needs a bit of work, but it's got bags of character and... our mortgage will be less than half of what it is now. It could be just the place to get back to where we need to be. So this house is going on the market tomorrow and, well, we'll see what happens.'

'It's where all our old friends live, too,' said Sofia. 'The ones we moved away from when we pretended we wanted more from our lives. I know we can't expect everything to go back to being the way it was before, and that wouldn't be the right thing to do anyway, but I hope when we explain why we did what we did, they might forgive us, in time.'

'I'm sure they will,' said Henry.

'It will be good, I think, to live in a hopeful way, instead of a hope*less* one, and if children come along, then...' Sofia broke off as her eyes welled with tears. 'Then I will be happier than ever... but if they don't then, in the meantime, I can give my friends a hand with theirs, whenever they need a break. The grass is always greener, isn't it? I bet they'll look at us – people who sleep for eight hours a night and aren't covered in baby sick– and think we've got it made.'

'They'll bite your hand off,' said Peg, smiling. 'And what about your job, Adam?'

'I'm still going to teach,' he said. 'Teach, but that's all. No management roles, nothing which will take me outside of the classroom. I'm going to do what I love, part-time too, if we can afford it. Maybe four days a week, leaving me with a day free either to write or... maybe take some qualifications in creative writing. That might sound naive, and I've got to get another job first, but...'

Henry leaned forward and patted his son's knee. 'Nothing naive about it. And I can't tell you how pleased that makes me.'

'It's bonkers,' Adam replied. 'We grew our life around us

like a protective shell, thinking that it would keep us from hurting. But we never realised how hard and unyielding it was. How much it separated us from everything which was important.' He shook his head ruefully. 'I can't believe it's taken us so long to understand that there only needs to be one thing in your life that isn't working, and it doesn't matter how rich or poor you are, how many things you have, or none, your life will never feel happy or fulfilled. In fact, if anything, all it does is highlight what you *don't* have, not what you do.'

'And perhaps even longer to admit to it,' added Sofia. 'I wanted something in my life to care about. Something which would swallow me whole and take away the empty feeling inside. I thought that if we had the kind of life everyone wanted, that if we started moving in the right circles, that my business would be a success and I'd have something to fill my days, instead of ceaseless longing. But it hasn't done that at all. All it's done is prove that you can't run from the things you actually want, and you can't buy endless stuff in the hope of burying them either.'

'You two still have a lot to discuss,' said Henry. 'But it's exciting, isn't it, thinking what the future could hold?' He swung a glance at Peg, and this time she held it. It was high time she started taking her own advice.

Sofia reached forward and pulled the plate of sandwiches towards her. 'Come on, Peg, tuck in. They're just cheese and chutney, but it's a nice one.' She grimaced. 'From the local deli admittedly, but it's not bad. And I've got some chocolate fingers in the fridge for afters.'

Peg edged a sandwich off the plate and took an appreciative bite. Sofia was right, the chutney *was* good, although it wasn't a patch on hers. Not that she'd say anything, of course... besides, she had a feeling that in a few years' time, the young woman sitting in front of her might be making her own...

. . .

Two hours later, Peg fastened her seat belt and, putting the car in gear, slowly pulled away from the kerb, waving until Adam and Sofia were out of sight.

From beside her, Henry sighed. 'You know, this is the first time I've left that house and haven't felt like I was making an escape.'

'Feels good, doesn't it?' replied Peg, glancing across at him before returning her attention to the road. It was very different for her, but even she felt the same.

'It does. We make a great team... although that should come as no surprise.'

Peg could feel Henry looking at her, and she knew without checking what his expression would tell her.

'Go on,' she said, smiling. 'It's obvious you have more to say.' She slid him an amused glance.

'You told me yourself what the problem was, don't you remember? I know I've mentioned your issue with your fictitious downstairs bathroom before, the one I had in my "dream", but you told me then that Adam and Sofia were unhappy. That they were finding fault with all sorts of things in their lives because they were ignoring the real problem. Are you sure you've never had a downstairs bathroom?'

Peg laughed. 'I'm sure. And I still stand by what I said before. I don't think it was me who was wise at all, more like your own subconscious working things out. You're the wise one here.'

'Perhaps... but I think my explanation is far more in keeping with the spirit of the season. Are you really going to deny me my miracle?'

Peg tutted, amused, but she had no answer for him. She was still very conscious that she was pushing away Henry's fantasy. Was she ever going to stop doing that? Mim used to tell her when she was little that just because she didn't understand something, it didn't mean it wasn't true. And she had to admit it certainly felt as if a miracle had taken place. Possibly even several of them.

'In any case, I want to thank you,' added Henry.

'Whatever for?'

'Oh God, Peg, where do I even *begin*?'

She dipped her head, still smiling, but still unable to find any words. She drove on. Hadn't she recently told Sofia to make room for hope in her life? When every day Peg spent *her* time making sure that she had no need of it, no need of anyone else – running away from possibility and never making it welcome? She could see hope glimmering everywhere, knowing that if life had taught her anything it was that there was always some to be found. So why did she resolutely turn her head away from it? Why did she refuse to see that Henry was her glimmer? She swallowed.

'Before we go home, could we go for a walk? Just a little one, if you feel up to it.'

'Peg, I feel fine... more than fine. Better than I have in a long while, so yes, of course we can.'

'It's just that there are too many ears at the house...'

He nodded, and she steered the car on past the green, past her cottage and up towards the church, the one Henry knew of old.

The churchyard was deserted, still and silent in the early afternoon sun, as Peg walked along the path she had trodden so many times before.

'My daughter tells me I should talk to you,' she said. 'About Julian.' She didn't need to point out where they were standing, whose gravestone was in front of them; Henry would be only too aware.

'Do you want to?'

'Part of me does. The sensible part. The logical part which knows things have to move on. But my heart doesn't make it so easy. It's scared, you see, of what might be said. What might be invited into my life and what it might not be able to cope with.'

Henry was silent for a moment, ostensibly looking at the place where Peg's husband was buried, but she knew he was thinking about her words. Thinking, but saying nothing.

She let the seconds tick by, her heart beginning to thump in her chest. She had started, but she had no idea how to carry on.

'I notice you haven't put yourself in that sentence,' said Henry after a moment more. His eyes were gentle. 'And I do understand why not, how hard this is.'

She gave him a quizzical look.

'The sensible part... my heart... *it's* scared... what *might* be said. Not *I'm* scared, what *I* might say...' He held up his hand. 'You're trying to protect yourself, and I get that, I really do. I can see how hard this is for you, Peg, and the last thing I want is to make it any harder. There's no need to share any of what you're feeling if you don't want to.'

Peg shook her head, harder than she intended, and took a deep breath. She needed to say this now, before it was too late, before she lost Henry as well.

'Do you know why I like gardening so much?' She tipped her head at him, carrying on before he could reply. 'It's because it's easy with plants. You can pull them into the light, feed them, water them, show them some love and they'll respond. But people don't, not always. Sometimes, despite your best endeavours, despite all the love you can show them, and all the care you can give them, they choose not to listen. And Julian was one of those people.

'He shouldn't have died when he did. We're all going to die, I know that, but Julian's death was... senseless. Unnecessary. Stupid and selfish... He was diabetic, but he absolutely refused to listen to anyone – not me, not the doctors – especially not the doctors. He said he wasn't going to let an illness rule his life, but ironically, trying to ignore it meant that it *very much* ruled his life. They call it diabetes burnout – when the relentlessness of living with it becomes too much, but I'm not sure that was the case with Julian. He barely even acknowledged he had the disease. And so over the years, his health deteriorated, rapidly towards the end, and then he had a stroke. I think you know the rest. We talk about grieving when someone dies, but I grieved for Julian when he was still alive. I had all that love and nowhere for it to go. I still do...' She trailed off, letting the tears come. It was time to stop holding them back. 'And so I don't know where that leaves me when it comes to someone else. When it comes to you...'

Wordlessly, Henry took a hanky from his pocket and handed it to her. Then he simply stood beside her, and she was grateful for his reassuring presence. Grateful that he didn't try to put words in her mouth.

'Have you ever gone walking at night?' he asked a minute or so later. 'And seen little snapshots of people's lives through the lighted windows of their houses? Dusk is the best time, when no one has their curtains closed yet. I used to walk our dog and wonder about all the lives in those houses – what the people were doing, how they had spent their day – who they were with, and what they were talking about. And in all the times I watched them, I never once thought they were unhappy. I always pictured them warm and cosy, without a care in the world, and it hurt because I wasn't one of them and I never thought I would be again.'

Peg nodded. 'For me, it was people holding hands in the street, or the way a couple would smile at one another, looks so filled with tenderness, so full of love for their shared life, that the pain was almost unbearable. I felt as if I were the only single person alive on the planet. And it wasn't that I wanted that kind of feeling with anyone else, just that it was a reminder that I'd had it, once, and lost it. That I would never feel that way again, never share in something so powerful it defied anything which stood in its way. The stupid thing was I don't even think that's what I had with Julian. We had a good marriage, don't get me wrong, but that's what hurt more than anything when he died – that he could give up on us, give up on our shared life so easily, and it made me see that he never even realised how powerful love could be.'

'Perhaps he was afraid of it,' offered Henry. 'Thought himself unworthy.'

Peg swiped a hand across her cheek. 'Perhaps,' she agreed. 'At times, I think I've hated him for that, but now all it does is make me sad, because he never understood it was there for the taking.'

Henry scuffed his feet in the gravel at the path's edge. 'Thing is though, Peg, that wasn't all I saw when I looked at those houses. My place isn't like yours – I live in a street, among a row of houses, which backs on to another row and looks out on another, and another, and another. And sometimes at night, I'd stare out across the rooftops, all those little boxes filled with light, like stars in the sky, all separate and never touching. But every now and again, I'd see something different. I'd see a tiny golden filament stretching from one to the other. I'd see lives connected, interconnected, and that gave me hope because I knew that we weren't all destined to be alone forever.

'Sometimes lives don't stay separate. Sometimes they touch, and once they do, they become bound together, at first by just a tiny thread, but then, if they touch again, the thread becomes stronger. Lots of those lives won't ever meet, but there are some who are drawn together because they can sense that thread just waiting to be picked up. I think that's what we are, Peg.'

Peg stared down at the ground. The same ground where, four years ago, she had stood to say her goodbyes. To a man who had been a part of her past, yet one never destined for her future.

'That's the difference between us,' she said. 'Once upon a

time, if I'd seen those boxes, all the little lights in the sky, the lives they held would have just run on endlessly into the night. Parallel. And never touching.' She turned to Henry, lifting her face to his.

'And now?' he asked, vulnerable, his heart open and undefended.

Peg smiled and slipped her hand into his. 'Now, I see hope,' she said.

27

The cottage looked different somehow as they approached – as if Peg was seeing it for the first time – the tiny but perfectly formed front garden which, come summer, would be filled with hollyhocks and larkspur, the bright green front door which always looked so warm and inviting, the deep mullioned windows which gave it such an air of permanence, and the rosy glow of the building itself, all the things which she had fallen in love with on the very first day she and Julian had come to view it.

She stopped on the path, guarding herself against the doubt she expected to feel, the pain of her loss which, during moments like these, always came to the fore. She waited, but it didn't arrive, and in its place was a small but growing burble of happiness, and she hugged it to her, precious and so very welcome after such an age without it. She hadn't been happy for a long while, she realised. Only fooling herself.

Opening the back door, Peg felt as if she was holding her breath. She was scared that if she started to breathe normally again, what had passed between her and Henry would be lost. She wasn't even sure what it was yet, but the thread was there, just as Henry had said it was, pulling them together, tightening their bond. And it was the most scary and exhilarating thing all at once. Perhaps that's what it was – she felt breath*less*.

And she was certain that Mim would notice. Mim, whose shrewdness was like a weather gauge and could sense any change in the atmosphere, but miraculously she didn't comment, only asked with concern how Adam and Sofia were faring.

'Remarkably okay,' answered Peg. 'And I think Blanche can expect a call from her daughter very soon. It's not for me to say why, but I reckon Sofia has quite a few things she'll want to share with her mum.'

'Well, thank goodness for that,' replied Mim. 'She's been beside herself with worry.'

Peg nodded. 'It's early days, but put it this way: I don't think the threat of redundancy is the disaster it first appeared to be.'

'Your family has had quite the ordeal over recent weeks,' said Mim, turning her attention to Henry. 'It's about time your luck changed.'

Henry smiled. 'You may well be right there, Mim, and who knows, maybe it's changing as we speak.' He flicked Peg a glance which made her stomach give a girlish skip. Honestly, anyone would think she was a teenager. She shuddered; she couldn't think of anything worse.

'I was thinking I'd make some tea,' added Henry. 'But would you mind if I took mine up to my room? The spirit is willing, but the flesh is decidedly longing for a nap.'

'It's been quite an afternoon,' said Peg, turning to face him. 'I don't blame you. Are you sure you're all right? Not overdone things?'

Henry shook his head, smiling. 'Just tired.' He paused. 'Are *you* okay?'

'Desperate for a cuppa, but other than that...' She smiled, shy, at the thought of what might yet pass between them. 'Shall

I bring you up a snack as well? You didn't have much to eat at lunch.'

'Can I just pinch a couple of biscuits for now? I think I need sleep more than I need food.'

Peg fetched the tin from the pantry and handed it to him. 'Take it up with you. If you don't, I'll only eat them. I'll bring your tea in a minute.'

She watched as Henry padded from the room, virtually soundless in his socks, his worn corduroys and bobbly jumper by now a familiar sight. She was suddenly reminded how out of place she'd felt in Sofia and Adam's modern, sleek house. And it was just the same for Henry. But here, in *her* house, he was the perfect fit.

A few minutes later, she sat down at the table, her tea in front of her, as yet untouched. A new emotion was clamouring for her attention, and she was having difficulty deciding exactly what it was. Her head wanted her to believe it was doubt, was *still* trying to convince her that's what she should be feeling, but it wasn't doubt, it was something more restless, something more anxious, more urgent... Her eyes widened in shock. She was *scared*. Not about Henry, or not in the way she thought she ought to be feeling anyway. She wasn't scared about having someone in her life again, about making room for him in her life, she was scared of *losing* him.

Because now, just at the point where she thought her life might be about to change, when fate had brought her and Henry together, and the thread which bound her to him was pulling them closer, that same fate was about to send them in opposite directions again – she moving to be closer to Mim, and Henry moving to be closer to his son.

Her hand flew to her chest, covering her heart as if seeking to protect it. Her eyes sought out her laptop, still on the table from where Henry had left it earlier. He'd been in the middle of looking at properties before they had left to go to lunch. Might he have left a tab open? Had Henry already found the perfect place to live? She opened it up, desperate to know how far he had got with his research, but what she saw on the screen made no sense at all.

She stared at the page in front of her, at the sales details for a house she knew well, a house she had been in a very short time ago. Mim's house.

Heart thudding in her chest, she carried her laptop through into the living room where Mim was sitting beside the fire, drinking her own cup of tea and eating a piece of cake. She set it down on the coffee table and swivelled it towards her aunt.

'What's going on?' she said. 'Why is your house for sale, Mim?'

Her aunt looked like she'd been caught with her hand in the cookie jar. But only for a second. Then her expression changed to one of consternation.

'Oh, honestly,' she said, tutting. 'Trust you to spoil the surprise. You were just like that as a child, tearing open tiny corners of your Christmas presents to peek inside.'

'I did not!'

'Oh yes, you did,' replied Mim, laughing. 'Your mother had to hide them in the loft because she knew it was the one place you were too scared to look. And not just *your* presents either. Don't you remember the year when you said "you can open your pyjamas now, Auntie Mim"?'

Peg did remember – they had teased her about it for years. She shook her head. 'That's not the point, as well you know. What's going on, Mim?'

Mim gave her a coy smile. 'Well, isn't it obvious? It's not Henry who's moving, it's me.'

'You?'

'Yes, me. I'm buying a flat at Athelstone House.' Mim folded her hands in her lap and gave Peg a triumphant grin.

Peg shook her head. 'But how on earth did you manage that? You—'

A creak on the stairs behind her gave the game away. 'You'd better have a good explanation for this,' she said without even turning around.

'Actually, it *is* pretty sound,' said Henry, moving into her line of sight. He at least had the grace to look a little ashamed.

He took a seat on the sofa, eyebrows raised, and she frowned. Was he mocking her now?

Swallowing, she sat down opposite him and indicated the computer screen. 'Well... start explaining then.'

'Oh, for goodness' sake,' muttered Mim, rolling her eyes. 'Your generation think you're the only ones who can organise things, with your laptops and your mobile phones.'

'To be fair, Mim, we did borrow Peg's laptop, and we did use my phone,' said Henry.

'Don't split hairs,' Mim replied. 'The point is that I can remember Dot's phone number, her *landline* number, without the aid of all these fancy gizmos, and she has a key to my house, so—'

'Of course she does,' murmured Peg.

Mim ignored her, darting her niece a fierce look. 'And so I rang her and told her that a nice young man from the estate agency would be calling and she was to give him the key.'

'And what did he say, this nice young man?'

'That I have a very desirable property which he thinks will sell quite quickly. He was particularly taken with the garden, apparently.'

Peg stared at her, desperate to find some fault in Mim's statement, but it was clear she'd been comprehensively outmanoeuvred. 'But you always said you didn't like old people. You said that Athelstone House wasn't your cup of tea.'

'I don't like old people. But Blanche isn't bad, I rather like her. As for it not being my cup of tea, I was *acting*, dear.' She leaned forward to pat Peg's knee. 'Have you *seen* the place? It's like Downton Abbey. They even have a proper dining room where you can order a fancy dinner if you don't feel like cooking, and they have wine with their meals. And a lady who comes in and does hair and another one who does nails. Blanche gets hers done every fortnight.'

'Does she?' said Peg, shooting Henry a look. 'That's all very well, Mim, but how can you even afford it?'

'Because my Bernard left me quite a lot of money, dear, which you must remember, because you were the one who sorted everything out for me – the executor thingy, of his will, whatever you called it. Anyway, I've had nothing to spend my money on for all these years, so what do you think I've done with it?'

It was true, Peg had been the executor of Bernard's will, but Mim's husband had died fifteen years ago. She just assumed... She checked herself. That's exactly what she had done – *assumed*. 'I didn't think there'd be any of it left,' she said. 'I thought you needed it.'

'What for?' asked Mim. 'There's only been me, and I don't eat much. The birds don't eat much either. So it's stayed in the bank, in some fancy account or other where the lovely lady who works there said I should put it. So now there's rather more than when I started. And it's plenty enough to buy a little flat. I don't want anything bigger because you know me, dear, and I hate dusting.'

Peg allowed herself a small smile.

'But your house, Mim... You love it there. You told me you never wanted to leave it. You wouldn't even come and spend Christmas with me, for goodness' sake. In fact, you wouldn't have if you hadn't broken your wrist. Seriously, Mim, I don't want you to feel like you have to move. I promised you could stay in your own home and I meant it. We can sort something out.'

Mim stared at Henry. A helpless look. An exasperated one. 'Honestly, Peg, aren't I allowed to change my mind?' she said. 'Besides, I thought you knew me better than that, so you should know that I don't do anything I don't want to.' She lifted her chin.

That, thought Peg, was most certainly true.

Something else occurred to her, and she swivelled to face Henry. 'You've been helping her with all this, haven't you? You and Blanche. Helping her and keeping it all secret from me. Worse, made out that it was you who wanted to move.'

Henry held up his hands. 'Guilty as charged.'

'But why? Why couldn't you have just been honest with me?'

'Because Mim was only too aware of the promise you'd made to her. A promise she knew you would stand by because that's what you do, no matter the sacrifice to yourself. She's not daft, Peg; she knew that might mean you moving from here. So buying this flat had to be *her* idea, and hers alone, with absolutely no involvement from you. Otherwise you would feel like you'd pushed her into her decision, even when that wasn't true. Worse, you'd convince yourself of it, feeling guilty when there was absolutely no need. And no one would be able to argue otherwise.' Henry raised his eyebrows. 'Apparently, you can be quite stubborn yourself.'

'*Did* you know I was thinking of moving, Mim?' asked Peg.

Her eyes widened in shock.

'No,' said Henry, answering for her. 'I knew *you* would never say anything to her and so I didn't either. Because again, if Mim *had* known what you were planning, that would have given you every excuse to say she'd decided to move in order to spare you from having to. This was Mim's decision, Peg...' He drew in a breath. 'And I helped because I knew how much leaving this place would hurt you. And I...' He swallowed. 'I couldn't bear that.'

Peg could feel warmth flooding her body. Moving up from her toes, making her fingers tingle and her cheeks flush. 'Oh,' she said. She didn't seem to be capable of much more.

'Yes, *oh...*' said Mim, eyes heavenward as she heaved an exasperated sigh. 'Now we've got that out of the way, can you two please, you know...' She pursed her lips as if to kiss someone. 'Sort yourselves out.'

Peg slid Henry a glance, terrified for a moment that she was going to burst out laughing and he wouldn't, but as soon as their eyes met, she could see that wasn't the case at all. They both understood each other perfectly.

She pressed her palms to her cheeks, which were now hot for a totally different reason, but then she groaned as a sudden thought came to her.

'Wait a minute... this still doesn't resolve anything. Ten minutes ago I was railing at a universe which was just about to have me move up to Stoke while you were moving down here. Now I don't have to move, a thought, incidentally, which makes me want to sing the "Hallelujah Chorus", but in case you've forgotten, that's where *you* live, Henry. We're *still* going to be miles apart.'

Mim gave a delighted chuckle. 'It's very simple,' she said. 'Henry can be your live-in lover. For a little while, at least. Until you get married and then—'

Peg practically choked. 'Mim!' she exclaimed. 'You can't go around saying things like that.'

Mim waggled her head in amusement, her eyes twinkling. 'Sorry, dear. You know what us old ladies are like – we simply can't be trusted not to embarrass you. We've quite taken over the role which used to belong to your children.'

Peg stared at her, her mouth hanging open.

'And are you going to tell her the rest, Henry?'

'You mean there's *more?*' Peg wasn't sure her heart could beat much faster.

'Oh yes. It's really quite delicious.' Mim tapped Henry on the arm. 'Well, come on then, out with it. Tell her what happened on the day I broke my wrist. Tell her why you thought I'd died.'

Henry looked suddenly bashful.

'I knew it,' said Peg. 'I knew there was something more to it than what Blanche had told me. You did, didn't you? You both believed Mim had died.'

Weakly, Henry nodded. 'Because when I heard from your neighbour what had happened, all I could think about was what you'd told me – about when Julian had died and why Christmas was such a difficult time for you. And you were all alone, Peg, I couldn't bear... I thought that maybe you could use a friend, so I –' He broke off as Mim clapped her hands together in delight. 'So I went to see if I could find you.'

'He drove up to Stoke, to the hospital, can you believe it?' said Mim.

Peg shot her a look. 'And you accused me of spoiling the surprise...' She turned then, looking at Henry, smiling at him, telling him she was ready to hear what he had to say. 'Did you really do that?' she asked. 'For me?'

He nodded, and then pulled a wry smile. 'Bit silly actually, 'cause when I got there I hadn't reckoned on my not being able to find you. Hospitals are *really* big places...'

Peg frowned. 'Then I still don't understand why you thought Mim had died.'

'Because I *did* find you. Just as I was about to leave. You were sitting in a tiny room, all by yourself, crying as if your heart was breaking. What else was I to think? I wanted to hug you, so you'd know you weren't alone, but how could I, Peg? When I didn't even know you. When I thought you'd be angry with me. Even that it was a bit creepy or something, and...'

Peg sat up slightly, as the penny finally dropped, although it might have been her heart thudding. 'Oh, Henry... I *was* crying, but with *relief*... I'd been so stressed, thinking about Julian, and terrified I was going to lose Mim as well, that when she was finally taken to have her wrist put in a cast and I knew she was okay, it just came over me – all the fear, all the anguish, all the grief... It just came out, in an almighty bawl, right in the middle of a corridor. I had to dash into the nearest room before I made a total fool of myself.' She sniffed, feeling tears begin to well in the corners of her eyes. 'It was probably just as well you didn't find me. I was one big snotty mess.' She smiled. 'But I still would have been very glad if you had... I think that's the nicest thing anyone has ever done for me.'

Henry held her look. 'I'm sure it can't be. I mean, Julian bought you a wood...'

Peg's gaze drifted to the mantelpiece where she had propped a piece of paper quite a few days ago now. A piece of paper which held something quite extraordinary. It was her drawing. Her drawing and the poem Henry had written there. The essence of them both, combined to make something far bigger than they could ever accomplish alone. But it was also a gift, because *he* was a gift. And a promise. Her miracle man with dark hair and dark eyes... one who she knew without a shadow of doubt would always, always strive to make her world a better place.

'*The way a crow shook down on me, the dust of snow from a hemlock tree, has given my heart a change of mood, and saved some part of a day I had rued...*' She leaned forward and slid both her hands into Henry's. 'Julian isn't here,' she said. 'But you are.'

And then she kissed him.

A LETTER FROM EMMA

Hello, and thank you so much for choosing to read *One December Morning*. I hope you enjoyed reading it as much as I enjoyed writing it. If you'd like to stay updated on what's coming next, please do sign up to my newsletter here and you'll be the first to know!

www.bookouture.com/emma-davies

I'm not sure whether you're the kind of person who always reads authors' dedications and acknowledgements, and so on, although I guess if you're reading this, you probably are! But I'm someone who always does. I love to wonder about them, about the messages they contain and the names they mention. Wondering who those people are in the author's life, those people who are the story behind the story because, trust me, every book has one. And this being true, you might already be wondering who the young man is that I've dedicated this book to… Well, let me explain.

Some years ago, when my children were doing the rounds of university open days, we paid a visit to Norwich, a city we'd never been to before. And reader, we fell in love… Fast-forward a few years later, and although university in Norwich was not to be, our love of the city didn't dwindle and so, some years ago we decided to take a break there, just before Christmas. Being a creative family, our visit was timed to take advantage of a weekend of makers' markets, and we had such a great time, our seasonal visit has become something of an annual pilgrimage. Being so close to Christmas, the weather has been varied, but that very first year, it was perfect – crisp clear air, bright sunny skies, and on the morning we drove home, just as it was for Peg, there was the deepest hoarfrost I think I've ever seen... The world was transformed, and our sadness at leaving was in some part allievated by the gorgeous scenes outside the car windows as I drove.

The only trouble was that with everything so icy, keeping the windscreen clear was a difficult job. Washer jets were frozen solid and as the miles under my wheels grew, so the screen became increasingly dirty. I stopped at a petrol station to clean it and when I returned to the car, having paid a visit to the shop, there was another car alongside mine having exactly the same trouble. It was a young man, driving a red Mini. After a few moments, he plucked up the courage to ask for help, and, being young and I expect not having been a driver for that long, he didn't know that the tiny holes just at the base of his windscreen were the washer jets. Long story short, I showed him how to clear them, and we wished each other a happy Christmas before I drove away. Cue quite a few miles of driving later and, as I slowed to stop at a roundabout to give way to traffic, in the lane beside me was, yes, you've guessed it, the red Mini... At which point, the writer in me became very excited as I realised what a wonderful way this could be for two people to meet. *One December Morning* is the story that followed, so you see, there is *always* a story behind the story...

So, not only am I very grateful to the young man for giving me the perfect opening to my book, but also to my wonderful publishers, Bookouture, for agreeing that it was. As always, a huge thank you goes to the whole team, whose names you can see listed separately, for their input into getting *One December Morning* ready for publication. Particular thanks go to my wonderful editor, Cerys Hadwin-Owen, for her sage advice in making Peg and Henry's story the very best it could be.

And finally, to you, lovely readers, the biggest thanks of all for continuing to read my books, and without whom none of this would be possible. Your support means the world to me. I also love hearing from you, so if you'd like to contact me then the easiest way to do this is by popping by my website, where you can read about my love of Pringles, among other things. You can also follow me on Facebook, or over on Substack where I share my writing, together with other thoughts, on my publication *At the Still Point*, subscribing to which is free.

I hope to see you again very soon and, in the meantime, if you've enjoyed reading *One December Morning*, I would really appreciate a few minutes of your time to leave a review or post on social media. Every single review makes a massive difference and is very much appreciated!

Until next time,

Love, Emma xx

www.emmadaviesauthor.com

atthestillpoint.substack.com

facebook.com/emmadaviesauthor

PUBLISHING TEAM

Turning a manuscript into a book requires the efforts of many people. The publishing team at Bookouture would like to acknowledge everyone who contributed to this publication.

Commercial
Lauren Morrissette
Hannah Richmond
Imogen Allport

Cover design
Ami Smithson

Data and analysis
Mark Alder
Mohamed Bussuri

Editorial
Cerys Hadwin-Owen
Charlotte Hegley

Copyeditor
Jenny Page

Proofreader
Helen Hawkins

Marketing
Alex Crow
Melanie Price
Occy Carr
Cíara Rosney
Martyna Młynarska

Operations and distribution
Marina Valles
Stephanie Straub
Joe Morris

Production
Hannah Snetsinger
Mandy Kullar
Nadia Michael
Charlotte Hegley

Publicity
Kim Nash
Noelle Holten
Jess Readett
Sarah Hardy

Rights and contracts
Peta Nightingale
Richard King
Saidah Graham

RAISING READERS
Books Build Bright Futures

Dear Reader,

We'd love your attention for one more page to tell you about the crisis in children's reading, and what we can all do.

Studies have shown that reading for fun is the **single biggest predictor of a child's future life chances** – more than family circumstance, parents' educational background or income. It improves academic results, mental health, wealth, communication skills, ambition and happiness.

The number of children reading for fun is in rapid decline. Young people have a lot of competition for their time, and a worryingly high number do not have a single book at home.

Hachette works extensively with schools, libraries and literacy charities, but here are some ways we can all raise more readers:

- Reading to children for just 10 minutes a day makes a difference
- Don't give up if children aren't regular readers – there will be books for them!

- Visit bookshops and libraries to get recommendations
- Encourage them to listen to audiobooks
- Support school libraries
- Give books as gifts

There's a lot more information about how to encourage children to read on our websites: **www.RaisingReaders.co.uk** and **www.JoinRaisingReaders.com**.

Thank you for reading.

Made in the USA
Monee, IL
17 November 2025